A DANGEROUSLY FASCINATING MAN
AND THEN THE HAUNTING ALLURE
OF THE SUMMERHOUSE . . .

"Meggie, what is that strange little building?" I cried, turning toward the bluff. Then, immediately, I knew it to be the summerhouse, although it was far from my expected vision of an open-sided, airy dwelling to while away a summer afternoon. This was a solid house, old and weathered, with windows boarded up. A wooden porch looked newer than the rest, but it also showed signs of neglect. Vines and cobwebs straggled everywhere and weeds grew tall and thick.

Fascinated, I moved closer until Meggie called to me, sounding agitated, and looking back, I realized she had stayed behind on the main brick path that wound around the rose garden.

"Come back, Miss Courtney, *please*!" She was torturing the edge of her pink cape between her hands. "We don't go up there. It's ___. it's dangerous."

I retraced my footsteps slowly. "Dangerous? Why should it be? It's just a neglected little house."

"It was *hers*. She used it before she—anyway, no one's allowed there now."

I knew who she ___ ___ 'as it some kind of shr

The Summerhouse

MARION CLARKE

A DELL BOOK

Published by
Dell Publishing
a division of
Bantam Doubleday Dell Publishing Group, Inc.
666 Fifth Avenue
New York, New York 10103

ISBN: 0-440-21181-6

Printed in the United States of America

Published simultaneously in Canada

February 1992

10 9 8 7 6 5 4 3 2 1

RAD

1

Last night I came to Castlecove. And for the first time, I dreamed of Dugan MacInnis. The dream came many times thereafter, but that was the beginning.

It was midnight in my dream. I seemed to be running through the rose garden, the towered Scottish castle a shadowed backdrop to my flight. My destination was the forbidden summerhouse, a place of weathered wood, shuttered windows, and tangled, neglected weeds. It was not a welcome sight yet somewhere within might lie the answer to my quest.

But before I reached it, I heard someone call my name. I whirled around, my white night shift fluttering against my body. Behind me on the path stood Dugan, feet spread arrogantly apart, fists clenched upon his hips. His russet hair and dark eyes were dredged of color by the moonlight, but there was no mistaking that angry Scottish burr.

"Didn't I warn you, woman? Don't you know the danger here?" His voice grated. "What must I do with you?" Moving swiftly, his arms reached out and jerked

me up against the hardness of his body. My breath
caught in my throat while strange emotions flooded
me: excitement, fear, and . . . something else I
couldn't even name.

I gave a gasping cry as his hands came up and
clasped my neck.

Then he forced a searing, grinding kiss upon my lips.

Next morning, when I awoke in the canopied feath-
erbed, my heart was still pounding wildly, my mind
beset with questions and dismay. Why had I dreamed
about a man who alternately attracted and repelled
me? Dugan MacInnis was the epitome of ruthless male
domination. Hard-faced, cold-voiced, his eyes were either icy as the Scottish peaks or burning with savagery
like the rocks and tides surrounding Castlecove.

And yet, he filled my thoughts. Too much. Ever since
the moment we had met on the doorstep of my London
house.

Shivering, I burrowed deeper beneath the comforter
and watched the gray dawn seep between the garnet
brocade drapes covering the tall windows.

Dugan MacInnis must not concern me, I told myself
with desperate firmness. I was here on an important
matter. That was why I dreamed about a summerhouse where Paul had worked when he lived here. I
was determined to carry on the last part of his research if at all possible. I owed it not only to his
memory, but to the love and help he had given me so
generously at a time when it was sorely needed.

The threads of fate that had led me to this castle had
started out so innocuously, spreading, tangling together, then intertwining to become a rope binding me
to the promise I had made. My mind went back to the
beginning, wondering if I had overlooked some clue
that might help me now.

* * *

I had met Paul Dunburn at my father's Copy House in London where I worked as a copy writer on legal documents or any other paper that needed the benefit of my clear script.

Paul was a writer and had several books on Scotland's history to his credit. Now he was working feverishly on a manuscript laid in the Scottish Highlands and had decided to employ my services to transcribe his scribbled pages before sending them to his publisher. It seemed that an urgent need for haste had overtaken him. Perhaps even then he had a premonition of his fate. A little of "the Sight," as his Scottish ancestors would have called it.

Paul was a distinguished, gray-haired man of fifty with an overwhelming dedication to his work. As I read his well-written pages, I also was caught up in his enthusiasm and looked forward to each new installment. Thus it wasn't long before our business relations ripened into friendship, even though there was such a wide discrepancy in our ages. I had few friends of my own, working as I did, and before my father's illness, my parents and I had been a constant threesome. Now, I welcomed Paul's attention, and when he started taking me out to tea several times a week, it became an eagerly awaited interlude in my life.

I found Paul to be a cultured, interesting man, well read, and with a growing reputation in his field. He told me that he had married late in life, and when his wife died in childbirth, he was left to raise a little son named Tommy.

He sounded lonely. I also faced a rather barren future at that time. My father and mother were preparing to leave England for a warmer climate, which, hopefully, would aid my papa's lung condition. The Copy House already had been sold, but I would continue to work for the new owners. I knew it would be a difficult time for me, but I could not add to my parents' financial burden by going with them.

I was young and healthy, and in these modern days of 1860 when industry was on the march, many women besides myself were tiptoeing into the working field as clerks, artists, writers, and even factory operators of Singer's new clothing machines.

I knew I must become independent and conquer any trepidation I was feeling. When I discussed it all with Paul, he listened to me with his usual quiet understanding. Though sometimes I caught a thoughtful gleam in his gray-blue eyes. And a rather tender smile upon his lips.

One day, instead of going to a public house, he invited me to his home for tea. Filled with a pleasurable anticipation, I donned a foulard gown of *raisin d'Espagne*, a lovely purple hue. I added a new inset of handmade lace at my throat and pinned on a cameo given me by Mama and Papa on my last birthday when I turned twenty-four. Then I draped a fur-edged cape, the best I owned, around my shoulders and topped it all off with a bonnet trimmed with green gooseberries and white ostrich tips.

Satisfied that I had done everything possible to improve my appearance, I indulged in the extravagance of a hansom cab, going to Paul's home in style instead of taking a public omnibus, which was my usual mode of transportation.

I found that he lived in a modest dwelling with only one live-in servant who evidently filled the requirements of cook as well as keeping an eye on Tommy. Paul had told me that he also had a maid-of-all-work who came in by the day.

When I arrived, Paul met me at the door and led me into his parlor, complimenting me gracefully on my appearance before summoning Mrs. Barker. She was a white-haired lady of a comfortable girth who carried a laden tea tray and smilingly bobbed a curtsy upon being introduced.

A young lad of about five years bounded in behind her. He was an appealing child, blond and slim, with Paul's own bright, intelligent gray-blue eyes and a natural, friendly manner.

"Come meet my friend, Miss Courtney Larson." Paul put out a hand and drew his son forward with obvious pride. "This is Thomas Dunburn, the future laird of Castlecove."

I smiled at Tommy and shook his little hand. "A future laird? How wonderful that will be." Actually, I knew very little about the duties of a laird but hesitated to confess my ignorance.

Tommy nodded, saying eagerly, "Someday we'll be going back to Scotland. I've never seen the land we own."

His eyes rolled toward the tea tray, and distracted by the goodies on it, he licked his lips and edged closer to the table, obviously anxious for the social amenities to be concluded so we could begin to eat.

Mrs. Barker left us after Paul asked me to pour the tea, and a little self-consciously, I rose and filled the cups. Then I handed out the plates of cucumber and tomato sandwiches, salmon patties in crust, slices of rich plum cake oozing raisins, and hot buttered scones complete with strawberry jam and clotted cream.

I took a seat on the brown velvet couch next to Tommy while Paul smiled at us from a leather chair across the glowing hearth.

"I had no idea you were a chieftain in Scotland, Mr. Dunburn," I remarked, sipping from my gold-rimmed china cup.

"You agreed to call me Paul, remember?"

"Yes, *Paul*." I laughed.

He smiled. "Well, Courtney, as to being a chieftain, I relinquished my claim when I left Scotland. So as next in line, the title probably will go to Tommy. My parents may have been disappointed when I left, but Dugan—a younger, orphaned cousin—has made his home at Castlecove and manages the estate. Sheep and cattle are the main industries there and well support the family and many crofters living on the land."

Tommy gave a restless bounce. "Papa, tell her about the book you're writing now about Bonnie Prince Charlie and—" Suddenly, he paused and gave his father, then me, an uncertain glance. "That is—I know you told me it was a secret—"

"I already know something about the Bonnie Prince," I told the little boy. "I've been copying your father's book for several weeks, but so far it doesn't have an ending."

"Ah, yes, the ending. That still presents a problem." Paul stared into the flames, looking grave. His slender face was a handsome one and certainly belied his years. Today he wore a gray velvet jacket edged in darker braid with a blue satin cravat tied at the collar of his ruffled shirt. Evidently he had taken pains to look his best on this day when I was first invited to his home.

A riffle of uneasiness—no, rather puzzlement—swept over me. Was it possible that Paul was . . . courting? Oh, surely not. He was almost the same age as my father.

In any case, why would such a courtly gentleman as Paul want me? He was a talented, well-known writer, and had been raised in castled halls, son of a Scottish chieftain.

Apart from our convivial tastes and the fact that he might be lonely, I knew I had no sparkling wit or any flaming beauty to entice an important man. I was too slight of stature, too quiet and reserved, my face merely ordinary with long, pale hair and light blue eyes that were a heritage from some undistinguished Swedish ancestor.

I looked away when Paul caught me staring at him, and a little flustered, I hastened into speech, turning toward his son. "I know part of your father's book concerns a lost treasure hidden by the prince at Castlecove, but the ending will not be revealed until the book is ready to be published."

Paul nodded. "That is true. I was troubled when notice about the nature of my book was recently inserted in a literary journal." He frowned. "I suppose it won't be long before I will be pestered by the curious and greedy."

"Is the lost gold of such great value, then?" I asked, wondering if this might be the usual, often exaggerated family legend.

Tommy burst out excitedly, "Oh, yes, there's lots 'n' lots of gold. Prince Charlie left it all at Castlecove before he went away and no one's ever found it. But we're going to, aren't we, Papa?"

His father laughed indulgently. "I see I have fired Tommy with my own enthusiasm. Can you tell Miss Courtney something of the prince's history, laddie?"

Tommy sat up straighter. "He was Charles Edward Stuart. His grandfather, James II of England, was made to give up the throne because he wanted to bring back the Roman Catholic religion and—and make everyone obey him." He glanced at his father, who nodded encouragingly. "Then Mary and William of Orange became the rulers but lots of people wanted another Stuart on the throne. And when Bonnie Prince Charlie was born, he became their hero," Tommy crowed. "He was ever so handsome and brave, wasn't he, Papa?"

"Yes, the Young Pretender, as he was called, was extremely charming, also bold and ambitious. He raised his standard in the Scottish Highlands, asking for their loyalty. The clans responded eagerly, ever ready for a good fight in a good cause. Charlie also expected that a large force would rise in England to support him."

Tommy's blue eyes sparkled. "He stayed at lots of castles in Scotland and Castlecove was the last one. People gave him money for the cause and it's still hidden there. Just think of that!"

"The prince expected to come back and get it, of course." Paul sighed. "But he was defeated at Culloden, where the English supporters failed to rally in sufficient numbers."

"Didn't he escape, though?" I asked, caught up in the exciting tale played right near Paul's ancestral home. My tea and plate of cakes remained neglected on my lap.

"Yes, the Bonnie Prince escaped. He had to flee for his life and didn't dare return. A huge price was on his head, but he never was betrayed even though the Scots were viciously persecuted by England because of their support of him. For a long time, tartans were forbidden as well as bagpipes, clans, the Gaelic language, and everything that meant a Scottish heritage."

"Are you certain that Prince Charlie left the gold behind in Castlecove?" I asked.

"Oh, yes. I've read many old diaries and letters and everything points to the fact that Charlie had no chance to take it with him and he never told where it was hidden. I used to spend hours studying and researching in a little summerhouse at Castlecove that was beloved by Charles. I have a feeling that it holds a key to the mystery. If I'm right, think what an ending for my book that will be. I have to return to Scotland, however, and prove my theory."

"Oh." I felt a sudden pang. "Will you go soon?"

He gave me a keen glance, probably considering my reaction. "Perhaps I should. Now that word of my project has been exposed, other writers as well as treasure seekers may be on my trail. There might be danger for me here."

What did Paul mean? How could the book be such a danger? What did it actually contain? Some hidden meaning? I maintained a thoughtful uneasiness while Paul and Tommy talked at length about the prince. Finally, when I picked up my cup of tea, it was too cold to drink.

The little parlor had grown full of evening shadows. The firelight flickered on the dark wood-paneled walls and wrinkled black leather chairs. Through the monk's cloth draperies, a sudden flicker of gaslight bloomed outside in the street.

Paul pulled a nearby cord to summon Mrs. Barker for some hot tea, but before she came, his face grew more stern than I had ever seen it and his voice dropped to a whisper. "Listen to me, both of you, there must not be a word to anyone about this matter we've discussed today. Already, too many hints are leaking out. Men have been killed for clues to such an important historical discovery." He raised a long, lean finger as he eyed us. "Now, do I have your promises for secrecy?"

Tommy and I both nodded solemnly.

2

I was half-inclined to believe that Paul had developed a melodramatic fixation where his family legend was concerned. But, of course, I honored his request and didn't even tell my parents about the Prince's Gold. I merely said that Paul must go to Scotland pretty soon for more research on his book, which caused them to exchange a worried glance.

Paul now invited me to his home more and more often. He also started sending me flowers because I once said that I loved them so much and had no garden of my own. The ones he sent were often delicate sprays of pink hawthorne, early daffodils from the Scilly Isles, or a little pot of lilies of the valley, whose meaning I later learned meant "new love."

I should have realized what was happening, but I didn't.

One morning I was perched on my high stool at a slanted desk, complete with inkwell, steel nib pens, and several documents awaiting my transcribing, when a delivery boy arrived. He handed me a sealed envelope from Paul and a most extravagant bouquet of purple hothouse violets. I sniffed the flowers with delight, then slit the sealing wax on the accompanying note. I read it with a feeling of dismay and astonishment that mounted with each word.

My Dearest Courtney:

Lacking the courage to make this declaration in person, I must acquaint you with my heart's desire in this cowardly fashion. I trust you will forgive me.

Whether you are aware of it or not, my high regard for you and enjoyment of your company have deepened into love and now I wish with all my heart to have your hand in marriage. Are you surprised, my dear? Or dare I hope that you return my sentiments? Oh, how I long for that most felicitous state of mutual love for us.

Now that this note has taken the edge of shock from my proposal, please come to tea today and we'll discuss it further. If you are amenable—and do not think that I am too old for you—I will call upon your parents and formally request your hand in marriage.

Yours in love and hope, Paul Dunburn.

I sat very still for a long moment, staring blankly at the sheet of paper, my mind awhirl. I was hardly able to absorb its contents and continued to read it over several times. Finally, I slid down from my stool, removed my paper cuffs, and darted up the rear stairs to the private living quarters that my family and I shared.

I found my father seated beside the window, his legs wrapped in a woolen rug, while he sipped a steaming cup of chamomile tea. His eyes turned from the noisy city street below to regard me with a welcoming smile.

"Come here, my dear. A group of boys are playing a

game of mumblety-peg. Watch them flip the knife. They're very good—"

"Not now, Papa. I—I have something to show you." I set the violets on a table and held out the note to him. "Just look at this."

He peered at me, bald head to one side. "The flowers are from Paul, I wager. But the note—you are not smiling. Is he perhaps about to leave for Scotland? I recall you mentioned the possibility."

"No, Papa, he is not leaving yet. But he sent me this letter just now. Please read it."

I watched him anxiously as he adjusted a pair of steel-rimmed spectacles on his slender nose and read and then reread the note from Paul, his tufted eyebrows elevating.

"By Jove!" he exclaimed. "Did this take you by as much surprise as it does me?"

"Oh, yes. Yes, it did." I clasped my fingers tightly. "Paul never even *hinted* at anything like this. We've become close friends and enjoyed some lovely visits, but—but—" I shrugged helplessly and shook my head.

Papa studied me. "Do you love Paul Dunburn enough to marry him? It's a woman's most important decision, my dear, and you must be very sure you want to spend the rest of your life beside him."

I bit my lip and looked away. "Papa, I don't love Paul. Not—not like that."

I went to the window and drew back the lace curtain, barely aware of the clattering of hooves on cobblestones, vendors' raucous cries, the sudden chiming of the new Big Ben . . .

"I don't know how to tell him. He's been so good to me." My lips trembled as I spoke. "How can I hurt him? And yet . . . I fear I must. . . ."

Papa raised his voice. "Lily, dear, come in here for a moment. I have a letter to show you."

Mama hurried from the kitchen, a small, gray-blond

person with a careworn, though still pretty face. Her first glance was a quick survey to see that Papa was all right, then reassured on that score, she turned to me.

"A letter? Has the buyer of the shop changed his mind?" A constant worrier, was Mama.

"No, no, Lily," Papa answered soothingly. "This is an entirely different matter. Don't be alarmed. Paul Dunburn has declared himself to Courtney. Read his letter."

Mama gave a little gasp. "Oh, daughter—a—a declaration?" Her eyes dropped to the note. Like Papa, she read the contents twice.

Then she looked at me, her eyes alight, the rosy ribbons on her mobcap suddenly aflutter. "Oh, heavens— why, Paul Dunburn is a splendid man. He does you great honor, Courtney. What is your answer going to be?"

Her voice was hopeful and I knew that both my parents would be so relieved if I could be delivered into the safekeeping of a good husband before their imminent departure.

"I know how fine he is, Mama. And how much honor I've received. I—I'm very fond of him, but— but—"

"She doesn't love him, Lily," Papa stated flatly. "And, besides, the man is old enough to be her father. Courtney is so young, so inexperienced with men. This is her first proposal. There will be others, never fear."

"Of—of course." Mama nodded, her face falling. I could tell that she suppressed a sigh.

"Mama, Papa, perhaps I could think about it . . ."

Mama glanced up quickly. But Papa knew better and shook his head with quiet understanding. I wanted desperately to send them away happy without worrying about me: a young woman alone in a wicked city with no other relatives.

But marriage was so . . . final. And it carried with

it all the intimacy and subservience that a woman must give her lawfully wedded husband. It gave me a hollow feeling of dismay even to contemplate it. A marriage without love would be like a prison.

"At least you and Paul can stay close friends, can't you?" Papa asked.

"Oh, yes! Yes, indeed," I answered, thankful that I could reassure them on this point, at least. "I value Paul's friendship more than words can say."

"Many a good marriage started out with less," Mama ventured.

"I'm really sorry. I know how much this alliance would have pleased you both." I smiled wistfully. "Well, I must get back to the shop. Please put these violets in some water, will you, Mama? I'm having tea with Paul today and I'll wear a few of them."

I turned away and started down the stairs, feeling as though a stone lay in my breast where a beating heart should be. But how could one force love, even for such a worthy man as Paul?

"Tell him we—" Mama called after me. I heard Papa murmur to her. "Just tell him we send good wishes," she amended.

Oh, Paul, I thought, how I would like to be in love with you. Someone so kind, so dependable, so talented and respected. A handsome, intelligent man of impeccable background. What was I looking for? Romance such as that found in fiction tales? Those heroes who appeared in *Jane Eyre* or *Wuthering Heights?* Men whose fiery glance created such a passionate response that all the world was lost for love?

I knew that was utter nonsense and I thrust the idiotic notions from my mind. But it was hard for me to concentrate on my work that day and I made several ink blots that required a whole clean start.

Finally, we closed the shop and I went apprehensively to tea, wondering what to say so that Paul would not be hurt too much. I had pinned some of his lovely, fragrant violets on my fur collar to show how much I valued them.

That was a mistake.

My heart was thudding and my mouth felt dry when I joined Paul in the firelit parlor. The tea tray already was in place, a quilted cozy enveloping the pot and linen napkins covering several plates. Tommy was not present.

Paul greeted me, dressed in fine array. He eyed the flowers on my shoulder with an eager flush of pleasure.

Oh, how I hated to erase that smile from his dear face! Then he looked into my eyes and the happy look faded to resignation even before I spoke.

"The answer is no, isn't it? My dear, don't look so troubled. And please don't cry." He took my trembling hands in his and pressed them gently. "I never meant to upset you, Courtney dear."

I brushed my eyes, and for a moment, it was hard for me to speak. "Paul—I—I'm so honored and I wish with all my heart that it could be otherwise. There's no one else, of course. And perhaps there never will be. Not as fine as you. But though you are my very dearest friend, I'm just not—not—"

"—in love with me." His smile was twisted. "I guess I dreamed a foolish dream. How could you return my feelings? I am twenty-six years older than you, a dedicated writer with a child. And you are so young, so sweet, so innocent and lovely. And, yes, in your heart, romantic. Am I not right? I am fully persuaded that you dream of a young man, strong and virile, who will sweep you off your feet someday."

I turned my face away. "No, Paul, I have no such foolish, romantic dreams. I'm past that time, if I was ever in it. But I feel that if I agreed to marry you, I would be cheating you. Instead of just friendship, deep affection, and admiration—which is all I have to give —you should also have a woman's complete love and warm response—to—to her wifely duties."

I flushed because I had been so frank and stole a glance at him. Seeing his downcast expression, my heart smote me afresh and I said impulsively, "Perhaps I might change my mind. Can you give me a little time to—think it over?"

His smile was rather wry. "I doubt if I'll suddenly appeal to the romantic side of your nature. But there, don't worry, dear. For now, we'll just stay friends and say no more about it."

He raised my hands to his lips, and for the first time, kissed them. His touch was as dry and fleeting as a moth's wing and I felt suffused with pity.

At any rate, I thought, I had been honest with him. He wouldn't have countenanced a lie. Paul was a worldly man and easily could have seen through any pretense of love that I might make.

At least, we were to keep on seeing each other. I clung to that comforting thought as we sat down to tea. Paul, with his unfailing kindness and understanding, tried his best to put me at my ease. He almost succeeded as we ate and talked of other matters.

So the most momentous day of my life—so far— drew to a close.

I didn't know it then, but the first skein had been woven that would eventually take me on my way to Castlecove.

3

I hardly had any time to ponder Paul's proposal in the days that followed. Events moved swiftly as my parents packed for their trip, saw me established in a nearby guest house, and finished negotiations with the Goughs, new owners of the Copy House.

The Goughs were a large, rather coarse-featured pair and I felt uneasy at the thought that soon I would be working with them. Mr. Gough constantly studied my face, hair, and person with a thoroughness I found most unsettling, while his wife eyed us both with inimical suspicion.

I kept all my worries from my parents, however. They had enough to handle with preparations for the move to Spain where my mother's cousin, a recent widow, had offered them a home. The warmer clime was expected to work wonders for my father's cough and all of us were filled with hope.

Naturally, my parents felt sad to leave me, but Paul had promised them he would look out for me and they were greatly comforted by this. I knew that Mama, at least, still harbored a romantic hope for me—that I would become so lonesome I would change my mind and turn to Paul.

Paul never referred to his proposal, but after my parents left, I knew he grew increasingly worried about my welfare. When he viewed my new drab quarters in the dismal guest home where I now slept and ate unsavory meals, he arranged to bring me to his house each day for supper, afterward sending me back in a hansom cab when darkness fell. I felt extremely grateful for his kindness and did not refuse, telling myself it would be only temporary until I had adjusted to my new life.

However, Paul's concern for me also extended to my employers. And I was very apprehensive about them, too.

Mr. Gough was becoming more of a problem every day. I felt certain that here was a rough bully who would prey on any female that he could. He hovered over me, pressing close, and touching whenever possible. But he had to evade the eagle eye of Mrs. Gough, and at first, her attention to us seldom wavered.

Finally, seeing how my cold reserve held her swinish mate at bay and the close watch Paul kept on me, she unfortunately relaxed her constant vigilance.

That led to one disastrous day.

Mrs. Gough had left that afternoon for a visit to the dentist and her husband and I were alone in the front shop. I was busy copying a Last Will and Testament for a client, while Mr. Gough bent over an open book of the accounts. I observed uneasily from the corner of my eye how frequently his head turned toward me.

I kept as still as possible, hoping to evade his further notice while I wrote quickly. Perhaps in a few minutes, I could slip out on an errand until Mrs. Gough returned.

It was becoming more and more apparent to me that

soon I would be forced to seek another position. However, first I intended to save as much money as possible so I could take my time while looking for new employment. I never would work for people like the Goughs again.

Perhaps Paul could help me find a place. Now, there was a good idea. I put down my pen and stared thoughtfully at the wall. It was time to confide in Paul about my problem, anyway.

I had confirmation of this when I heard a faint noise behind me and a big hand dropped heavily upon my shoulder. I gave a start of fear.

"Hey, are you dreamin' about your sweetheart, then? I'll bet you have some cozy times now that Ma and Pa are gone." Gough's coarse chuckle smote my ear, his breath smelling of ancient ale. "I can give you good times, too, my girl. What say? We got a lot of space alone today and—"

"Take your hand away." I spoke between gritted teeth, my fingers clasping the edge of the desk with whitened knuckles. "At once! Do you hear me?"

"Naw, then, don't act hoity-toity with me. I'm not so bad. In fact, in certain ways, I'm very good." His thick finger drew a suggestive path along my spine. His other hand jerked at the snood confining my long hair, allowing it to tumble down around my shoulders. The next instant, I was horrified to feel his hot, wet mouth pressed against my neck, rubbing back and forth.

With a shriek, I sprang to my feet. The stool crashed backward and the inkpot tilted on the floor, spattering his trousers.

He uttered an obscene oath and grabbed me savagely, turning me so that one of his hands was free to tear at the buttons on my blouse, before plunging it in against my flesh.

"You owe me something now," he snarled, squeezing fiercely. "And, by God, I'm gonna have my due. Back here we'll go—"

Twisting and pounding, I tried to rake his skin, kick his shins, while screaming threats into his reddened, panting face. Nothing fazed him. My blouse gaped open to the waist, the hair streaming over my bare shoulders as he dragged and shoved and half-carried me toward a curtained alcove in the rear.

Almost out of my mind with frenzied fear, I could hardly believe it when the fiend's arms suddenly fell away and he staggered back, yelling and clutching at his head.

Mrs. Gough stood behind us, an iron-headed, furled umbrella in her hand. Her fiery glance transfixed her husband. "Up to your old tricks, you blasted bugger? I'll fix you!"

Whimpering and wiping blood from his head, my attacker cringed from his avenging spouse like the craven coward that he was.

Without looking at me, she spat: "And you, missy, pull up your clothes and get out of here. And don't come back. We won't be hiring a pretty, young one next time, that's for certain."

"My—my wages—" I gasped, dragging my blouse up to my neck and fastening it as best I could.

"Take the money in the drawer. Then get out!"

She advanced on the cowering bully. "How far were you about to go, old beauty? And with a young virgin, too!" She raised her weapon, and with yelps and howls, the pair fled up the stairs.

Though I was trembling in every limb, and feeling both sick and faint, I managed to secure my cape, stuffing the wages in my reticule before I left. Then down the street I fled, just one destination in my mind.

A hansom cabby called out to me. Perhaps he thought I was a prostitute from my disheveled state.

Other people stared. I didn't care or even glance at them. Almost running blindly, I tore on until I reached Paul's house. How I prayed that he'd be home!

Mrs. Barker opened the door and her mouth fell open as she took in my condition: tousled, unbound hair, torn and rumpled gown, fevered face . . .

"M-Mr. Dunburn—" I choked, stumbling inside. "Is he at home?"

"Yes!" She put out her hand. "Oh, miss, are you all right? Can I get you something?"

"N-not just now, thank you." Trying to subdue my labored breaths, I stepped to the hall mirror, pushing my hair in place as best I could, smoothing down my clothes. However, there was nothing I could do about my ashen face, my wide and staring eyes, the shaking of my hands.

I left the hall and found Paul seated by the fire in his book-lined study, gazing absently at a small coal fire. He dropped his quill and stood up quickly with a surprised exclamation when I burst in.

"Oh, Paul, I had to come—it was so awful! That Mr. Gough—he—he—"

Instantly, Paul had me in his arms, but before my head dropped to his shoulder, I saw his face whiten with a look I'd never seen before.

"What happened?" he whispered hoarsely.

Desperately, I fought for self-control. "He—he tried to take advantage of me today while his wife was out. She returned unexpectedly and—and stopped him just in time."

Paul's arms tightened and he cried, "I'll take a horse whip to him!"

"No, no, it's all right now. I'm quite unharmed—just frightened. I'm never going back there, though."

"Indeed, you're not!"

After a few minutes, while he held me tight against him, we both grew calmer. Then, divesting me of my cape, Paul put me in a chair close to the fire. He summoned Mrs. Barker, speaking softly to her in the hallway.

When he sat down again, I filled him in as briefly as possible. I noticed that his face looked stern and hard, quite different from his usual mild expression. As for myself, I now felt drained of all emotion and wished that I could just sit here by the fire with Paul. Forever.

"Would you like some brandy?" he asked, after a moment. He rose, going to a sideboard. "I know I would."

I declined and watched Paul quickly quaff the amber contents of a crystal glass. I felt surprised. I hadn't even known he kept strong spirits in the house. He must be very affected by what had nearly happened to me today.

"I thought at first I could handle Mr. Gough on my own, but he's been getting bolder and bolder." I shivered and held my hands out to the fire, still feeling cold. "Just before this happened, I had decided to seek another position and ask your help in finding one. I hope I didn't do wrong—visiting my troubles on you."

"Of course you didn't do wrong," Paul answered almost roughly. "Who could you go to for help except the man who loves you? I don't want you to hesitate for a single second if I can aid you. Whatever the reason, I stand ready. Do you hear?"

"Yes, Paul. Thank you."

He leaned down, his expression softening. Perhaps he intended to kiss me. But his eye fell on my torn lace collar, the bruise upon my neck, the buttons missing from my poplin waist. His fingers bit into my shoulder. *"Did he do this?"*

I touched his cheek. "Paul, let us forget it now. Please! I'll never see the Goughs again. I'm quite unharmed except for the fright he gave me. And I think he'll have a very sore head before his wife is finished with him."

Paul gave a groan and drew me up into his arms where he held me closely. "Oh, my dearest, can't you change your mind now and marry me? I would take such good care of you. We'd go away to Scotland soon—"

I felt so tempted then, I almost yielded to his wishes. But I cared too much for Paul to take advantage of his love.

"Oh, Paul, you're so good—so dear to me," I whispered. "I wish I could marry you, but I—it still would not be fair to you."

He sighed. "You don't feel the slightest stir of passion for me. I know that. But perhaps in time . . ." He held me off. "We could be wed, but make it a marriage in name only for a while. Do you know what I mean?"

My face flushed. I looked away and nodded. I understood his meaning and the kind spirit that prompted it. However, I also knew that in time he'd want a marriage in truth. He was too much in love with me to wait forever.

Marriage with Paul as a real husband—what would it be like? Mama had talked to me in her hedging, roundabout fashion, but I was worldly enough to know what she was trying to say. You couldn't live in the heart of London and be ignorant of certain facts.

Fortunately, Mrs. Barker entered then with tea and Paul didn't pursue the matter. He talked about his book, his home at Castlecove, a recent visit to the zoo in Regent's Park where Tommy had a memorable ride on a live elephant.

But just before I left in a cab hailed by Paul, he said one more thing. Probably the last argument that he could think to summon. "Tommy would love to have you for a stepmother. He has said so. He talks about you frequently."

"Perhaps, perhaps," I stuttered.

He put his hand upon my arm. "Not now, my dearest. You are still upset. Don't worry about a thing. Rest and then tomorrow come to tea. I'll be here and I promise that nothing more will be said about my proposal for the time being." He brushed my forehead with his cool, dry lips before handing me into the cab and slipping some coins into the driver's box.

I lay back on the worn, black leather, drained and weary. So much had happened recently: the wrenching departure of my parents, the lonely existence in the guest house, the daily apprehension I experienced working for the unsavory Goughs. And then today! Thank heaven, it was over.

That's what I thought. But I was wrong.

As I started up the walk toward my door, a figure detached itself from the shadows. For some odd reason, the nearest streetlamp was unlit and all I could discern was a long, black cloak, a wide-brimmed hat.

Then came a hissing voice. "Miss, wait . . . I have an interesting proposition for you."

I heard no more. My feet flew up the steps and I burst through the unlocked door before the shadowed figure even budged.

I shoved the latch in place with shaking fingers, then put my eye to a crack beside the window shade. All I could see was a black cape swirling across the street as the figure disappeared around the corner.

I was certain it was Gough. He knew the address where I lived and was not going to let me get away so easily. Trembling in every limb, I flew upstairs to bed.

The next day, I agreed to marry Paul.

4

A few days later, Paul and I were married in a simple civil ceremony at the Registry Office, attended only by his son with Mrs. Barker and another clerk for witnesses.

Tommy was in the highest spirits for which I was very grateful. He immediately began calling me "Mama Courtney." Since he didn't remember his natural mother, I promised in my heart to fill that vacancy to the best of my ability. I knew that already a strong affection bound us close.

Paul was becoming dearer all the time. It was so wonderful to be cared for, surrounded by every comfort, and also to know that my parents were delighted. There was no question of their coming to the wedding, but they wrote to each of us at once, sounding ecstatic in their congratulations.

Paul also sent the news to his family at Castlecove. After several days a warm reply arrived with congratulations and the hope that the three of us would pay a visit to them. Paul had several reasons for the trip to

Scotland, not only to see his parents and the ancestral home but also to research his book. Preparations soon were underway. Tommy would come with us as he had never seen his grandparents. Mrs. Barker (who had accepted me with apparent pleasure) was to take care of the London home until our return.

Paul gave me a wedding band, a string of pearls with matching earrings, and then bought me clothing to keep out the northern chill of Scotland: a fur-lined, hooded cape, stout half-boots, dresses of fine wool, others of rich, thick velvet. He also insisted on buying me some more elaborate gowns of silk and satin and I couldn't refuse, not knowing what my life might entail as a guest in a laird's castle.

When the garments arrived from the Bond Street seamstresses, my bedroom was a bower of color and delight and I felt very happy. Fervently, I hoped that Paul was happy, too. He had given me so much. In return, I had brought him only my fond companionship. I was sure he entertained a hope for future wedded bliss and after a while I wondered . . . was it now the time to become his wife in deed as well as fact? My heartbeats quickened. Surely Paul would be a gentle, patient lover. And at Castlecove we probably would be assigned one room as newlyweds. What would we do then?

The next night, I made up my mind to accept my wifely duties and tried to subdue my quivering apprehension. I bathed, brushed out my hair until it formed a pale gold curtain on the shoulders of a white silk shift that fell in clinging draperies about my form. I slid my arms into a brocade outer-robe woven in tones of bronze and peach, also a recent gift from Paul.

Drawing a deep breath, I stared into my full-length pier glass, noticing that my face looked fevered and my eyes had a most unusual glitter. What should I say? How must I act? Perhaps the words would come to me and Paul would understand what I was trying to convey.

Finally, I left my room, trembling as I started down the stairs. Paul was working late, as usual, in his study. I wondered if he had to drive himself to a point of fatigue so he could sleep, unmindful of the young virgin wife lying in her bed just beyond his door.

Poor Paul . . . he had been so good to me. It was time that I reciprocated.

I had nearly reached the lower hall when the doorbell rang, startling me so that I froze, clinging to the banister. Fear jolted through me. It was ten thirty. Who could be calling at this hour? I still had moments when I feared that Gough would find me.

The doorbell jangled once again, and when Paul emerged from his study, his name fell from my lips.

He glanced upward briefly. "Go back to bed, my dear. This is someone I expected. A certain professor interested in my work."

Not Gough, then. Someone else. As I retreated upward into the shadows, Paul opened the door and I caught a glimpse of a bearded figure in a large, black cape, a wide, soft hat obscuring his upper face.

Could this be the man who had accosted me at the guest house? What had he tried to say to me? Something about a "proposition." Now he was here, late at night, and Paul had ushered him into his study.

Uneasily, I crept closer, trying to hear their voices, but the door was shut fast and I couldn't make out any words. However, I still waited on the stairs.

At last, the study door burst open. The cloaked figure swirled into the hall, his back toward me as he jammed the black hat on his head. He jerked open the front door and the cold night air swept in.

Paul called after him in a loud, agitated tone, "I'll never change my mind, so don't return!"

"We'll see," a deep voice shouted in reply.

Then the door banged shut and Paul stood back against it, breathing deeply.

I ventured close, but I had to touch his hand before he was aware of me. "Paul, what is it? Who is that man? I think I saw him one night near that guest house where I stayed. He called to me, something about a 'proposition,' but I was alarmed and ran inside."

"Is that so?" Paul straightened wearily. "Well, he is one of the vultures who learned about my book. He wanted to *collaborate*. His information for mine. As though I'd let anybody share my triumph!"

His eyes flamed angrily, then he made a conscious effort, it seemed, to relax. "Why aren't you in bed, my love? It's late."

I dropped my head as my hair swung forward and I put my hands upon his chest. "Paul . . . I thought . . . perhaps tonight . . . you'd like to come to me." My voice dropped to a whisper in an agony of shyness. "Tonight, you could become my real husband . . . if you want to . . ."

Paul brushed back my hair and put his hand beneath my chin. Then he smiled. "Thank you, my lovely girl. You make me very happy. But, dear heart, I'm not a young man anymore and tonight I have a lot to do. I realize now how important it is that I go to Castlecove and prove my theory so I can get the facts published as quickly as possible."

I must have looked rather daunted after all my preparations and the effort of winding up my courage.

Paul gently kissed my lips. "I do love you very much. Perhaps I'll be up later. If not tonight, it will be soon, I promise you."

But though I stayed awake, tossing anxiously for many hours, Paul never came.

And after that night, it was too late.

* * *

The next day, two policemen arrived at the front door. Paul lay between them on a stretcher, a bandage on his head. A doctor followed close behind carrying a cross-marked satchel.

I must have cried out for the little man thrust forward and caught my arm. "Mrs. Dunburn? I am Dr. Fraser. Your husband had an accident a few blocks away."

"Bring him in," I managed to gasp. "Oh, dear heaven—"

The men carried Paul to the parlor couch, and if they spoke, it didn't register with me at all. I was dimly aware that they had left as I bent over Paul. "He—he isn't dead, is he?" I whispered in agony.

"No, not yet. But I fear it won't be long."

I pressed a hand against my heart. "What—what happened?"

"I saw him stumble off the curb into the path of a wildly running pair of cart horses. They vanished down the street and the area became a swarm of people. When I reached your husband's side, I could see that he'd been struck on the head and spine by hooves and it was no use taking him to the hospital. He managed to give me his name and address, then lapsed into a semiconscious state. I assure you he is not in any pain."

"There's nothing you can do?" I cried, dropping to my knees beside the couch.

"No. I fear he hasn't long to live. Steady now, my dear. Do you have some person to be with you? Would you like a sedative powder?"

"No, thank you." I choked. "S-somebody will be here soon." Mrs. Barker had taken Tommy to the market with her and I expected they would be back shortly.

I pulled myself together enough to thank the kindly

doctor, then when he left, I sponged Paul's face, drew an afghan over him, and sat down by his side to wait.

Dearest Paul, I prayed, oh, please don't die! Don't leave me now. But in my heart I felt there was no hope and tears streamed down my face unchecked.

Finally, his eyelids fluttered open and Paul spoke to me in a breathy whisper that I had to bend down close to hear.

"Dear heart, you must be brave. I know I haven't long to live—"

"No, no," I sobbed. "Don't worry, dearest, everything will be all right."

His hand fluttered and I enfolded it tightly against my breast. I smoothed his hair, managing to control my voice as best I could. "What can I do for you? Is there anything you want?"

He then spoke clearly but with the greatest effort. "My love, I heard what the doctor said. Listen carefully. We have so little time—"

His voice faded and I put my ear down to his lips. "Don't go into mourning—too young—"

"I won't," I answered huskily.

"You'll take care of Tommy?"

"Of course. Always!"

"Go with him to . . . Scotland . . ."

"What?"

"Yes, yes, you must prove my theory . . . and finish my work. Promise . . . promise . . ."

"But I don't know how—"

"My notes . . . all there . . . search the beloved place . . ." His breath grew labored. "Water . . ."

I started to rise. "You wish a drink?"

But his hand caught mine with a fevered grip, the last surge of his ebbing strength. "No! By the water . . . summerhouse. Find . . . gold . . ."

I felt his fingers slacken and terror swept me like an avalanche of ice. "Paul! Paul!" I screamed.

"Farewell, my dearest love." He smiled, closed his eyes with a deep sigh, and died.

Sobbing wildly, my head dropped on his chest.

5

Our household now was engulfed in grief, but I was forced to keep a strong grip on my emotions to help Tommy face his loss. The poor child was so frightened and bewildered. I tried to find chores for him to occupy his young mind and Mrs. Barker was a great help in this matter, taking him for walks, keeping him busy in the kitchen baking sweets, and having him visit other children.

For the sum of two shillings, I sent a message about Paul's death via the Electric Telegraph Company to his family in Scotland. Since the line went only as far as Edinburgh at this time, I didn't know how soon I'd hear from them.

I also informed my parents of the sad news, stating that I didn't need them to return. There were people helping me and soon Tommy and I would depart for Scotland on a visit to his grandparents. I told them that Paul had urged this with his dying breath.

I had to arrange for Paul's interment and regarding this I visited his lawyer. I had met Mr. Humphrey when Paul had him draw up a new will just after our marriage. He now told me that Paul's first wife was buried back in Scotland but Paul had wished to be buried next to me in London and had made provisions for this. Therefore, I had Paul's body carried to a funeral establishment. I was puzzled that no answer had come from Castlecove regarding Paul's death, but I'd heard how erratic telegram and letter service could be. After three days passed, I went ahead with a simple burial service. His publisher, Mr. Holt, attended, as well as Mr. Humphrey, Mrs. Barker, Tommy, and myself.

Though everybody was exceedingly kind and helpful, I now felt that much depended on me alone. I think I grew emotionally a great deal at that time. Grief and horror still gripped me, tears fell when I was alone, but decisions must be made. I also had Paul's dying wishes to consider.

Carefully, I began to sort his manuscript and try to make some sense of his last notes. There were lots of Gaelic words, references to Scottish history, but nowhere a clear-cut pathway to the Prince's Gold.

It was too much for me to fathom in my present state. Wearily, I locked his original copy away in my trunk. I knew I must undertake the Highland journey soon. Tommy and I had been nearly packed before Paul died and now the trip would be a welcome distraction for us both. The family at Castlecove had sounded quite sincere in their desire to see us.

I purchased first-class tickets for the train trip to Edinburgh. After that, we would have to hope for help from Castlecove or hire some conveyance to carry us across the Grampian Mountains. Perhaps a boat would go around the waterways called firths and we could arrive that way.

Sometimes, in my weaker moments, it seemed almost too much and I would wake with tears upon my cheeks after dreaming about Paul. How glad I was that I had offered him my love before he died. The least I could do now was try to carry out his wishes and somehow establish his authority about the legend of Castlecove.

With that in mind, I visited his publisher, Mr. Holt, a lean, gray-haired man with a shuttered face. I raised my widow's veil, my only sign of mourning, though my gown and cloak were of sober hues, my wedding band the only piece of jewelry.

I took a seat, then stated my business calmly and succinctly. "Before he died, Paul asked me to prove his theory regarding the lost gold donated to the cause of Bonnie Prince Charlie. My husband was of the opinion that it was still secreted somewhere at Castlecove."

Mr. Holt bent a keen eye on me. "I must admit that I have been concerned about the ending of Paul's book. I knew that he hoped to prove his theory, but after word leaked out that he believed the treasure to be intact at his ancestral home, he suddenly became very secretive. He refused to divulge his findings, only saying that he must prove them first. Then publish." He stared at me narrowly. "Do you know the answer, Mrs. Dunburn? Did Paul confide in you at the end?"

I sighed and shook my head. "He only said that I must read his notes. So far, they have told me nothing." I cleared my throat. "Perhaps the book will have to be published just as it is with the mystery unsolved."

Actually, I had no intention of not complying with Paul's last request and would do all in my power to prove his theory. But hadn't Paul stressed secrecy?

Mr. Holt fiddled with a silver inkwell, but his eyes did not leave my face. "An unsolved mystery would drastically affect the book's potential sales. It is scheduled for our fall printing so there is not much time. Could not another person go over Paul's last notes?

Perhaps someone knowledgeable in that field? He might discover what you have missed."

"A collaborator? I think not yet." I recalled Paul's feelings in that matter, his agitation with the strange, cloaked figure who had suggested such a thing. "I have placed his notes in safekeeping and probably will carry them to Scotland. In a few days, I am traveling to Castlecove to see Paul's family. When I return, we'll discuss this further."

"Good. Something may develop there to aid you in your search."

I rose, drawing on my black silk gloves. "That's very doubtful, Mr. Holt. At any rate, Paul wished Tommy to see his grandparents. That's the main reason for my journey. The boy needs a change of scene. His father's death was very hard on him." My own lips quivered for a second.

"And on you, also, Mrs. Dunburn, being so newly married." Mr. Holt sounded warmer than he had so far and his eyes gave me a rather masculine appraisal. "I know Paul cared a great deal for you. He was so happy when he told me about his coming nuptials. And I certainly can see why."

I couldn't speak. My throat suddenly was too full for words.

"Do you need any funds at this time, Mrs. Dunburn? An advance, perhaps, on Paul's new book?"

Lowering my veil, I thanked him and declined. There was a fair-sized bank account in my name and I could draw on that.

But as I left the building, I wondered uneasily about my future earning capacity. I now had Tommy to support, the house to maintain, as well as Mrs. Barker. What would I do when the current funds ran out? Should I try for work in another copy house? Penmanship seemed to be the only talent I possessed.

Well, I would deal with that on our return from

Scotland. Too many other matters demanded my immediate attention. Sometimes it all seemed overwhelming. At other times, a sort of desperate courage filled me and I vowed I would carry out my new responsibilities the best way I knew how.

I took an omnibus and hurried home. When I reached the house, as I turned the key in the lock, I became aware of heavy, determined footsteps that halted when I spun around. Fear darted through me. Could it be—Gough?

"I'm sorry," said a deep, Scottish voice. "Did I startle you? I'm a relative of Paul Dunburn."

"I—I thought that I'd been followed."

I lifted my veil and our eyes locked, both studying the other. Though he wore a conventional British suit and short Inverness cape, I believed this might be Paul's cousin who managed the estate.

Confirming this, he doffed his gray top hat. "I am Dugan MacInnis. Are you my cousin's widow?"

"Yes. Come in, please." I felt a great relief that someone had come at last from Castlecove.

In the hallway, my visitor placed his hat, cape, and a small valise on a chair, then followed me into the parlor where I rang for Mrs. Barker, requesting that she fetch some tea. Before observing Mr. MacInnis in any detail, I excused myself and hurried upstairs to remove my wraps and smooth my pale hair back to its dark blue snood.

Curiosity mixed with excitement sped my feet down to the parlor where I found the large Scot sipping calmly from a glass. "Your housekeeper kindly fetched me a wee dram. Will you join me—er—Mrs. Dunburn?"

I shook my head. There had been a noticeable pause before my name and a coolness in his Scottish tones.

He was a very strong-looking man, almost overwhelming, with a craggy face, and eyes of an extreme darkness, heavy-lidded, yet keen and searching. But it was his hair that struck me most, being of a glorious deep russet like a burnished autumn leaf.

As the silence stretched, his eyes never left me and I felt that he now knew every detail about my appearance from head to toe in just this short observation.

I cleared my throat. "Did the family receive my telegram, Mr. MacInnis?"

"Aye, and the letter that preceded. My aunt sends her apologies for not answering more fully, but the roads were impassable for a while and her husband has been very ill."

"I'm sorry to hear that. Is he better?"

He nodded, sipped his drink, eyeing me over the rim, then drawled, "I bring you our condolences."

"Thank you." Had he come all this way just for that?

"Where is Tommy?" he asked abruptly.

"Visiting a child nearby. He'll be home soon."

Another silence fell. I wished desperately that Mrs. Barker would hurry up and bring the tea.

Suddenly, he leaned toward me. "The news of your marriage came as a great surprise. Even more surprising since I've met you."

"Why?" I shifted in my chair and drew back from his close regard.

"You are so very young. And quite pretty. Also an obvious gentlewoman—or a clever actress." His voice grew harsh. "Why did you really marry Paul, a man probably thirty years your senior? Did you love him?"

I stared at him in quick resentment. How should I answer this rude man? What did he mean "a clever actress"?

He leaned back in his chair and crossed his legs. "You do not answer. Why not the quick, glib lie? Perhaps you recognize that I can't be lied to. Is that it?"

Fortunately, Mrs. Barker entered then and left us with a well-filled tea tray. Dugan MacInnis rose and helped himself. I took only a cup of tea, annoyed that the cup rattled in its rose-sprigged saucer.

After a few reviving mouthfuls, I was able to reply in a stiff voice. "I really cannot conceive how the relations between Paul and myself are any of your concern. I will say that Paul and I cared deeply for each other. And if you think I married him for gain, I will tell you that his bank account will only last me about a year. Half of everything is for Tommy and I am charged with caring for him."

"It must have been a bitter blow when Paul's earning powers were cut off." He eyed me with his glinting, half-shut gaze, then added softly, "However, there is still the Prince's Gold, you may be thinking."

"I am aware of the lost treasure."

"Of course." His full, strong lips twisted. "But a fairy tale it is at best. The gold's long gone in my opinion. Nobody believes in it at Castlecove."

I pressed my lips together and didn't answer. I was not about to tell him of the mission I had undertaken, and in silence, I watched him consume his sandwiches and cakes.

After a few minutes, he rose and filled his cup again, then spoke to me across his shoulder. "I have come to escort you and Tommy to Castlecove. When do you propose to leave?"

My eyes widened. "Day after tomorrow, but there's no need for you to wait—"

"Och, but there is." He turned and strode to the window, gazing through the lace curtains at the street. It was the first hint of emotion I'd heard in his deep voice with its rough Scottish burr. "Paul was a fine man. And he was my cousin. Tomorrow I wish to pay a visit to his grave. Will you take me there or—"

"I'll take you," I answered quickly, my manner softening. "And if you'd like to spend the night here—"

"I would." He parted the lace curtain. "Here comes young Tom."

I hurried to the door, pleased that Tommy had arrived to ease the rather strained relationship that seemed to have developed with Dugan MacInnis. Perhaps when I knew him better . . .

Tommy's eyes lit up after I introduced his cousin. "Papa told me about you. Have you come all this way to take us back to Scotland?"

"Aye, lad." Dugan shook his hand, quite man-to-man. "Sit here by me and I'll tell you about Castlecove."

I hovered for a minute, then murmured an excuse and left to confer with Mrs. Barker. My thoughts whirled. There would be a whole day to spend with Dugan MacInnis before the *Flying Scot* departed. And two nights. There was only Paul's bed for him to sleep in, right next to my room. And no key to the adjoining door. But why should I need one? The last thing this dour Scot evinced was any pleasure in my person.

After I had told Mrs. Barker about our plans, I went up to my room. I could hear Tommy's piping voice in a constant chatter and the deep answering rumble of his Scottish cousin. This might be a good distraction for Tommy, and for that much, I felt thankful.

However, Mr. MacInnis seemed to believe that I didn't love Paul since I was so much younger and thought that I had married him for gain. I sighed. Well, wasn't that the truth? I had sought to gain security. I sank down on the edge of the bed, lost in thought. I had loved Paul only as a dear and trusted friend and had married him because I was so lonely and afraid of Gough.

But to my credit, I had been honest with Paul. He knew how I felt and he had wanted our marriage just the same. Perhaps he hoped that living together—and eventually sleeping together—would bring about the desired response from me. Well, we had nearly achieved that felicitous relationship when, unfortunately, he was killed. Now, I would never know if he'd been right.

Not for the first time, I wondered if Paul had been pushed deliberately into the path of the thundering team of horses. Someone might have been after his notes about the Prince's Gold, and when the cloaked "professor" couldn't get them one way, he had followed Paul and tried another. With Paul out of the way, he might think I would be more accessible.

It would be no use going to the police. There was not a shred of proof. Dr. Fraser had not voiced any suspicions and had written it off as an accident. As for myself, I had no idea of the professor's whereabouts. Or even what his face looked like. I could only hope fervently that I would never lay eyes on him again.

But later on that night, we had another visitor.

6

When I came downstairs for dinner in my brown Venetian silk trimmed with a cream net inset and short puffed sleeves, I was again subjected to a studied survey by our Scottish guest. His narrowed gaze went from the tiny pearl drops in my ears, past the form-fitting, round-necked waist, to the billowing ruffles sweeping around my velvet slippers.

I had felt satisfied that my attire was elegant yet subdued enough to withstand any criticism. But I was wrong.

"I see you do not wear mourning, madam."

I set my teeth. "Paul told me not to. And, personally, I am of the opinion that an outward show can indicate little about one's inner grief."

"Especially if there is none."

I opened my lips on an angry retort, but it was cut off by the entrance of young Tommy, who went right to his cousin and began to chatter. As the only child of a lonely man, Tommy was far from fitting the popular concept of children who were better "seen but not

heard." Someday I might have to admonish him when
there was company coming, but this was not the time.
I was all in favor of whatever would help the little
fellow through this trying ordeal. I was also relieved
that Tommy's talking helped me to avoid the constant
dueling between MacInnis and myself.

I smothered a sigh of relief when Mrs. Barker signi-
fied that dinner was served. However, before I could
move away, Dugan MacInnis clasped my bare arm in
his large, strong fingers and propelled me from the
room. Color seeped into my face and I knew that he
was looking at me when we settled at the table.

Then, without so much as a by-your-leave, he filled
my wineglass from a silver decanter of Madeira near
his place. "I think you need something to steady your
nerves," he said. "They seemed to be jumping when I
took your arm just now."

"There is nothing wrong with my nerves, Mr.
MacInnis. I am just . . . tired."

"Och, aye?" he drawled.

Whatever the reason, I was glad to sip the wine
while I ate. Mrs. Barker had outdone herself on the
meal, which proceeded from a creamy soup of chicken
reine to turbot with salmon sauce, a saddle of mutton,
potato sprouts, and new peas glistening in mint jelly. I
discovered I was ravenous, and ignoring the dictum
that says a hostess must converse, I applied myself to
the food almost greedily. And silently.

"I see that apparently nothing has spoiled your appetite," Dugan observed dryly.

I took another sip of wine, staring at him over the
golden rim. If anything could, it would be you, I
thought grimly.

Tommy took over at that moment, since he had
cleaned his plate twice. "Cousin Dugan, tell me all the
names again of the people living at Castlecove."

"Can you not remember any that I told you?" Dugan

asked mildly. While not exactly warm with Tommy, he gave him an adult attention that the little fellow seemed to relish.

"Let's see . . . there's Grandpa Hugh, sick in bed. Grandma Margaret. Nora and Davy, your wife's sister and brother. Uh—is that right?"

"Aye, right so far." The red head nodded, glistening in the candle glow.

"Oh, are you married?" I exclaimed, putting down my fork.

"Why? Do you find the idea incomprehensible?"

"Not at all," I lied, and lifted up my glass.

"You didn't tell me your lady's name," Tommy continued. "So I don't know that. But you said there was your girl named Meggie. Will she like me? How old is she?"

"Meggie's eight. And it will depend on you whether or not she likes you."

Not necessarily, I thought. Not if she takes after her father.

I had many questions of my own and wondered if I could get some answers after Tommy left us. He was suddenly nodding sleepily and couldn't even finish his cherry fritters with whipped cream, a favorite dessert of his.

"Come, Tommy, I will take you up to bed," I said.

But MacInnis forestalled this. "Let Mrs. Barker do it." He summoned her by jerking on the bellpull and gave his instructions with a lordly air that I found decidedly irritating. Mrs. Barker didn't seem to mind at all. Maybe she thought he had more rights here than I did. Or at least as much. Perhaps he did, but I resented it just the same.

I was the next person to receive orders from him. "If you are finished, madam, let us adjourn to the parlor. Naturally, I have some questions."

"So do I." My words were brisk and his eyebrow quirked.

As soon as we were seated on the sofa, I wished he had not chosen to sit so close. Probably he thought it gave him more power over me.

He began at once. "Your telegram stated that Paul fell beneath a horse. Were there any witnesses? What were the exact circumstances?"

"A certain Dr. Fraser saw it and brought Paul home after doing all he could for him. The doctor said Paul fell into the path of a team of horses careening wildly around the corner. Such things are all too common in London's crowded streets. Paul felt no pain and died shortly after coming home."

I spoke woodenly, not giving way to my sudden surge of grief. I kept my gaze below Dugan's face, concentrating on the well-tailored gray serge suit, black satin waistcoat, and a cravat tied at his throat in a mixture of blue, red, and yellow.

"Is that a clan plaid?" I asked, forcing my mind away from thoughts of Paul.

"It is the Dunburn plaid. Since I am a relative through my mother's family, I am entitled to wear it."

"Are there quite a lot of relatives at Castlecove?"

"A few. But it is a large estate with many crofters." He folded his arms across his chest and I knew he no longer was going to be diverted from his inquisition. "Now, I would like to hear how you met Paul."

I drew a deep, heaving breath, which he observed with a downward flicker of his heavy eyelids. Why did he unnerve me so? He was just a man and had no jurisdiction over me. Yet he made me feel that, somehow, he might control my future destiny in a way I wouldn't like.

I steadied my voice as best I could. "Paul came to my parents' Copy House, where I was working. He was in a hurry and wanted his manuscript copied in a good, clear hand before sending it to his publisher."

"Was the book finished?"

"Not quite."

"So what will you do with it now that Paul is dead? Fling it in a dustbin?"

"Of course not." I hesitated, turning my gaze toward the fireplace. "I might try to finish it myself. Or perhaps his publisher will know what to do."

"Did Paul think he had solved the mystery of the famous Prince's Gold?" There was a distinct sneer in the Scottish burr.

"I believe he had the solution in his head, but it was not written down and he was very secretive about it. I can discern no clues in the manuscript thus far."

"Perhaps I'll just have a wee glance at his notes tomorrow."

I frowned uneasily. "I don't know . . . Paul said his theory must be kept a secret until he was ready for publication." How could I protect it from this man's prying eyes? "Mr. MacInnis, Paul left his manuscript in my care and asked me not to show it to anybody."

"I see."

Indeed, his narrowed, glittering gaze did seem to see —too much. The whole day had wearied me and I was in no condition for fencing. "If you will excuse me, I fear I must retire. Tomorrow, I'll answer any other questions you may have and I'll also take you to Paul's gravesite. If you need anything further tonight—"

"—I'll ring for Mrs. Barker." We both stood up. "She said I would be in Paul's room—next to yours."

"Do you know the way?"

"She showed it to me."

"Good night, then." I managed to step around him.

Unfortunately, he was not through with me yet. "Paul's first wife, Charlotte, was his own age. A sensible Scottish woman he had known for years. He must have become daft as he grew older to marry someone as young as you."

Thinning my lips, I glanced back over my shoulder. Were all Highlanders as insufferable as this? I had read the novels of Sir Walter Scott and formed an impression of a warlike, roistering, extremely masculine society, freedom-loving and wench-loving. Even the famous Scottish poet Robert Burns had fathered a number of illegitimate children and ruined his health by drinking.

Dugan was now helping himself to a "wee dram." He raised his glass sardonically. I flew upstairs to wedge a chair beneath the knob of our connecting door.

Three hours later, we were both back downstairs in the hall.

I had been awakened by the sound of something falling. Immediately, I sat up in bed, wondering if MacInnis was searching for Paul's notes? A board creaked and I knew the sounds came from the study.

Quick as thought, I pulled on slippers and a dark velour robe and crept down the narrow flight of stairs, straining my eyes and ears for all their worth.

On drawing closer, I observed a flickering light such as a shielded candle makes. "Who's there?" I called out loudly.

At once, the light went out. I heard the sound of running footsteps, the screech of a raised window, and my heart gave a leap of fear.

When I peered cautiously into the study, it was empty with just a faint light coming from the street-lamps and wind billowing the curtains of an open window, a window I was certain had been closed before. I stumbled across the room and looked out, but the area was deserted.

The floor seemed to be filled with tumbled books and papers, which was borne out when I lit a lamp and stared around. Everywhere I looked, I saw astounding havoc.

Suddenly, I gave a yelp of fright before I recognized Dugan's growl behind me. "Whisht! Who's been at the place?"

I whirled around. "I have no idea. I thought at first it might be you!"

"Devil take it, woman! Do I look the sort to creep around destroying things at night?" He strode forward, tossing the end of a tartan shawl across one bare shoulder. The other end was wrapped around his middle. He was a large, arresting sight, but I had no time to waste on admiring muscled arms and tousled auburn hair.

I stared around the room uncertainly. Had someone been searching through Paul's papers? Some midnight intruder?

"Look at yon window. Do you suppose that's where the villain went?" Dugan peered out at the night, then he shut and latched the leaded panes, jerking the draperies back in place.

He turned around. "Well, woman, what is missing?"

"I don't know." I began a search of all the scrambled papers. Drawers had been emptied on the floor, books taken from their shelves . . .

At last, I was forced to admit aloud that the manuscript pages of Paul's book were gone.

Dugan put his fists upon his hips. "Do you have another copy?"

"Yes, I packed the original notes to take to Scotland with me."

His gaze narrowed. "Do you realize what this means? The thief was looking for the last pages about the Prince's Gold. Some fool got wind of Paul's idea and believes the bloody fable."

"Someone came here to see Paul one night who believes it." I described the black-caped professor who had upset both Paul and me.

Dugan nodded thoughtfully. "It could well be the same."

"Well, there's nothing we can do about it." I sighed wearily and began to gather up the books.

"Leave that for the morning," Dugan ordered curtly. "Let's go back to bed."

The words sounded suggestive though I knew it was quite unintentional. But it gave me an almost hysterical urge to laugh, which helped to ease my tension.

"First, I'm going to check all the doors and windows," he informed me.

This time, his high-handed actions were well received. "I would be very grateful. Thank you, Mr. MacInnis."

"Woman, I'm thinking you should call me Dugan."

"Not if you continue to call me *woman*," I answered with asperity.

He gave a kind of grunt that might have indicated anything.

That night I was very glad to have him in the house, and in spite of the alarming incident, I soon fell fast asleep.

7

The Scottish countryside rushed past our window at an alarming rate, but since the scenery was so fascinating, I felt only minor fear of the unnatural speed at which we traveled. Tommy, of course, was ecstatic.

We had a private compartment on the *Flying Scot*, and though Dugan had obtained one for himself, he spent most of the time with us, pointing out the sights.

" 'Tis a bonnie day," he said with satisfaction, gazing at sunlit fields with their peacefully grazing herds, the spring flowers in shades of lavender, white, and yellow, the new-leaved trees, the sparkling streams and lakes . . .

"This is Border Country," he informed us, "scene of many a bloody fight in days of yore, first with the Romans, then with the English. Yet right now, you'd never know it."

I wondered if he still harbored an animosity toward England and its people, the old enemy of Scotland. Maybe that was why I was the recipient of so many dark and enigmatic looks.

After our shared experience in the study when he had told me to call him Dugan, I had expected there would be more harmony between us. But the visit to Paul's gravesite seemed to depress him and he often was as curt to me as ever. I just couldn't call him "Dugan" to his face though it was the name I used to myself whenever I thought about him. Which was quite often.

However, he still was patient with Tommy. On the train ride, apparently he was not averse to imparting knowledge to his inquiring little cousin.

I also listened avidly to Dugan's explanations and even asked some questions: "What is that body of water we passed?"

We had left the rolling farmland and a great deal of beautiful water now met our eyes. "That's a loch, the Scottish word for lake," he stated. "Soon we'll be beside the river Tweed."

"Can we swim in the rivers?" Tommy wanted to know. "Can we catch fish?"

"I think you'd find the waters rather cold this time of year, laddie, though I swim in the cove come summertime. As for fish, it's everywhere. There's nothing like a good Scotch salmon."

"I'm hungry, Mama Courtney." Tommy bounced up and down on the hard plush seats. "I want to eat—right now."

I shivered, drawing my fur-edged cloak tighter around my shoulders. "Perhaps some hot tea would be nice. Isn't there any heat in these trains?"

Dugan's heavy, white lids raised briefly. "In the late springtime? Woman, are you daft?"

However, he went into the corridor and collared a man selling hot tea while I opened the big basket packed by Mrs. Barker. It contained hard-boiled eggs, sandwiches of ham or beef, wedges of yellow cheese, a bag of apples, various jam tarts, and several bottles of lemonade and ginger beer.

Everyone was now ready to eat and we fell to with good appetites. At last, replete and considerably warmer, I asked Dugan about the rest of our trip.

"We'll spend the night in Edinburgh at a hotel," he replied. "The next day we'll hire a coach to take us to the west. It's no' too far."

By your standards, I thought. "Do we have to cross the mountains?"

He shrugged. "Aye."

"Oh, champion!" Tommy cried.

I recalled pictures I had seen. "The Grampians look very big and rugged. I suppose the road is safe?"

Dugan bestowed an exasperated glance on me and nodded briefly.

I said no more about the ensuing journey, but I was very glad that we would break this long train ride with a night in a big, warm hotel with some big, warm meals.

Tommy tugged at Dugan's arm. "Tell me some more about Scotland. Why do they call our people 'clans'?"

"Tommy," I interrupted, "perhaps Mr. MacInnis wants to rest. You've been after him all day."

Dugan quirked an eyebrow. "Now why should I be needing rest? What else are we doing on this trip, pray tell?"

Silenced, I turned my attention to the scenery, but I couldn't help listening when he spoke.

"Tom, I'm thinking your papa must have told you about the clans. You know they're a group of people with a common ancestor."

Tommy nodded. "Yes, and the laird is the chieftain and makes the rules for everybody."

"Not exactly. Only the important decisions."

"I'll be laird someday."

"Aye, quite possibly."

"Will I meet all the clans pretty soon?" Tommy demanded. "I want them to kneel down and say . . . something. What would they say?"

"Scots will not kneel to any man, although they may bow and greet the laird." Dugan then added sternly. "Which is your *grandfather*, laddie. Not you. Not yet."

"What is he like, my grandpa?"

Dugan didn't hesitate. "Kind and just and good. But his heart is weak right now so he bides in his room a lot. He is a Scottish baronet and is called 'Sir Hugh.' Your grandmother has a courtesy title of 'Lady Margaret.' "

Tommy frowned thoughtfully. "Yes, I remember Papa told me that, but it's been a long time since he lived at Castlecove."

I turned my head around. "Strange. He didn't talk to me about the people living there though some must have come after he left Scotland. I never knew his father was a baronet."

"Did you not?" Dugan eyed me sardonically. "You really fell into the jam pot when you married Paul, didn't you?"

Haughtily, I raised my chin. "I expect nothing from the grandparents. This is just a visit because—"

"Oh, Mama Courtney—" Tommy interrupted. "No, no! We're going to live at Castlecove *forever*. Aren't we, Cousin Dugan?"

"You might. But your stepmama may have other plans."

"They may not wish me to remain," I answered. "At any rate, I must take Paul's manuscript back to his publisher as soon as I compile an ending for it." I sighed, thinking of the burden reposing on me. I felt that I had little talent for uncovering a more than hundred-year-old mystery. The idea was preposterous. But try, I must.

I cast a considering glance at the large Scot who

was our companion. Should I confide in him? Would he give me any help?

"Do you live in the castle, Mr. MacInnis?" I ventured, trying to sound charmed by the idea. And evidently failing.

"Afraid you'll see too much of me? Sorry, but I do. Daytimes I'm out with the flocks of sheep, overseeing matters. We also raise good Angus beef that require a lot of care. But I warn you, I take most meals with the family." He stared at me with a deceptively mild and sleepy glance that roved across my face, then drifted downward.

He's trying to embarrass me, I thought furiously, feeling my face flush as I turned toward the window.

I was relieved when Tommy shouted, "Look, there's a castle! Is ours like that?"

Dugan folded his arms and shook his head. "Castlecove is much smaller and newer. It was built about 1645, just a hundred years before Bonnie Prince Charlie stayed there. I was born at Castlecove, and after my parents died, I continued living there."

Tommy tilted up his head. "Does your wife like it? What is her name?"

"Aileen." Dugan's face grew still and he continued to stare out of the window. "She drowned in the waters of the cove two years ago."

"How terrible," I gasped. "How did it happen?" I was sorry the instant the words passed my lips. I could see by the hard set to Dugan's face that it was a painful subject and he was a long time answering. Then all he said was: "No one knows for sure."

In the silence, Tommy touched his sleeve and gave his own sweet smile. "But you have a little girl. She's left for you to love."

Dugan nodded absently. His somber thoughts evidently were on the not-so-distant tragedy. Perhaps it explained his grimness and frequently harsh manner.

He probably had loved her deeply, this young wife who had died so horribly.

I studied him covertly, wondering how he acted when love swept away his iron reserve. Was he fierce and demanding, impatient to enforce his will? I couldn't picture him as soft and hesitant. No . . . not at all.

An odd wave of heat suffused my body. I had to shut my eyes and lean back in the seat, aware that my heart was thumping. Why did I think about such things in connection with this man? What ailed me? I hated blatant, overwhelming masculinity. Unfortunately, that was one of Dugan's less charming characteristics.

For a long time, I pretended to be asleep so that I wouldn't have to look at fiery russet hair, heavy-lidded eyes in a rough-hewn face, and a strong, male body straining at the fine cloth of his suit.

When we reached Edinburgh, twilight still filled the city even though it was late at night. As we stumbled wearily from the train, I could see the stretch of beautiful, sunken gardens with Edinburgh Castle beyond them on a huge gray rock. A mile farther down the hill, Dugan pointed out the palace of Holyroodhouse.

"Mary, Queen of Scots, stayed there," he said. "Also the Bonnie Prince."

"I want to go up there," Tommy whined, "right now!"

Everyone was far too weary. For once, Dugan and I were in accord. We ate supper in the hotel, then I bathed in the enormous tub and climbed into the raised bed, cozy with thick comforters and feather pillows. Tommy chose a trundle bed beside his cousin in another room. Already, the boy was leaning more toward Dugan, I thought a little sadly.

Greatly refreshed next morning, I was treated to my

first Scottish breakfast: porridge with thick cream, finnan haddie, which was a kind of smoked haddock, scrambled eggs, fried potatoes, hot rolls with Scotch marmalade, and several pots of strong, delicious tea.

However, that was the last pleasant interlude in a day spent bouncing over a winding mountain road in a rented coach drawn by two huge grays. A wildly yelling Scot kept cracking the whip above their heads to keep up speed. When I looked out of the window, the sheer drop made my stomach lurch.

We ate lunch at midday in a roadside inn. Then on we tore as though the Hounds of Hell were at our heels. They weren't, of course, it was only Dugan's impatience to reach home and discharge his obligations.

Tommy was as excited as the driver, but when the long journey neared its end in a chilly, greenish twilight, he gave in and slept, his head against Dugan's arm.

I must have slept also because I jumped when Dugan shook me and said in a loud voice: "We are at Castlecove. Get out."

"Must you shout so?" I muttered.

He carried Tommy out of the coach and I stumbled after them, blinking and trying to prod my numbed senses to take in the strange surroundings.

Had I stepped into a fairyland? Against the dusky sky, a towered, turreted stone castle seemed to shimmer with golden light from its many windows. Everywhere, I saw green lawns edged with beds of flowers bisected by the graveled drive. Hills rose in a purple haze and a copse of trees encircled everything. Mingling with the fresh, cool scent of grass and blossoms, I detected a whiff of sea air from the cove, which probably was below a cliff.

"It's beautiful." I sighed and swayed as, suddenly, my senses seemed to fade away. Immediately, Dugan shifted Tommy higher and put his arm around my waist. It felt as hard and impersonal as the branch of a sturdy tree, but I was very grateful for his support and leaned wearily against his stalwart body.

We mounted a wide flight of stone steps to a massive, open door. Strange faces swam before my vision and a dialect difficult to understand came indistinctly to my ears.

A woman drew me away from Dugan and led me down a long hallway, up uncarpeted stone stairs, to a big, high-ceilinged room whose furnishings I was unable to absorb.

"I doubt you heard my name below. I'm Nora Kern, Dugan's sister-in-law."

When I nodded and tried to smile, she continued. "Here is your maid, Polly, who will see to you during your stay. Is it food you're wanting?"

"No, thank you. Just sleep," I whispered.

I had no memory of getting into bed, but weary as I was, that was the night I dreamed of Dugan kissing me.

8

After I awakened from my disturbing dream, I knew I must thrust the thoughts about Dugan MacInnis firmly from my mind. The dream meant nothing . . . it was merely a ridiculous image created from being in his company for several days. Now, I probably would see very little of him and could pursue the problem of unraveling the location of the Prince's Gold.

Unfortunately, when light grew stronger in the room, no matching light exploded in my brain as I went over all the events leading up to my present position at Castlecove.

I remembered clearly Paul's words as he lay dying: summerhouse . . . water . . . beloved place . . . Somewhere by the cove must be a house I should explore. I couldn't contain a groan. The idea that I, untrained, unscholared, and so new to sleuthing, should attempt to find what others couldn't was daunting, to say the least. If only Paul had left me more to go on! Still, I had his notes and must try my best. I had given him my promise.

When sunlight fell more brightly on the red-and-gold-patterned carpet, I sat up and surveyed the room with curiosity. The furniture was dark and rich with ornate carving on the bedposts supporting a white lace canopy. By the windows stood a little desk, a beautiful thing of inlaid, painted scenes and gilded wood. Two crimson-covered chairs flanked a fireplace faced with green-veined marble. All spoke unerringly of wealth and taste.

As a breeze stirred the floor-length draperies, I grew impatient to see more of this domain, and flinging back the covers, I ran to the window and pushed it wide.

The view below was breathtaking. In a sheltered garden, walks of brick and emerald grass interwove between waving trees, fountains . . . and roses, roses everywhere! Cream, gold, apricot, crimson, and pale pink. For an enchanted time, I feasted my eyes, then closed my lids, feeling the warm sunshine on my face and throat, and leaning on the sill, I inhaled deeply of the delightful fragrance drifting up to me.

The crunch of gravel failed to alert me, but when a voice called, "Good morning," my eyes flew wide. I looked down to see two men staring up at me. One was blond and handsome; the other was the subject of my recent dream.

Remembering it, a wave of embarrassment swept over me so strong that I could hardly speak. "I—I was just admiring the view," I faltered, pushing back my tangled hair.

The blond man laughed and gave a graceful bow. "So are we. May I say that it is as unexpected as it is lovely."

"Dinna stare so, Davy," Dugan drawled. "Have you never seen a female clad only in her sheer nightwear?" His lips curved down sardonically as he surveyed me as thoroughly as did his companion.

Suddenly aware of my attire, I gave a horrified gasp and darted back into the room where I leaped into bed, not even waiting to close the window. From below, I heard the sound of masculine laughter diminishing in the distance.

I felt terribly shaken until I realized that I had done nothing wrong—unless unawareness was an error. However, the men's conduct had been rude in the extreme. What could one expect from Highland barbarians! Gritting my teeth, I determined to treat them both with the utmost cold indifference in the future.

I rang for Polly, ordered tea, and sipped it in my bed. With the window now closed and a fire crackling in the hearth, I soon felt warm and calm.

"Where is my stepson, Tommy?" I asked, as the freckle-faced, red-haired girl briskly laid out my clothes and poured water into the tub of an adjacent bathing room.

"Och, he's downstairs with the others about to break his fast. I saw him with the governess, Miss Grey, and thought him a fine, wee laddie and verra friendly."

It sounded as though Tommy was settling nicely into his new abode. "I must hurry and join them," I told Polly. After performing my ablutions, I let her brush my hair and fasten the back buttons on my dress. I had chosen a long-sleeved, dark blue alpaca, its severity relieved only by a white ruching at neck and wrists. My appearance must do nothing to encourage lewd, male laughter.

"Who is that young man with blond hair?" I questioned Polly. "I saw him down in the garden this morning."

"You must mean Davy Kern, the puir dead lady's brother. A great one for the gurrls, he is. His sister works here also, Nora Kern, ye ken."

"What a lot of people to sort out! Was Aileen MacInnis an employee, also?" Since Polly did not seem averse to gossip, shamelessly I decided to encourage her. In this unfamiliar household, I needed all the information I could get.

Polly shook her head. "Not Miss Aileen. Davy is a sort of record-keeper for the estate and Nora runs the household. Their sister came here to visit them and right away she wanted Master Dugan. Quick as a cat can lick its ear, the two were wed." Polly sighed dramatically. "Then two years ago she died."

"Her death must have been a terrible shock to everyone. I imagine her husband still broods about it."

Polly drew the brush through my long hair and began to wind it skillfully upon my neck as I sat before my dressing table. She nodded thoughtfully. "Aye, a sad, hard man he seems. Just imagine! She died in the sea and her body was never found!"

"Never found?" I exclaimed.

"Neither hide nor hair."

This was a tragedy, indeed. As I rose and followed Polly down the stairs, I couldn't help feeling sorry for Dugan. Perhaps there were extenuating circumstances for his curt behavior.

When I reached the breakfast room, I saw him seated there with several others, but my eyes passed over him quickly as I hovered uncertainly in the doorway. The room was circular in shape with uncurtained windows along one wall disclosing a charming garden view. At the big, white-damasked table, people were eating, drinking, and chattering. Servants hovered in the background by a serving table.

When I cleared my throat and quavered a "Good morning," the noise all ceased abruptly and every eye turned toward me.

Dugan rose at once and came to my side. Whatever his opinion of me, he evidently knew his duty. "This is Courtney Dunburn, Paul's widow, everyone. I'd like to introduce you all to her. I doubt if she caught any names last night.''

Tommy leaped up and started toward me. "I know everybody, Mama Courtney. I can intro—intro—"

"Not now, laddie," Dugan said firmly. "Sit down and just be quiet."

I stood stiffly at Dugan's side, but with his usual arrogance, he grasped my arm and propelled me forward. An unobtrusive attempt to twist away was not the slightest help.

He led me first to a small, plump woman with curly white hair and a pretty face. "This is Lady Margaret, Paul's mother."

I wondered if I should curtsy, but she leaped up at once, enveloping me in a sweet-scented hug, her powdery cheek pressed against my own. She was dressed in a lavender cambric basque, or morning dress, worn over a heavier white skirt. A cap with floating ribbons matched the top.

When she drew back from the embrace, tears stood in her blue-gray eyes, which were so like the son I'd married. "I'm so sorry about Paul. I felt terrible when I heard about Paul's death. We tried to send a telegram, but the unusual storms this spring have made some mountain roads impassable and then my Hugh became so ill—"

"That's quite all right. I trust your husband is better?"

"Yes, dearie, but still in bed a great deal of the time. You can see him later. I also want to have a nice long chat with you."

"I'd like that," I answered warmly as she resumed her seat with a sunny smile.

"Davy Kern, at your service," was the next voice in my ear.

I felt my cheeks flush as I recalled our last encounter. But the young man was all politeness. He bowed suavely, murmuring a welcome.

"My brother-in-law," Dugan added. "He works as factor on the estate."

I nodded stiffly without speaking and moved on.

Nora Kern addressed me next. "You and I have already met. Are you rested? Do you need aught in your room? I am in charge of all housekeeping matters at Castlecove."

She was a tall, thin young woman with dark hair and a rather harassed expression. There was not much warmth in her manner and I thought she seemed completely different from her flirtatious brother, Davy.

"I'm fine," I told her. "The room is very comfortable."

"With a lovely view," the incorrigible Davy murmured just loud enough for me to hear.

Dugan growled something at him underneath his breath and steered me around the table where a little girl stood waiting.

"This is Meggie," Dugan said in a softened tone, "my daughter." I was surprised to see him rest a large hand briefly on her red-gold braids. Perhaps he liked children better than adults. He certainly had a way with Tommy.

Meggie was a round-faced, freckled child, a little on the plump side, with an eager friendliness that drew me to her at once.

"Your boy is a verr-ry nice wee laddie." She put out her warm little hand to clutch my fingers. "I'm so glad you've come. Tommy and I will show you the gardens and—"

"But later, Meggie," Dugan interrupted. "Miss Courtney has not eaten yet."

Next, I met Miss Grey, the middle-aged governess who now would have Tommy in her charge. She had a kind face, but I thought she would need extra firmness to keep my sprightly stepson in line.

At last I was free to be directed toward the sideboard where I filled my plate with sausage, oat cakes, and some fruit preserves. As I slid into an empty chair, the conversation started up again. They all spoke a cultured form of English, but often a sort of dialect crept in that was hard to understand.

Lady Margaret's face showed grief for Paul whenever she mentioned him, but she did not wear mourning. However, Paul had lived in London for a long time and must seem like a stranger to the others.

They maintained a very informal atmosphere at the table. When people finished eating, they simply departed. Miss Grey swept up the two children to prepare them for their walk, but before she left, she bent down to me and whispered: "Pray, ma'am, do not think I make so bold as to eat with the family regularly. It was just today—because of the new arrivals, you and Master Thomas. A special occasion, one might say."

She didn't sound like a Scot. "Are you English?" I inquired, thinking it might be pleasant to have a fellow patriot in this Scottish stronghold.

"I haven't been to England for twenty years, ma'am. I consider myself a Scot." She backed away, eyes lowered as though in the royal presence.

How sad, I thought, as I continued with my breakfast. A governess is neither a familiar of the servants nor of the masters. Miss Grey might be rather lonely. I decided to seek her out and take tea with her some day in her rooms. Perhaps eventually I might be a governess myself if Tommy stayed here with his grandparents and I returned to England.

Thankfully, these somber thoughts were soon interrupted by Tom and Meggie, who came bounding back, both dressed in capes and hats, eager to be out exploring with me in the brisk and shining day.

I had finished eating so I ran upstairs to don a cloak and bonnet of my own. Polly was busily removing day dresses from my trunk, then spreading them upon the bed.

"I'll be ironing these now, Mrs. Dunburn," she said, rolling out her "r's." "After that, I'll hang them in yon wardrobe. Such lovely things they are—all soft and war-rum. 'Tis reet bonnie ye'll be looking."

I thanked her and hurried away down the wide stone staircase to the front hall where paneled walls were hung with softly colored tapestries. On carved oak tables, unlit candlesticks, thick as my wrist, stood by copper bowls of yellow gorse and purple heather. In spite of thick stone walls and enormous, dark-beamed ceilings, there was a warmth and charm about the castle—at least what I had seen so far.

Tommy ran up to me and tugged my hand. "*Come on*, Mama Courtney. There's lambs and cows here. I've never seen any 'cept from the train. Let's go—*right now!*"

"Och, Tommy," Meggie said severely. "You must be a good, wee laddie and mind us both."

"Mind you?" he shrilled. "Why, you're naught but a —a—*wee* girl yourself!"

"Now, calm down, Tommy." I straightened his cap and rebuttoned his belted jacket while he jiggled from one foot to the other.

Meggie was as neat as a pin in a wide-collared cape of pink cord, a matching bonnet tied precisely beneath her plump chin, and snowy gloves upon each hand. I wondered how these two opposites would get along. I knew Tommy had been overly indulged while Meggie seemed to be something like her serious father. Perhaps they would be good for each other.

"Take Meggie's hand," I ordered Tommy as we

stepped outside. He scowled but complied, while Meggie smiled at me, slipping her other little paw in mine.

"Do you have children to play with, Meggie?" I asked as we walked around the house on a wide brick path.

"Och, yes. There are lots. The crofters have many children. They live and work on our land but are— are—"

"Independent?"

She nodded, then drew her hand from Tommy's to point ahead. "Look, aren't the roses beautiful?"

"Oh, indeed they are." The well-kept beds that I had seen from my window certainly were a vision, rioting in every shade of pink to palest white and filling the air with a delightful fragrance. Around each plot were edgings of pansies, violets, or tiny daisies. Graceful stone figures peeked out from vines and shrubs. Somewhere a fountain tinkled and birds wheeled and trilled against the clear blue sky. I paused upon the path, drinking it all in.

Tommy looked around impatiently. Roses were not for him. "Where are the animals? I can hear them somewhere . . ."

"We'll soon be there," Meggie told him. "Then you can see baby lambs and—"

"Baby lambs? Oh, *champion!*" With a great shout, Tommy went pounding away across the garden.

"Come back here!" I cried. My entreaty was as useless as calling to the wind.

"Och, he'll be all right." Meggie shrugged. "We'll find him soon enough with Sammy in the barns. Or by my papa in the fields."

As we started walking, she stared up at me. "Miss— Mrs.—I dinna ken what best to call you."

"How about just 'Miss Courtney'?"

"That's a bonnie name. And you're reet bonnie, too."

"Oh, no, not really."

"*Aye!* I've never seen prettier hair. Or eyes so light and glisteny."

"Thank you, dear. You're very sweet. I like your hair, too."

"It's the same as—" Suddenly, the rosy, round face sobered. "Well, *she* had hair like mine."

"Your mother?" I asked unthinkingly, then changed the painful subject swiftly. Unfortunately, in the wrong direction.

"Meggie, what is that strange, little building?" I cried, turning toward the bluff. But then, immediately, I knew it must be the summerhouse, although it was far from my expected vision of an open-sided, airy dwelling to while away a summer afternoon. This was a solid house, old and weathered, with windows boarded up. A wooden porch looked newer than the rest, but it also showed signs of neglect. Vines and cobwebs straggled everywhere and weeds grew tall and thick.

Fascinated, I moved closer until Meggie called to me, sounding agitated, and looking back, I realized she had stayed behind on the main brick path that wound around the rose garden.

"Come back, Miss Courtney, *please!*" She was torturing the edge of her pink cape between her hands. "We don't go up there. It—it's dangerous."

I retraced my footsteps slowly. "Dangerous? Why should it be? It's just a neglected little house."

"It was *hers*. She used it before she—anyway, no one's allowed there now."

I knew who she meant, but it puzzled me. Was it some kind of shrine to the dead Aileen? I stared down at Meggie as we headed for the belt of trees. "Why do you say it's dangerous? It appears solid enough."

Her little face looked as stubborn as her father's. "I dinna ken, but my father said—" She swallowed.

"Yes? What?"

"Not to go near it or we might get hurt. I do what he says."

"I'm sure you do," I muttered. Had this been Aileen's secret hideaway?

"And he told me not to ask questions about it." Her blue eyes rolled up at me, pleading for understanding.

I squeezed her hand. "I can see you are a most obedient little girl. Your father must love you very much." And probably never tells you so.

Meggie beamed, however, happiness restored, as she led me through the copse of beeches beyond which a big green meadow stretched right up to the high hills dotted with giant rocks and purple clumps of heather.

I caught my breath. It was a scene beautiful enough for a master painter. Beneath the azure sky, a flock of white, black-faced sheep were jumping stiffly, chomping grass, running, butting, and baaing. They were mostly babies with mothers and a ram or two gazing at them benignly while a couple of black and white collies watched attentively from the sidelines.

Tommy was right there in the middle, shouting and chasing, trying vainly to capture one of the elusive little creatures. As I watched, Dugan came toward him and placed a tiny lamb carefully in Tommy's arms. Meggie left my side and ran to join them. They all spoke together, Dugan evidently showing Tommy how to feed the animal a bunch of clover.

When the children were completely absorbed in this, Dugan straightened and came over to me. He now wore corded breeches, leather boots to the knee, and a brown jerkin over a white shirt open at the throat, the sleeves rolled to his elbows. The sun glinted on his sun-darkened arms and tinged the hair blowing carelessly across his forehead with a fiery sheen.

"Do you want to see the other animals we raise?" His eyes on me were calm, his manner more relaxed than I had ever seen before. Judgment on me might still be pending, but right now, there was none of the sneering or open hostility that had marked our former encounters. Perhaps the beauty of his native land had soothed him.

"I'd like to see everything," I answered, determined to meet him at least halfway.

We headed down a path edged by tall green trees with buttercups and daisies rioting in the underbrush. Beside a fenced-in field, he leaned against the rail and gestured at a herd of great, shaggy, red-coated beasts. "Aberdeen Angus beef, the best there is."

"Goodness, they certainly are huge," I exclaimed.

"And verr-ry expensive."

A pleasant silence enveloped us. Then I had to go and spoil it all.

"I was very interested in a little summerhouse I saw this morning, but Meggie told me it was off-limits."

"That's right." His face darkened. "It's quite dangerous. About to slide into the sea some day, I fear. The storms have loosened the foundation. If the place belonged to me, I'd tear it down."

"But Prince Charlie liked to go there so it may have a certain historical value."

He muttered stubbornly, "Even so, the cliff around there is not safe."

"Is there another way to the beach?"

"Aye, but don't venture down alone. The cove can be a place of rough tides and sharp rocks. 'Tis best not to go out in a boat unless you are a fisherman or with somebody who knows his business."

He probably was remembering Aileen and I regretted mentioning the cove. "At any rate, I enjoyed the rose gardens. I've never seen anyplace so lovely."

Dugan's voice was gruff. "I'm thinking I must apologize for Davy. He's a wee bit young and brash. Not above a bit of fun with a pretty girl and ofttimes he goes too far."

"I—I didn't know anyone was there," I said huskily.

He turned his head, smiling coldly. "Did you not? Was that how you entrapped my cousin, with loveliness displayed with such pretended innocence? A poor but ambitious girl who thought Paul might be rich?"

Fury flooded me and I clenched my fists. His change of mood was all the worse because he had seemed friendly so short a time before.

"How dare you sit in judgment?" I sputtered. "You don't know anything about it. If I told you—"

He gritted his teeth, then grabbed my shoulders, jerking me close so that only a few inches separated us. "If you told me, would it be the truth?"

He drew in a ragged breath, his face flaming with some strange emotion. Then his heavy lids flicked me up and down with an assessing insolence as though he still saw me in the revealing night shift. "Aye, you could cast spells to seduce a man, couldn't you?" he muttered thickly.

"I don't know what you mean," I gasped. "What are you talking about?"

He shoved me back so hard, I stumbled. "You had best not tarry long at Castlecove," he ground out. "There's danger for you here. And that's a warning!"

Spinning on his heel, he vanished through the trees and left me standing there, pulses pounding and every nerve end tingling.

9

Calming myself with an effort, I tried to brush off Dugan's angry warning as I walked back to my room. Danger? What danger? From him? What nonsense! His strong masculine attraction might alarm me, but he wouldn't do me any physical harm, I felt sure of that.

The only danger to me would come if I discovered the Prince's Gold and someone found out about it. Even that unlikely event would only anger another seeker who wanted the prestige of discovery for himself (or perhaps a chance to steal it!). But no one at the castle seemed to believe Paul's theory. Hadn't Dugan dismissed it as a fable?

However, just then a vision crossed my mind: a large man wearing a slouch hat and black cape. A "proposition" for me. And an angry rejection from Paul. If that mysterious person should suddenly materialize here like a phantom in the night . . . yes, that man could mean danger if he guessed my mission here. Because he probably was after the same thing: a chance to win acclaim for the discovery of the gold. In my case, it would mean the triumphant conclusion of Paul's last book and the fulfilling of my promise.

I was very anxious to explore the castle and make some discreet inquiries of the inmates; therefore, I was delighted when Sir Hugh sent a request that I visit him in his chambers that afternoon.

Lady Margaret, clad in a trailing tea gown of apricot silk and rose-point lace, came to my room to escort me. We traveled along several winding corridors, one of which had an arched doorway disclosing dozens of portraits. It was a long, narrow room with polished walls covered by large oils in gilded frames. I stared curiously and slowed my footsteps. "Are these the Dunburn family?"

"Yes, dear," Lady Margaret answered. "Several hundred years of them. The earliest ones are farthest back."

That meant that the portraits of Paul's and Dugan's wives were closest.

When I made no effort to move on, Lady Margaret lit a candle from a nearby taboret, and holding it aloft, stepped inside. "Of course you're curious. Look, then. Here is Paul's first wife, Charlotte. She lived on a neighboring estate and they were longtime friends. There was no romance between them until Paul returned from Edinburgh University and even then it was a while before they married and finally left for England. The poor lass died in childbirth there."

I gazed with pity at the small, dark-haired woman with her good, plain face and wondered how much Paul had been in love with her. His portrait hung next to hers and showed a younger, more vibrant man than I had ever known though he had the same intelligent eyes and sensitive, thin lips.

I'm here to carry out your work, my dear, I told him. The best way that I can.

Seeing my sad expression, Lady Margaret took my arm and urged me along. "Here is Dugan. He was my dead sister's child and is like a second son to us, so dependable and strong. This portrait was painted fifteen years ago when he was twenty-one. He's changed in looks, hasn't he? But still a bonnie man."

"He looks quite different now," I murmured, gazing up at his face. He looked amused, as though he were about to laugh. The hair was redder, the eyes more wide-open. But he was still large and determined-looking.

"He always was a strong-willed lad, but good and hard-working, too." Lady Margaret mused. "If he had a fault, it was that he teased the lassies overmuch and wouldna settle on any one until he met Aileen when she came to visit Davy and Nora. That's all it took. One meeting."

Her voice was suddenly flat and cold as she pointed to the next portrait. "And there's Aileen herself."

I gazed enthralled. Here was a stunning beauty with red-gold hair and a luscious figure rising from a daringly low-cut gown of sea-blue froth. She had long-lashed eyes of the same hue as a large sapphire surrounded by diamonds that hung on a silver chain against her surging breast.

"She died two years ago," Lady Margaret informed me stiffly. When I glanced at her, another question on my lips, she was staring up at the portrait with a strange look on her face. "There's an old Scottish proverb: 'They that deal wi' the deil get a dear penny-worth.' "

Seeing my puzzled expression, she forced a laugh. "My mind's a-rambling like my tongue. Come, my dear, let's not tarry any longer. Sir Hugh is waiting for us."

She started briskly down the hall and I moved silently beside her, many questions churning through my mind that I knew I had no right to ask. The truth was that Aileen MacInnis and Dugan intrigued me greatly. But this was a distraction I couldn't encourage and firmly I thrust it from my mind as we entered the bed-sitting room of the laird of Castlecove.

Lady Margaret drew up two ladder-back chairs and placed them beside a big, four-poster. Sir Hugh made scarcely any bulge beneath the covers. He had thin, white hair, his face looked waxen, the blue-veined eyelids closed. I wondered, with a startled pang, if he had passed away while sleeping!

But then his wife spoke to him and touched his face. "Wake up now, dearest. Paul's widow is here to see you."

At once, the old man's lids flew wide and I saw that he was far from dead. His light brown eyes stared avidly at me. Then he smiled, struggled higher on his bank of pillows, and extended his hand.

I clasped the thin, skin-covered bones. "How are you, Sir Hugh?"

"Much better, thankee, lass. I'm so pleased that you have come to us." His voice was clear and fairly strong. He looked at Margaret. "My dear, would you see to some tea and cakes? Make sure it's what we like."

It probably was an excuse for us to be alone. After the door closed, he eyed me carefully. "So you are Courtney. When Paul wrote that he had remarried, we were very happy. He told us all about you."

I doubted that he had told his father "all." "He wanted me to come here," I said. "Have you seen Tommy?"

"Aye." The old man chuckled. "He's a young limb, that one. Wanted to know about everything in the castle and asked a mort o' questions about the legend of Prince Charlie's gold. I wager he has more spirit than

Paul ever had at his age. My son was always a romantic dreamer.''

"Yes, but he was also very talented," I said firmly. "A most respected writer."

"Och, aye. I've read each book he wrote."

"Then . . . you didn't resent his leaving home to write in England?"

"Nae, nae. I told him he should go." The lively gaze dimmed, straying past me at some grim memory. "He didn't realize the danger here. But I could see it."

"Danger?" I repeated.

His eyes returned to my face. "I won't speak ill of the dead, lass. So dinna ask me. Now, then, have you seen the inside of the castle?"

"Not too much, but my room and the halls are charming and the gardens are magnificent, especially the wonderful roses, my favorite flowers."

"Mine, too. Perhaps you'd pick some for my room when you have time?"

I thought this probably was a ploy to see me again and I felt flattered and quite willing. "I'll bring some every day. We can visit then, if you are feeling up to it."

"Och, I would enjoy that. I must say that Paul didn't exaggerate. You are very kind and sweet, young and lovely, too. I can well see how he would want to marry you. Even though he was somewhat older—" He cleared his throat. "But that's no matter—"

"Sir Hugh, I know some people wonder why I married your son. We had become dear friends before he ever proposed to me. I told him when he first asked me to marry him that I wasn't sure. Later, when he asked me again, I accepted because . . . because I needed him. He said he thought in due time I would come to love him as a husband wishes."

"And did you? Nay, lass, I shouldn't ask that." His frail white hand fluttered upward from the quilt.

I took his hand in mine. "It's all right. I think I would have very soon. Only . . . Paul died. But I've never known a finer, dearer man, except my father."

"Tell me about your father," Sir Hugh said brightly, changing the subject just as Lady Margaret entered with a maid carrying a laden tea tray. "Paul wrote that your parents had gone to Spain for your father's health."

After that, we all chatted together while Sir Hugh sipped minted tea and ate a plain sponge cake. His wife and I consumed strawberries with brown sugar and clotted cream, crumbly, rich shortbread, and the most delicious chocolate cake I had ever tasted.

I told them about the copy house and how I had met Paul and worked on his last book because he was in a hurry to see it published. I patted my lips with an embroidered napkin. "He didn't finish it because he wanted to return to Castlecove for the ending of his book."

Sir Hugh smiled. "Paul always was intrigued by the story of Charles Edward Stuart, the Young Pretender to the throne of England. It was a very colorful time, I grant you, filled with derring-do, brave fighting, high romance, and then the legend of the lost gold hidden here at Castlecove."

"Which someone probably stole many long years ago," Lady Margaret said briskly. "But always these silly rumors will persist."

"Aileen thought that Paul was on to something," her husband mused. "Do you remember how they were always at that summerhouse, reading old letters about the uprising and so forth?"

"I remember fine," Lady Margaret snapped, looking as though she recalled some unpleasant memory.

My ears had perked up at the mention of "old letters." "I wonder, would it be possible for me to read those letters you say Paul studied? Some way I might contrive an ending to his book."

They both looked rather skeptical, then Lady Margaret shrugged. "Of course, you may see them. They're in the library under lock and key, quite valuable, you know."

I thanked her with a surge of hope. When I went back to my room, I wondered if there had been something in the old letters about the gold? If there were something that compelled Paul to return to Castlecove for the ending of his book?

Had Aileen encouraged him in his theory about lost gold simply because she was bored? He might have been flattered by her interest and even felt a growing infatuation for the exquisite young woman. Perhaps that was why Sir Hugh, seeing the danger in Aileen, had urged his son to take his wife and move to London.

I studied Paul's notes again, but as before, found nothing. I could hardly wait to read the letters that Lady Margaret had promised to show me. And sometime I must investigate the little summerhouse when no one was about to warn me away.

I felt too tired to venture out right now. It had been a long, exhausting day filled with new sights and new people. Wearily, I dropped down on the bed and slept until it was time to dress for dinner. Polly helped me into a gown of pale blue silk, which called for the addition of a rose or two. Since the dinner warning chimes had not rung yet, I slipped outdoors into the garden.

The sun's warmth still lingered in the perfumed beds and I sauntered slowly up and down the paths, selecting a few special flowers for the basket on my arm that Polly had procured for me. The sky was softly lavender, the time of day the Scots so lyrically called "gloaming," when shadows lengthened but night was slow to come.

I was just about to retrace my steps when Dugan's voice grated in my ear, causing the usual acceleration of my pulse.

"Och, woman, did you ask Auld Angus if you could strip his special roses?"

Why on earth did this man seek me out if he found me so constantly annoying? I wheeled around, scratching my finger on a bush in the process. "Who's Auld Angus? And taking four or five roses from this overburdened spot is hardly stripping!"

"He's the head gardener. And blood is dripping from your finger." He stepped close and took my hand. "Whist, you've caught a thorn!"

Ignoring my protests, he propelled me to a nearby fountain where he made me sit on a wide stone rim while he extracted the thorn, then plunged my hand into the clear, cold water.

"Thank you, but really it's not necessary—"

"Ofttimes a thorn can be a wee problem." He wiped my hand with a clean white handkerchief. "You are a guest, after all, and must be taken care of."

He sat down beside me, his eyes resting on my face. "Do you want those roses in your hair? It seems to be the style with ladies now."

Before I could reply, he bent down to my basket and lifted out the deep pink flowers I had picked. The next thing I knew, he broke them off short, pulled off the thorns, and began to thrust them into the coil of hair upon my nape.

"Oh—oh—" I fluttered, putting up my hands. "N-never mind, I'll do that—"

"It's done. Ah, we have one left." He eyed my bosom edged in the soft blue silk.

"No—"

"Well, then, in your sash." Deftly, he thrust the last rose in the ribbons at my waist, then leaned back to eye the effect, not speaking, merely nodding.

My pulse was pounding as I stared at him, unable to think of anything to say. What a strange man he was! So changeable. Would I ever understand his moods? The dying sun had caught fire in his hair and glinted in his narrowed gaze. He was dressed for evening now in gray and white, sleek and elegant, quite different from the booted farmer with his sheep but every bit as masculine and virile.

"What are you thinking?" he demanded suddenly. "With that wide-eyed stare?"

I caught my breath and answered without considering my words. "I'm wondering if I'll ever understand you."

A smile glimmered briefly around his chiseled mouth. "Try. What do you think I'm like?"

I cleared my throat. "I think . . . you are probably dependable and honest with a strong sense of duty. That's why you came for me in England and brought me here against your better judgment."

"Go on," he ordered silkily, clasping his knee in both long-fingered hands. "Do you dare to list my bad points? Or can't you think of any?"

The arrogance of the man! I tilted up my chin. "I think, rather, *I know* that you have a temper. You also are stubborn and prejudiced."

That made him frown. "Prejudiced? About what?"

"Me—for one thing."

"I had cause," he growled.

"Why? Because I was a lot younger than Paul and still we married? Do you want to hear how it came about?"

A silver chime rang out and Dugan said, "No, it's dinnertime. I don't want to hear about your romance with Paul. It's sufficient that you married him. We'll never know how it would have turned out, will we?"

I didn't answer. How could I?

He took my arm in his hand as we both stood up, his

fingers pressing where the skin was smooth and bare. "My guess is that you would have left him," he said softly.

"How can you possibly guess that?" I protested indignantly, trying unsuccessfully to twist away from his disturbing touch.

Dugan looked down at me from beneath his heavy lids. "I believe you didn't feel any passion or desire for him. You have recovered too quickly from his passing. And the more I know you, the more certain I am that you'll be wanting that kind of passion from a man some day."

His eyes ran up and down my form. "The time will come. I am convinced of that. You wear seductive nightwear and you respond with trembling nerves when I touch you. Are you not aware of that?" He drew his hard fingers slowly down my quivering arm.

My agitated breath was shallow, fluttering in my throat, and it was a long, pulsating moment before his knowing smile gave me the strength to break away.

"Why don't you just leave me alone?" I cried, then ran into the house as though escaping from some terrible danger behind me in the garden.

10

I managed to avoid being alone with Dugan for the rest of the evening, but next morning he was in the breakfast room along with Davy and his aunt.

Lady Margaret greeted me cheerily. "My dear, we are going to have a dinner party in your honor in a couple of days' time. Just some of our neighbors in the glen, about a dozen people. Nora is now conferring with cook about the food and if you have any preferences—"

"Oh, no, thank you, but I wish you would not go to such trouble on my account." Out of the corner of my eye, I noticed Davy grinning at me. Dugan kept his eyes upon his plate.

"Nonsense, child," cried Lady Margaret. "We Scots dearly love a party, don't we, laddies? And a houseguest such as Courtney deserves the best."

"That's right." Davy nodded. "Lady Margaret, I'm wondering if you would like me to show Miss Courtney around the castle? I'm sure she would need a guide and everyone's so busy today. Dugan, didn't I hear you say you were going to the village to buy supplies?"

Dugan muttered something.

"Thankee, Davy lad. I'm sure Courtney would enjoy that." Lady Margaret beamed at us both.

I accepted graciously as I was very anxious to see the castle. However, I hoped Davy would not attempt any familiarity and shifted uneasily as I noted his surveying study. Because the day was warm, I wore a simple nainsook gown patterned in lilac blossoms. The sleeves were short, the corsage collarless coming to a scalloped point below my neck. I wished now that I had also worn a concealing shawl.

As soon as I had finished eating, Lady Margaret left and Davy sprang up, holding out his hand. "If you are ready, Courtney . . ." Already, he was dispensing with the "Miss."

Dugan rose. "Wait outside, Davy, and review our little talk. I wish a word with *Miss* Courtney."

"Alone?" Davy laughed. However, when Dugan didn't answer, he shrugged and winked at me, then strolled out to the hall.

When I stood up, Dugan took a stand in front of me. What now? I wondered nervously and braced myself.

"Now, then," Dugan said, inhaling deeply. "Yon laddie will be all right if you don't tease or flirt with him. Do you take my meaning?"

"Oh, for heaven's sake, don't be ridiculous. I'm not one bit of a flirt." With an impatient gesture, I tried to move past him, but he stayed stolidly in place, arms crossed, legs spread arrogantly apart.

"Are you not?" he sneered. "Remember just the other day when you lolled out of your bedroom window clad only in a thin night garment?"

"How *caddish* of you to remind me! Aren't you ever going to forget that?" I flared. "And I didn't *loll!* It was completely unconscious on my part."

"So you say."

"You know it was! It is simply your perverse nature that delights in tormenting me." Gritting my teeth, I tried to shove against his rigid form. "Will you *please* let me by?"

He stood rock-solid. "You'll mind what I have said? I've seen young Davy looking at you, no doubt imagining—"

"Are you much better?" I hissed. "Always speaking to me in an obnoxious, suggestive manner?"

"I'm warning you today because it is my duty," he growled.

For a heated moment, our eyes locked. Then he stepped aside without another word and I swept angrily out of the room.

I discovered Davy lounging on a large hall chair. He leaped up with alacrity and had enough sense not to ask me about Dugan's private session. Perhaps he knew I wouldn't tell him. Or perhaps he had a pretty good idea what Dugan had said. At any rate, though he looked amused, he was all politeness as he led me forth to explore the castle.

There were a great many rooms, and while very old, they were all well cared for and quite beautiful since the carpets, draperies, and furniture were of the finest materials. Some of the high-domed ceilings had beautiful painted scenes of cherubs and flowers, others were carved and gilded. Crystal or china chandeliers hung in nearly every room with candles ready to be lit. Gas lines evidently hadn't extended this far yet and I really preferred the softer, fragrant light from oil lamps and beeswax candles.

After visiting a well-stocked library, a formal dining room, and a huge ballroom lined with mirrors, we came to a heated, damp conservatory at the end of a long hall where it evidently joined an outer wall giving access to the garden.

The conservatory had a high glass dome with palm trees and fleshy vines rising nearly to the roof. There were tubs of orange and lemon trees and many exotic flowers growing in banks of bark and earth. I recognized only a few, namely, orchids, violets, and camellias, but to see them this far north truly seemed amazing.

"You must have a wonderful gardener," I said to Davy, who then pointed out Auld Angus working in the corner. When we greeted him, he merely grunted and I decided not to mention the roses I was cutting.

But, suddenly, like a gypsy mind reader, he called out to me. "Meestress, ye kin hae the roses for Sir Hugh and make free with ma garden. Aye, the maids told me," he added sourly when I spun around. "But dinna gae to yon wee house upon the cliff. Or doon to shore."

"You mean the summerhouse? I know it isn't supposed to be safe. But what's wrong with the cove?"

"Just stay awa' from there," he shouted fiercely, shoveling earth into a large clay pot.

"He thinks he owns the place because all his forebears worked here." Davy grunted.

As we walked away, the gardener screeched, " 'Twas *her* place and nane gae there if Auld Angus knows aboot it."

"We're not going to the cove or the summerhouse," Davy yelled over his shoulder.

When we were once more back inside the castle proper, I turned to him. "Speaking of the cove, exactly how did Aileen die? I only heard that she had drowned. Was she swimming?"

"My sister couldn't swim, but she loved to go sailing. Glynnis Macrae was a close friend of Aileen's from their finishing school days in Edinburgh. They were a lot alike, both wanting excitement and attention. Glynnis was visiting here when Aileen and Dugan had their last fight, and in a fit of recklessness, the girls took out the boat even though a storm was coming up. Glynnis survived. Aileen didn't.''

Davy's voice had roughened. "Glynnis is coming here for a visit soon. She's a bold one. Her claws were always reaching out for Dugan. I suppose that's why she's returning now—to have another go at him.''

"Did Dugan respond?'' It seemed the words were forced out of me. "Didn't Aileen object?''

Davy shrugged. "My sister and Dugan were always fighting about something, but Aileen only seemed amused by Glynnis's tactics. I guess that was because Aileen had such faith in her own power over Dugan— when she cared to exert it. My lovely sister attracted every man she met. And, frankly, she was often bored here.''

"How about you? Aren't you ever bored?'' Immediately, I regretted my words, knowing that they sounded rather provocative.

But Davy seemed sobered by the discussion of his sister and answered indifferently. "I have friends—ladies—in the glen and I take frequent trips to Edinburgh for a little social life. Aileen did that, too. She and Glynnis liked to shop in London and go away for a few days. Otherwise, she told me that she couldn't bear her life. And Dugan wouldn't give her a divorce.''

These revelations were making me uneasy, but there was no stopping Davy. Even when I tried to comment on the rooms we passed, he kept reverting to his sister. "Aileen couldn't help attracting men. To her it was just a game, but it was the cause of all the quarrels with Dugan. He didn't try to understand her. And now she's gone.''

I could tell his voice was thick with unshed tears. He and Aileen must have been very close. I put my hand upon his sleeve. "I'm so very sorry, Davy.'' He merely sighed.

Finally, there was but one place left, which Davy told me was Aileen's tower room. Her private aerie where no one ever came without an invitation.

He opened a narrow door in the third-floor hall that disclosed a dimly lit, curving staircase hugging an inner wall. It didn't look especially inviting.

"What is up there?" I asked dubiously.

"Oh, beautiful things that Aileen prized." He picked up a candle from a hallway stand, struck a lucifer, and held the flickering light aloft. "Come on. I know you're awfully curious about her. Who wouldn't be?"

"Well, since we've come this far."

He gave a rather sardonic chuckle and led the way carefully up the winding, pie-wedge stairs. There was no railing on the outside to break a fall so I kept my hand braced against the damp, gray stone wall, holding up my skirts with my other hand and watching carefully where I put my feet.

At the top, Davy thrust open a heavily barred oak door and stepped across the threshold. Immediately, he gave a startled cry.

"What is it?" I gasped.

Not another sound came from him, and when I pushed around his rigid form, at first I couldn't see what had caused his alarm.

In the light from the flickering candle's gleam, I obtained the impression of a circular boudoir of remarkable beauty; the abode of a sybarite dedicated to sensuous luxury. Rich, ruby velvet hung above an emerald satin bed, the posts covered with gilded nudes from which I quickly averted my eyes. Glancing down, I saw the rugs upon the floor were soft, white wolfskins. Pillows of pink and green were strewn beside an empty fireplace, which was faced with rosy marble. Everywhere I looked I saw tables, chairs, and lamps clustered with various *objets d'art* in many beautiful materials.

But then as I advanced farther into the room, I saw what had caused such an agonized cry from Davy and my own breath caught tightly in my throat. All was not as it at first appeared. A mysterious deviltry had been at work. Pictures were slashed, seats and pillows ripped, gouges and stains were everywhere.

The room had been defiled. Or searched.

Davy moved slowly, like someone in a dream, cursing in what seemed to be the Gaelic tongue as he discovered broken mirrors and bric-a-brac, drawers spilled upon the floor, clothes from the armoire torn in shreds . . .

"What happened here?" I cried. "Who has done this?"

"I don't know!" His hands knotted into fists and his voice shook. "This place was so beautiful. I wanted it kept as a sort of shrine to her memory. Before she died, I came up here and it was all perfection and now . . . this . . ."

"Did someone hate her?" I whispered, horrified. "This much?"

Davy shook his head, bewildered. He didn't mention Dugan's name. But I felt sure this couldn't be his work, no matter how much her flaunted escapades might have angered him. Dugan was direct, open, forceful. He wouldn't vent his rage in secret. Or so I believed.

But if not Dugan . . . then, who?

"I'm going to look into this," Davy cried in a choked voice and rushed out of the tower, leaving me completely on my own. I heard him clattering down the stairs. I couldn't blame him. He was terribly upset and I was perfectly capable of finding my own way back.

But for a moment, I stood still, staring around, wondering. Then in the silence I heard an eerie sound break through. It was a chirping noise from the fire-place. At the same time, a shower of soot fell into the cold and empty grate.

"Birds!" I cried aloud. In London it had often happened that a wren or starling would become entrapped in the chimney and had to be forced upward with a great deal of broom shaking down below and terrified squawking up above.

Something plopped in the grate as I advanced and I saw it was a grimy, blackened book. I picked it up and put my head inside the fireplace. Sure enough, there was an empty hole in the brick interior where the book must have been kept.

At the top, a flash of wings arrested my attention and a final hoarse cry indicated that the bird was free.

I stepped back into the room, brushing ashes from my arms and bodice. My heartbeats quickened as I stared down at the object in my now equally blackened hands. There were two tarnished silver initials on the leather cover. When I rubbed them clear, I saw they were "A.M."

Without a doubt Aileen MacInnis!

I turned it over in my hands. It might be a diary, a journal secreted for a purpose. Should I hand it over to Dugan, unread? That would be the honorable course.

But then a sly voice whispered: You are here to find an ending to Paul's book. This might shed some light on all that researching in the summerhouse.

With a quick decision, before my nerve could weaken, I hid the book in the fullness of my skirts and made my way carefully down the pie-wedge stairs.

When I reached my room, I wiped off the diary and placed it, unread, beneath the mattress of my bed while I sat down in a chair, considering it.

It was odd that Aileen, given her reputation, hadn't tried to seduce Paul. His being married at the time would not have mattered to her. It might have only added spice. From all I'd heard, she sounded bored to death, out of love with Dugan, and trying her power on every man who interested her.

But perhaps in Paul's case, he was too honorable to respond. That might have been the danger Sir Hugh wanted to avoid. Or perhaps Aileen's main interest was in Paul's discovering the gold so she could steal it and run away.

I thought I understood Dugan a little better now. He saw me as another Aileen, only not so beautiful, of course. He believed I had schemed and caught Paul with seductive wiles because I expected him to have a lot of money.

All that day, I debated about reading the diary. Was it right to delve into someone's secret thoughts? Was it justified by the importance of finishing Paul's book?

That night after supper when I asked Davy in a quiet aside if he had found out who was responsible for the havoc in his sister's tower, he answered that no one admitted knowing anything about it. He thought it must have been some former disgruntled servant as she had a habit of flirting with the better-looking men and then discarding them.

After that, Davy flung away, his face tight-lipped and I knew it was better to ask no more about the painful subject.

But as I climbed the stairs to bed, a new thought struck me. Could someone have been searching for the diary in her tower?

11

When I woke up in the morning, I realized that I hadn't slept well with so many matters churning through my brain. Therefore, I asked Polly to bring a light breakfast of porridge, bannock cakes, and hot, strong tea to my room. When it arrived, I had her place it on a table by the window, but when I drew aside the heavy drapery, I saw that the day was filled with swirling fog, cold and gray. Shivering, I quickly closed the curtain.

"I'm thinking that Miss Macrae will have a dismal journey on this day," Polly remarked, stirring up a stronger blaze in my fireplace.

"Who's that?" I inquired, trying to place the name as I poured thick cream on my porridge.

"You have no' heard of Miss Glynnis Macrae? She who was a friend of Aileen MacInnis?"

"Oh, yes, Davy mentioned her," I said slowly. "She was in the boat . . ."

"Aye. The last person to see Miss Aileen alive."

Polly's freckled face assumed a mysterious expression laced with relish. "She'll be biding here a wee."

"Yes, I remember that he mentioned something about a visit."

Making slow work of tidying the room, Polly continued. "No doubt Miss Glynnis wants to test her chances again with Mr. Dugan, if ye take my meaning." She giggled and rolled her eyes.

This gossip was getting out of hand and, abruptly, I asked Polly to bring hot water for my bath. When she had gone, I continued eating, wondering about the coming visit. It would be distasteful to observe this woman flirting with Dugan and I hoped I could avoid her company.

After I had bathed, Polly helped me into a new style called a "Garibaldi" shirt, named for the famous Italian patriot. It was a belted tunic of blue and white checks trimmed with darker braid. My skirt was of plain blue in three deep flounces. The whole outfit was simple and comfortable. I smoothed my waist, glad that boned corsets were on the wane. Since women had become more active in work and sports, the vogue was now toward one such as I was wearing that snapped down the front and eliminated the long, front busk.

When my toilette was complete, Polly asked if I wanted a special gown freshened for the coming dinner party. "You may be sure Miss Glynnis will be wearing something in the height of fashion," she told me slyly.

In that case . . . I crossed the room to view my own gowns in the wardrobe, finally selecting a pink silk rep with deep flounces edged in lace and ribbon. The material with its narrow crosswise ribs was brand-new this year, so the London dressmaker had informed me. I had not worn it yet, but felt satisfied that it was smart and elegant enough.

Polly left then, carrying my gown away, and without hesitating, I extracted Aileen's journal from beneath my mattress, making up my mind to read it. During my restless night, I had wrestled with the problem, finally deciding that since Aileen was dead it could do no harm to read her diary. I couldn't afford to overlook anything that might contain a clue to the Prince's Gold.

I settled by the fireplace and riffled through the pages, noting there was a great deal about trips to Edinburgh and London, new gowns, parties, people whose names meant nothing to me. At last an entry arrested my attention and I began to read more carefully:

"Paul and I went to the summerhouse today. He had some old letters written by the Bonnie Prince that he wished to discuss with me. They must have historical value, but were not a bit exciting, mainly concerned with a dog he had grown attached to, a golden retriever.

"The wee doggie died just before the biggest battle. She was buried on the grounds and Paul seemed to find this very interesting. But I was bored. I tried to distract him with my new gown. But it was useless."

A few entries later, Paul had left Scotland and Aileen wrote:

"His father finally convinced Paul to take Charlotte to London and try to find a publisher there for the books he's written. I am persuaded that the main reason was Sir Hugh's desire to get Paul as far away from me as possible. He need not have worried. Paul only loves his writing.

"As for me, I don't care. I would have dallied with him, given the chance, but though sweet, Paul was really a wee bit stuffy. The new groom, Rory, is much handsomer and decidedly more aggressive. There's a hot gleam in his black eyes that I am very familiar with. Just so did "He" look at me on my last trip to London. But Rory is *here*. And "He" is *there*."

Two weeks later, Rory's name surfaced again and I could tell the diary's author was annoyed.

"I made Dugan discharge Rory for impudence and he has been sent back to the village without a character. I was glad to see him go. He frightened me with his roughness the last time that I let him come up to my tower, and goodness knows, I'm not a shrinking violet. Well, I have someone else and at least "He" is someone I can control."

That was the last entry. I closed the book with a shiver of distaste. It hadn't told me anything about the gold and I decided to return it to the tower room at once.

I was halfway across the room when, suddenly, someone knocked, and without waiting for an answer, opened the door and stepped inside.

"Dugan!" I exclaimed. "I might have known only you would be so brusque."

"What do you mean?"

"You barge in here uninvited! How did you know I wasn't bathing?"

"In your bedroom? You have a private bath."

"I might have been dressing."

"This late in the morning?"

The wretch had an answer for everything. "Well, what do you want—now that you're here?" I demanded.

"What a sweet and cordial greeting! What do I want? Why, merely to tell you that a friend of my wife's has just arrived from London. With a companion. I thought you'd like to meet them. He's—um—unusual and I'd like your opinion of him."

His eyes were snapping with excitement and I stared at him, bewildered. "My opinion?"

Before he could reply, his eye fell on the journal still

clasped in my hands. His brows lowered, a furrow creased his cheek, tightening his mouth. "What's that you have? It looks like—"

"Oh, yes, it's your wife's diary. I found it up in the tower when Davy showed me around." I swallowed hard and licked my lips, disturbed by the evident anger I'd aroused and feeling decidedly in the wrong.

He plucked the book from my limp grasp. "You have read it? Without so much as a by-your-leave?"

"Well—not exactly. Just a page or two where she mentioned Paul and—"

"They were no' lovers, if you suspected such," he ground out furiously. "I'm sure of that. A fine opinion of your husband you must have had!"

My anger flared to meet his own. "I never thought that about Paul. Not for a minute. But he and Aileen spent a lot of time in the summerhouse discussing the whereabouts of the Prince's Gold. And I was curious—"

"The Prince's Gold!" he spat. "Didn't I tell you that there is no gold?"

"How can you be so certain? Paul was sure—"

"Paul was a romantic writer, enchanted with the tales about a dashing, handsome prince fighting for the throne of England. Don't you think if there was any gold, it would have been discovered by this time?"

"Not necessarily. Those were troubled days. Anything could happen. The prince was defeated—to his astonishment—and he had to flee immediately. He had no chance to return here—not with English soldiers hot upon his trail."

Dugan crossed his arms and sneered. "And so what happened to the gold?"

"Paul said that he believed the prince hid it someplace in the castle or on the grounds. If it was outside, wind and storms and shifting earth might have completely covered it. But Paul was certain he had found some clues to its whereabouts which would make an exciting finish to his book—"

"You have not yet discovered these—clues?"

Too late, I realized that I had blurted out the secret of my quest. Well, what did it matter? I shook my head. "I must keep on looking, however. For a while, at least. I promised Paul."

"And if you are successful, what then? Would you claim the gold for yourself?"

"What are you saying! Of course not. It would belong to Sir Hugh or a legacy for Tommy. Or perhaps they would donate it to a museum. How do I know?"

Dugan stared at me and his belligerence faded into mere exasperation. "Go on then, woman, search. For all the good it may do you." He held out the journal and a corner of his strong mouth quirked upward. "Do you want to continue reading this? Perhaps you're curious to discover what Aileen thought about me as a lover."

I gave a shocked exclamation. *"No!* Never in my entire life have I met such an ungentlemanly person as you! Your crudeness is appalling!"

To my utter astonishment, he threw back his head and gave a shout of laughter. His dark eyes danced with a fiendish humor. "Aye, that's right. What did you expect from a rough Highlander? Am I not a rude, crude devil of a Scot?"

I pressed my lips together because, suddenly, I also felt like laughing. I took the book from him and placed it on a nearby table.

"Lead me to your guests," I told him primly. "I'll come down now."

At once, his features sobered. "You're going to be surprised, mayhap. So be careful what you say or do." He turned and strode into the hall.

"What on earth do you mean?" I asked, gathering up my skirts as we went down the wide stone stairs. I could hear voices coming from one of the lower rooms. A woman's high, affected tones. And the gruff deepness of a man.

I halted, my hand gripping the banister. "Who is it?" I whispered.

"My wife's friend, Glynnis Macrae."

"And—?"

From the step below, he turned and faced me. "She has traveled here with a companion from London. A certain Professor Harden."

"A *professor?*" My startled eyes met Dugan's, which narrowed, reflecting my own concern.

"Aye. A professor with a keen interest in Scottish legends."

My hand flew to my throat. "Is—is—it—"

"Our intruder?" he asked softly. "There's no way of knowing yet. But it's not beyond the realm of possibility."

"Why has he come here? Did he follow me? And what is Miss Macrae's part in this?"

Dugan shrugged. "Who knows? He wrote asking permission to visit Castlecove for some historical research, so I've been told. As for Glynnis, an old friend is always welcome at a Scot's hearth. Or a friend of a friend."

He put his hand upon my arm. "Now, woman, watch your tongue. Play it cool and canny. No excited accusations, mind."

"I never would," I hissed, flinging off his hand.

"Och, aye?" he drawled, and arched an eyebrow at me.

We proceeded downward until we reached the open doorway to the parlor and I stared inside with an accelerated heartbeat.

12

Nora and Lady Margaret were seated in the parlor, welcoming the newcomers. Everyone was sipping from little crystal goblets and it looked quite cozy and innocuous with the crackling fire warming the damp day and glinting on the sleek, black curls of a fashionable young lady seated on a nearby gold velvet settee.

My eyes skimmed past her rapidly for it was her companion who aroused my keener interest at this moment. Big and heavy-set, he was past the first flush of his youth with a florid kind of handsomeness that bordered on the coarse. He had a clean-shaven face except for dark sideburns low upon his cheeks. Without the cape, hat, or beard, this man bore no resemblance to the one I had seen in London. But the coincidence of another large professor interested in Scotland was too much for my ease of mind.

Hewing to his usual line of duty, Dugan first introduced me to the female guest, Glynnis Macrae. I now observed her more carefully, this woman who supposedly wanted Dugan. She was not a beauty but her face had a predatory sensuousness that men might find intriguing. It was evident in the intently gleaming eyes, the wet look on her lips, and the tightness of her basque.

Her green eyes narrowed as they swept me, then I was dismissed as unimportant, although she said she was "delighted" to make my acquaintance and extended white, jeweled fingers to touch my hand for the briefest courtesy.

Next, Dugan led me to her companion, whose name was Max Harden. The professor stood and bowed, reached for my hand, then kissed it just a shade too long. We eyed each other, he with a little, tight-lipped smile that told me nothing. Quickly, I glanced at Dugan, who gave an infinitesimal shake of his head, warning me that this was not the time to query the professor. I thought he *could* be the same man . . . but how could I be certain?

Miss Macrae now claimed Dugan's attention by leaning forward so that the striped gray silk tightened on her prominent, full breasts. "May I have another little drop of wine?" she purred, holding out her glass and giving his other hand a quick, intimate squeeze.

"Certainly. Would you like some sherry, Courtney?" Dugan asked.

I accepted and moved back out of the circle, which was clustered near the huge carved fireplace with its beautiful stone statues at each end. The room, though large, had an attractive grouping of glowing Turkish rugs and ornately decorated tables, some draped with silken scarves, some covered with Dresden figurines, lacquer boxes, and artificial birds and feathers under glass. Deep green velvet draped the windows while the opposite walls held row on row of oils in massive frames.

As Glynnis Macrae had captured the attention of both the professor and Dugan, I moved across the room to take a closer view of a portrait of Prince Charles, the unwitting catalyst of my mission to the Highlands. He certainly seemed to be a charmer. In his red velvet coat and white peruke, he was the handsomest man I had ever seen, with a warm, bright-eyed smile that must have fired the loyalty of his many followers.

Suddenly, a low-pitched, rather gruff voice spoke at my side. "Underneath that white wig, his hair was a beautiful red-gold. Fascinating devil, wasn't he?" Hands clasped behind his back, the professor studiously eyed the painting.

I turned impetuously, unable to contain my curiosity another minute. "Have we met before, Professor Harden?"

He skirted a direct answer by merely saying silkily, "Perhaps. I have a great interest in Scottish history . . . as did your late husband. Am I not right?"

His gaze slid sideways toward my face before I could reply. "My condolences on the death of Paul Dunburn, madam. His loss will be keenly felt, I'm sure, in many literary circles."

"How did you learn that he had died?" I probed.

He shrugged. "A newspaper account in London, if memory serves correctly." Then his voice grew hard, though still pitched for my ears only. "Mrs. Dunburn, you and I have things we must discuss."

My pulse accelerated. He must be the same man! The one from whom I'd fled that night. The one who had angered Paul. And perhaps the one who had ransacked his library and made off with the manuscript.

I glared at him. "Indeed we do!"

"But in private," he hissed. Taking my arm, he led me farther down the long, elaborately furnished room, our footsteps muffled on the deep-piled, jewel-toned rugs.

"Is there a conservatory by the house? The Scottish

winters are so cold, they nearly always have one on a large estate."

"Yes, there's one, but—"

"We'll meet there at midnight. The conservatory will be deserted then. Can I count on you?"

Evidently he was as anxious for the meeting as I was —just as he had been anxious in London. If he had stolen Paul's notes, I wondered how much he'd learned from them?

"I'll be there," I told him.

He nodded and returned abruptly to the group around the fireplace. They had now risen and were moving toward the door.

A maid had been summoned, but before she left to seek her room, Glynnis told Lady Margaret that she would like to greet Sir Hugh a little later on.

Lady Margaret murmured something, then turned to Nora. "There'll be two more now for the dinner party tomorrow. About a dozen guests have accepted."

Nora nodded. "I must confer with cook again." She hurried away, looking worried and distracted. Was Nora ever gay and happy, I wondered? So far, I had never seen her smile or laugh. She certainly seemed different from her brother. And also from Aileen, of course.

Which brought my thoughts back to Aileen's friend, Miss Macrae. Just what was her relationship with the professor? I could hardly wait to see what I would learn from the midnight rendezvous although I could tell already that the man was very cagey.

I had deliberately dawdled behind the others and was still in the hallway hoping for a word with Dugan. He had escorted Glynnis to her room, but didn't tarry. Before I could start upstairs, he appeared at the top and hurried toward me.

"Come in here," he said in a low tone. Taking my arm, he led me into the book-lined library where he shut the door and escorted me to a padded window seat as far as possible from the hallway.

"I saw the professor talking to you. What did he say?"

Shrugging, I sat down facing him. "This certainly is an odd situation. He didn't give me a chance to find out anything, but I am almost certain he is the man from London who wanted to collaborate with Paul. Of course, he has shaved off his beard; however, I feel the coincidence of two large history professors interested in Castlecove is just too much. Besides, he wants to talk with me in private."

"Whisht! Where and when?"

"In the conservatory at midnight. Doesn't that prove he has something to hide?"

"It certainly sounds like it. I wonder if this is such a good idea—"

"I'm going," I said firmly.

"Och, 'tis a fine, brave lass you are."

Did he mock me? I brushed his words aside. "Dugan, I'm wondering about the connection between the professor and Miss Macrae, aren't you? Do you know how well they are acquainted?"

He shook his head. "I couldn't very well bombard guests with personal questions the minute they arrive. However, I may learn more tonight. I, too, have been invited to a rendezvous."

"With the hungry Miss Macrae?"

"Hungry?" He choked back a laugh and swept a russet lock from his brow. "Aye, perhaps you're right. Some women have considered me attractive." He leaned toward me suddenly with a wicked gleam in his brown eyes, and to my consternation, dropped his hand upon my knee. "What do *you* think?"

I was reminded of Lady Margaret's words that he "teased the lassies overmuch" when he was younger and I was not in the mood for any teasing games. I stood up quickly and headed for the door. "I must go—"

With a lithe movement, he stepped in front of me, his hands clamped on my shoulders. "Listen to me first. I want to warn you—"

"What about? You?" I cried shrilly.

He gave me a little shake, his face now grave. "Och, don't be daft! I want to warn you to be careful what you say around Professor Harden. Find out what he wants, but act as cool and canny as possible. Remember, he's a man of the world and probably hard and ruthless. Do you understand?"

I felt a stab of fear, but I answered calmly. "I'm not a child. Besides, what can happen to me in the conservatory?"

He stepped away from me, still frowning, but he didn't answer me. As rapidly as possible, I left the room and headed up the stairs.

In the upper hall, I encountered Lady Margaret. "Courtney dear, I've been looking for you. I want to give you these letters." She lowered her voice and glanced up and down the corridor before handing me an age-darkened book tied with a cord. "This is hollow. The letters are inside. One is from Prince Charlie and is a family treasure. I have no' read them for many years, but I ken fine that he wrote for us to give the gold away." She shook her head and sighed. "However, it was never found."

"Thank you so much," I exclaimed. "I'll be very careful with them, I promise."

Entering my room, I clutched the book to my bosom. Dear heaven, if the professor knew about these, he'd tear the house apart looking for them. That is, if he were the same man who had done that once in Paul's study. And the more I thought about it, the more certain I became.

I wondered uneasily if I would be in any danger

when I met him tonight in the conservatory. Then I brushed the idea impatiently from my mind. How could he do anything here? Besides, he probably wanted my cooperation and hoped I would be amenable to a "collaboration." His theories for mine. Would it be possible to effect some trade without giving him the upper hand? Perhaps I could sound him out, discover what he knew, then offer him a false lead or two. That should be "canny" enough.

I sank down at the window table and stared at the old, dark book, wondering what it would tell me. In tarnished gold, the lettering stated *Wonders of the Ancient World*. I untied the knotted cord around the outside and it promptly broke into a powdered, shriveled string. Fearing to do more harm, I raised the cover carefully. Inside, the center pages had been cut into a hollow to fit the size of the old letters, which I withdrew slowly. Unfortunately, there were no envelopes which would have added to the value, especially with a hand-struck stamp.

I saw that the writing was cramped and crisscrossed on many of them in order to save space. They seemed to have been written from one clan member to another, some of them here at Castlecove. A few mentioned "The Young Pretender" very discreetly without a word about the gold. But then I found a letter enfolded in tissue paper. It was a single, pale brown sheet with a signature that made my heart leap: "Charles Edward Stuart." The heading was "Isle of Skye, 1746" and it was addressed merely "To Castlecove."

I bid you all farewell, dear friends. I will carry the memory of your gallant fighting in my heart forever. And the tragic deaths will always haunt me. I love you all, none more than the dear, brave lass who helped me to escape disguised as her handmaiden.

Alas, I now must sail to Europe with the tide, a most unhappy exile. Take the gold given by my loyal followers and spread it among the widows of my ill-fated army. Remember the beloved place. God be with you all.

Tears slid from my eyes as I relived the heartbreaking tale. This letter made it all so real. "The dear, brave lass" was, of course, the famous Flora MacDonald. Like so many others, she had loved the handsome, dashing prince and it was her daring that had saved his life.

"Charlie's Year," Paul had called it; just fourteen months of high hopes and adventure and the rallying of the clans. All of it leading to the sad defeat at Culloden, where so many brave, true men went to their deaths. After that, the Bonnie Prince had found no joy in his escape, or the long years of his exile. Paul had included an old Scottish song in his book:

> The bonnie boat like a bird on the wing
> > Over the sea to Skye.
> > Carry the lad who was born to be king
> > Over the sea to Skye.

At last, I put all the letters back inside the book, placing it beneath my mattress until I could peruse them further. Aileen's journal still reposed there, also, but it had been no help to me so far.

Was everybody except Paul right? Had the gold been stolen over a hundred years ago? At that time, someone in the family might have known where Prince Charlie put the coins. Or was it possible that the gold had been distributed as he asked and knowledge of the transaction lost in the confusion of the times? Could there be an old family record hidden in a dusty file and long forgotten?

Suddenly, I wondered if Miss Grey, being a teacher, might not have an interest in the history of Castlecove? Perhaps she had delved in their ancient records at some time. I had meant to visit her but so far had failed to find the time. Jumping to my feet, I sent a maid to invite her to take tea with me today in my room.

She accepted with alacrity.

13

"Oh, yes," Miss Grey said, sipping daintily, little finger extended. "There are ledgers, records, account books from the old days all in locked boxes in the storage quarters." She preened a little, setting her cup down carefully. "Lady Margaret graciously allowed me to peruse them at my leisure. So kind of her. It was most educational, the prices paid for tallow and wax candles, wages for maids and footmen. Yes, yes, a fascinating glimpse of how a place like this was run, you know."

I passed her the plate of *gâteaux* and what the Scots called "crumpets," which consisted of jelly-filled rolled pancakes. In England, they were more like muffins.

"Have you seen the letters written during Prince Charlie's stay?" I inquired.

"Yes, I have indeed. Many times." She twittered delightedly over her selection from the tray. "Oh, thank you. So delicious."

When she was munching happily, I continued carefully. "You may have heard that my husband's last book was about Charles Stuart, the time he spent here, and the fact that the gold donated for his cause was lost after the defeat."

"How fascinating that sounds. I would love to read your husband's book."

"It was never finished."

"Oh?" She shot me a narrow glance. I detected a keen intelligence behind her show of humble deference.

I leaned forward and spoke deliberately. "Miss Grey, I am going to confide in you."

She raised her chin, evidently pleased. "I assure you, madam, it is safe to do so."

"Well, then, one purpose of my visit here is to find an ending to my husband's book. His theory was that the Prince's Gold remained hidden somewhere at Castlecove and was never found."

"Yes." Miss Grey's eyes glinted thoughtfully behind the steel-rimmed spectacles. "The family here were very loyal and fought beside him all the way. This was the last place Charlie stayed. He hid the money expecting to return, not knowing Culloden was his last battle. A loyal young woman helped him to escape to Skye and he never set foot at Castlecove again."

"I know that. In one of the letters he wrote from Skye, he asked the family here to distribute the gold to the army's widows. Is there any record of that?"

Absently, she reached for a chocolate-covered biscuit. "No, there wasn't any mention of such a distribution. That would certainly have cleared up the mystery, wouldn't it?"

She took a sip of tea. "Yes, I particularly recall that letter from the dear lad. So sad, was it not? That ending to all his hopes and dreams. He aroused such passionate devotion among his followers. And it was easy to see why when one studied the nobility of his character."

I leaned back in my chair, feeling discouragement creeping closer. "Then you think the gold was stolen?"

"Not necessarily. Who would have taken it? The Dunburns and all the other clans were honorable."

"Perhaps a spy or one of his followers grew greedy and learned where the prince had hidden it. Then after the defeat at Culloden, somebody became reckless."

"I don't think you believe that," she said. "You are playing devil's advocate, are you not? By arguing for the other side? I really think the prince would have been more careful about where he hid the gold and whom he trusted with the secret."

I had to smile. No fool, she. "You probably are right. In one letter from the clan, a mention was made of the 'beloved place.' Do you think they meant the summerhouse? Where lovers had their rendezvous?"

Miss Grey nodded.

"But Lady Margaret said the place had been a favorite searching ground for many of her ancestors who thought the gold might be hidden there. Eventually, all gave up in disappointment."

"Someone may still be searching in another area," I told her slowly. "The other day I saw a great deal of havoc wrought in Aileen MacInnis's tower room. Did you hear about that?" I eyed her curiously.

But her look was dumbfounded. "No! Who could have done such a thing?"

"There is no proof, but the theory is held that a disgruntled servant did it."

"Then it's doubtful if a servant was hunting for the gold." She was too discreet to mention any of the dead woman's indiscretions. We both left the words unspoken regarding a possible grudge against Aileen.

After a minute, she sank back, quietly accepting another cup of tea. "Perhaps you will just have to write an inconclusive ending to your husband's book. At least, the main part of the story will be a thrilling one."

She sighed. "How I would love to visit the museum in Edinburgh and view the prince's memorabilia. I imagine there would be a sword, his standard, mayhap some clothes. . . . And I would also like to explore the castle where he stayed—Holyroodhouse."

"You should go," I said. "Why don't you?"

She smiled slightly. "I don't have the 'siller' as the Scots say. I will have to leave when the children are sent away to school and I am saving every penny against that day."

"Maybe they'll keep you on to tutor them."

"No, Mrs. Dunburn. I don't have enough learning for that. The future laird will need the best of schooling."

I thought of Paul, who had given up his lairdship. How disappointed his parents must have been. But now they had Tommy to raise their hopes and I knew that the lively little fellow was looking forward to his future role as leader of the clan.

Miss Grey now made motions toward leaving, returning to her twittering obsequiousness with profuse expressions of her gratitude for my "graciousness" in having her to tea.

I wished she would accept me as an equal for I felt she would be a loyal friend. When I said as much, she colored up and blinked rapidly.

Then she stood up taller. "I would be very honored by your friendship. I knew your husband, Paul Dunburn, and thought him extremely kind and charming. I am so sorry for your loss." Her thin hand fluttered forward timidly.

I clasped it. "Thank you, Miss Grey. And we'll take tea together again very soon."

"Oh, lovely. Perhaps you could come to the nursery next time. It would be a little party for the children, don't you know." Her gaze grew thoughtful. "I also have something to show you. I am sure it would be interesting."

"Shall we say in two days' time, then? Tomorrow I'll be busy preparing for the dinner party."

I wished she also could be invited as there would be so many strangers present. But I felt certain that she would be too shy to enjoy such a gathering and probably was more comfortable with just one person at a time.

When Miss Grey left, I decided to gather some red roses for the gown I would wear that night, a simple white taffeta. I peered out of the window and saw that the fog was moving off and a watery sunshine now shone upon the garden down below. I donned a shawl, and with shears and basket, sallied forth.

For a while, I wandered idly, snipping here and there, gathering some blossoms for Sir Hugh as well. I was surprised that it was not as chilly after the misty morning as I had feared. Obviously, the Gulf Stream that warmed the western side of Scotland was drawing closer to the land.

The fountains were not turned on today and everywhere was silence, even the waves below the cliff were barely audible.

Then from behind a hedge, I heard two voices and the sound of advancing footsteps. It wasn't hard to recognize the rather strident tones of Glynnis, and with a jolt, I realized she was speaking about me.

I made no move to leave, although eavesdropping was not a pretty thing to do. However, neither was criticizing a person behind her back. Which was exactly what Miss Macrae was doing.

"Does that Courtney creature think she stands a chance with Dugan? How utterly absurd! After he has had a vivid beauty like your sister."

The other voice belonged to Davy. "She doesn't

seem to flirt with Dugan. Instead, they're often snapping at each other."

"Then why does she remain at Castlecove? You say that she came here to deliver the child, though why that was necessary when Dugan was along—"

"Perhaps she wanted to ease the path for Tommy. There's something else. Her husband, Paul, left an unfinished manuscript about Prince Charlie. Maybe . . . she's trying to write an ending for it."

Glynnis laughed. "That old legend of the gold gets them all. I know Paul was a fanatic on the subject."

I heard the crunch of footsteps moving off and I crept along until I could hear them clearly once again.

This time, Davy's voice was strained. "Glynnis, I've been wondering. Do you know anything about my sister's death that you haven't told? It was all so strange . . ."

She didn't answer for a minute. "I've told everything I knew. I was fighting for my life, wind blowing, waves crashing. I saw Aileen go under. I nearly drowned myself, but I can swim and Aileen couldn't. I would have tried to save her, but she never surfaced. I'm very sorry, Davy."

His voice was ragged. "Perhaps she didn't struggle. She and Dugan had just had an awful fight about that groom."

"You think Dugan's feeling guilty? He shouldn't. Forgive me, Davy, but you know how Aileen treated him, flaunting her affairs. Believe me, *she* never felt a speck of guilt."

"She was bored and wanted a divorce—which he refused."

"I know. Poor Dugan. I can't help feeling sorry for him. I'd like to distract him . . . if he'll let me."

Davy laughed harshly. "I know that's why you've come back."

"Well, he is quite attractive. And has inherited

wealth. He doesn't need to spend his life working with animals. He should travel, get away, have a romantic fling . . .''

Without being aware of it, I had come to the end of the hedge. Suddenly, we were all face to face. I was so surprised, I dropped my basket and we all stared at each other in consternation.

I could tell exactly what they were thinking: How long has she been here? How much did she hear?

I bent down and gathered up my flowers, babbling brightly. "I just slipped out to get some roses for Sir Hugh. I had no idea anyone else was here. You certainly surprised me. Well, I'll just run along—"

"Yes," Davy muttered, raking back his hair. "It's getting cold again."

Glynnis almost immediately regained her poise. She moved to my side and slid her arm through mine. "Courtney, I may call you that? What are you wearing tomorrow night? I've heard the dinner party's in your honor." Without waiting for a reply, she continued rapidly. "I have a new gown by Charles Worth. You've heard of him, no doubt?"

"Oh, yes, the Englishman who went to Paris and became the most famous couturier in the world." And the most expensive. No wonder Dugan's money was also interesting.

"I will look forward to seeing Worth's creation on you," I said. "I fear my own dress will pale by comparison. It simply came from an unknown dressmaker in Bond Street."

"I'm sure it is delightful. Paul must have been a generous husband."

"How is the research going on Paul's book?" Davy threw me a sly glance. "Have you managed to contrive an ending?"

There was nothing left for me except wiliness. "Paul thought the Prince's Gold might still be here. But I think that he was wrong. Everyone believes the money was stolen long ago."

Glynnis stepped away from me. "Professor Harden is very interested in Scottish legends. Perhaps the two of you should compare notes." Before I could frame a question, she vanished through the rear doorway of the house.

I turned to Davy. "What does the professor want here? Why did he come?"

Davy shrugged. "All I know is that he's a friend of Glynnis's from London and he's interested in Prince Charlie. He sent a letter to Sir Hugh asking if he might visit Castlecove. They barely had time to reply, I imagine, before he arrived."

"Odd that he knew Glynnis," I murmured.

We parted company then and I went upstairs to dress for dinner. My worries were certainly increasing. I could tell that Professor Harden was a clever, ruthless man. And if he discovered the solution to the lost gold he would publish his findings first and Paul's book would come to nothing.

I must do everything in my power to prevent that from happening and my eagerness for the midnight meeting with my rival grew apace.

14

I had heard some revealing statements behind the hedge today—though not much that hadn't been hinted at before.

There was just one thing: Dugan's possible sense of guilt. That might account for his dark and clouded countenance and the harshness of his manner toward me. He might often be consumed with anger toward all women. Especially someone like me who he had decided was a greedy, selfish person who had married for money and now was seeking to discover the Prince's Gold.

Well, he was right about one thing. I did most urgently want to find the gold or at least determine what had happened to it. To that end, I must follow every little clue and trail.

All the while I dressed for dinner, my mind dwelt on the coming rendezvous at midnight. I knew I wasn't very brave or clever. But I must try to match wits with the professor to the best of my ability. A false clue seemed to be the best idea (given with seeming reluctance). The ransacked tower or the deserted summerhouse leaped instantly to mind—places about which I could drop hints as possible locations for the gold. That should keep him occupied for a day or two.

If I was wrong and he actually did find the Prince's Gold or proof of its disbursement in the past, what could I do? Lock him in a room and flee to London with Paul's manuscript in a race to publish first? Or should I sidle up and try to convince him that I was willing to do more than "collaborate"? Perhaps some way I could distract him. . . .

I had to laugh then at my absurdities, and catching up my white lace flounces, I left the room, still chuckling. As a *femme fatale* or spy or ruthless villain, I knew I would be a complete and utter failure.

"Laughter becomes you," the professor drawled, coming up to me as soon as I entered the crowded drawing room. "With your pink cheeks and lips and the fragrant red roses at your bosom, you look utterly enchanting."

Oh, I thought, if he only knew what I'd just been thinking he wouldn't be giving me such fulsome compliments. Then I wondered, perhaps he was using the same technique on me that I'd been considering: devasting charm.

He lifted my hand to his full, red lips and murmured, "Don't forget tonight, my dear. The conservatory. At midnight."

His words reminded me of an exaggerated gothic thriller and I almost laughed again. I definitely felt giddy tonight. Biting my lip, I nodded to the professor and turned away, almost colliding with a maid who offered me a crystal goblet of sherry on a silver salver.

As I thanked her, I caught Dugan's quizzical gaze on me. He was leaning on the mantelpiece, a glass of spirits in his hand. The candelabra struck gleams of fire from his russet locks and shone silkily on his smooth black coat and trousers.

He beckoned me imperiously and I maneuvered around the other chattering people until I gained his side. "Tonight's the night," I whispered dramatically, narrowing my eyes and tossing a glance from right to left.

"Aye," he grunted, "and I'm wondering how the likes of you can handle such a person as the wily professor?"

"Fie on you, sir. A little while ago you called me a fine, brave lass. Have you changed your opinion of me so quickly?"

He shook his head at me. "Levity in this matter is quite misplaced, my girl. Has it slipped your mind how the London house was ransacked, probably by this same person with whom you intend to sally forth in a deserted hothouse at the stroke of midnight?"

I tossed my head. "What of it? Besides, the professor may be perfectly innocent. The person who entered the London house might only have been a street thief—er —searching—"

"For what? A manuscript to peddle on the corner? Are you daft, woman? You ken fine that was the only item taken."

"Well, what's your theory then?" I demanded, keeping my voice low with an effort. I glanced behind me. "Are you certain the professor was our intruder?"

"Aren't you?" he growled.

Just then, a soft chime announced the call to dinner. I downed the rest of my drink. Dugan placed his half-full glass on the overmantel and we both joined the exodus into the dining room. Tonight it glittered with crystal chandeliers, silverware, and damask napery. Silver epergnes filled with hothouse fruits graced either end of the table. Many-branched candelabra sent extra light spilling into every corner, outlining carved black walnut, green velvet draperies, and walls of murals depicting moors and castles in vivid hues.

The table itself was an arresting scene: the men in their elegant black and white setting off the colorful gowns the women wore. I particularly noted the azure silk adorning Glynnis. This was not the gown by Worth but its lace and pearls managed to make my own white flounces appear childishly dull and simple.

Lady Margaret sat at one end of the long table, Dugan at the other. The slow meal wended its way through julienne soup, Scotch salmon with mushrooms, veal croquettes, roast of lamb, then fowl. Every course was accompanied by an array of hot breads, wines, and various side dishes. And finally dessert: a quivering blancmange with chocolate sauce. I had never dined so regally and I relished every bite.

"You have a wonderful cook, Lady Margaret," I called down the table.

There were assenting voices from everyone except Glynnis, who touched a hand gingerly to her midriff, which evidently was tightly laced. No one with such a bosom could be so thin below it without a rigid corset, I thought cattily. As for myself, I continued eating smugly, my own undergarment being unboned and very comfortable.

As usual in a gathering like this, I knew the sexes separated after dining: the ladies to the drawing room, the men to sit at table over more wine, probably exchanging ribald stories. I had read many books and articles of the day so the social customs of the rich were not unknown to me even though I had never even partaken briefly of a life such as I was experiencing at Castlecove. I had to admit that I was getting accustomed to it very quickly and finding it extremely pleasant.

Glynnis expressed a desire to play the piano, so after supper, Lady Margaret, Nora, and I followed in her wake to the music room. There she spread her skirts upon a crimson velvet stool and began to play, a loud and lively tune that I didn't recognize. Evidently, when she couldn't be with the men in person, she was going to keep a reminder of herself clearly in their ears.

I wondered idly why such an avid creature had not found a mate? She certainly was attractive enough. Was Dugan the only love of her life? I recalled her words to Davy. It seemed that Dugan's wealth also held a lure for her. Like Glynnis, I, too, felt surprise that he labored like one of the field hands.

I finally spoke to Lady Margaret under cover of the music. "Do you think your nephew will stay here all his life? Or does he want a place of his own someday?"

"He'll leave, I think, if he ever decides to remarry. He doesn't really have to work at all, but he loves the farmland and beauty of this glen. I think he'll build his own house no' too far away." She cocked her curly head at me. "Do you also like it here, dear lass?"

"Yes, very much. I grew up in the heart of London and never knew how much I would like country living. I probably will hate it when I return."

"Why should you, then? As Paul's widow, this is your home now. You've become a dear part of our family. You must know that."

I smiled and thanked her but I knew I could not stay here forever. Dugan might not be able to wed until his wife was declared officially dead and I had no idea how long that took. But Glynnis probably was willing to become Dugan's mistress, and when that day came, I would have to leave at once. The idea of their making love was extremely unappealing to me and I didn't stop to wonder why.

Then Lady Margaret whispered low, "What do you think of Dugan? Do you like him?" She had a little arch expression on her face.

"Oh . . . yes . . . he's . . . he's . . ." I stumbled.

The door leading to the hall opened and I was spared the necessity of finishing my sentence. The three men entered and Glynnis's busy fingers stopped their play. The professor moved toward me, but Dugan immediately summoned me. "Courtney, will you step here for a minute?"

Unquestioningly, I rose and joined him.

He drew me into the hall and shut the door as the music started up again, Glynnis trying a tune of a more rowdy nature, evidently to please her new male audience.

"Miss Macrae is quite talented and has a wide repertoire," I remarked, recognizing a rather naughty music hall song called "Suzy's Saucy Skirts," "Perhaps she will sing and play for you alone tonight. Is your—er—rendezvous with her still scheduled?"

"Never mind that." He started briskly down the hall. "Come along. I want to visit the conservatory with you for a moment."

"Now? Whatever for?" I asked, quickening my steps to keep up with his long strides, and trying to hold my skirts out of the way at the same time.

"I'll tell you when we get there and can't be overheard," Dugan muttered, giving a swift glance behind him at several closed doors—all of which added distinctly to my feeling of uneasiness.

The conservatory, at the end of a winding passageway, was very dark. But Dugan had come prepared. He pulled a lucifer and candle from his pocket and picked up a pewter holder from the hall table. Soon wavering beams shone on the green-and-white tiled floor and glass-paned windows, now merely black oblongs in the night.

Slowly, Dugan began examining the place, moving among the ferny plant stands, enclosed terrariums, moss-covered rock gardens, and various chairs and tables of white wickerwork.

The odor of blossoming tuberose was so heavy on the humid air, I began to wish heartily that I had brought my fan.

"What are you doing?" I demanded. "Why have we come here?"

Dugan paused beside a trellis thickly covered with a concealing vine of green leaves and yellow bells. He pointed to a wrought-iron bench in front of it. "Tonight," he said softly, "you'll make sure to sit there. I will be behind the trellis."

"What!" I exclaimed. "That's not a good idea at all. Suppose the professor sniffs around to make certain we're alone? Anyway, why should you want to be here?"

"Because we don't know this man. Maybe he entered the London house and ransacked it. Maybe he didn't. When he meets you here tonight, immediately engage him in conversation so he doesn't have a chance to 'sniff around.' Anyway, he's acting very strange, I'm thinking, telling you to meet like this in the dead of night."

"Perhaps he was smitten by my charms."

Dugan pulled me around to face him, gripping my bare arms. "Don't make light of this matter. You may have undertaken a mission that's way beyond your capabilities. You told me you were trying to discover what became of the Prince's Gold. But I'm not sure why."

"I owe it to Paul's memory. I've told you that before."

"So you say. Since he failed to discover the gold, you're going after it. Is it greed that drives you or what?"

I jerked away from him and rubbed my arms. "You certainly have a terrible opinion of me, don't you? First, you think I married Paul for his money. Now you think I'm still driven by mercenary motives in everything I do."

"Aren't you?" he drawled.

"No!" I whirled away, pacing around a dry stone fountain. "Paul was very dear to me. He helped me when I was troubled and alone. When he was dying, he asked me to find an ending to his book and I could not refuse. That's *all I want*. An ending. There—does that satisfy you?"

I glared at him, but he did not reply. I wondered if he had even listened as he leaned against one of the tables, arms crossed upon his chest, the candle beside him sputtering low in the moist, almost suffocating air.

I observed him warily. He certainly was an enigma, his hard-hewn face unreadable as he slowly examined me from top to toe.

"Strange," he finally muttered. "You could pass for an angel if I didn't know better. All in white, pale gold hair, pale blue eyes so wide and innocent-looking. The rose petals soft and tempting against your snowy bosom."

I put a fluttering hand up to conceal my breast, feeling unnerved by his strange words and that devilishly shadowed face.

"What are you, woman?" he ground out harshly. "Saint? Or sinner?"

I drew an angry, trembling breath. "Neither! Just a *woman*, as you persist in calling me so often."

"No . . . not *just* a woman . . ." Slowly, he started toward me.

Pinned by the mystery in his dark gaze, I couldn't look away or move a muscle.

"What on earth are you two doing in here?" A shrill voice smote the air. There was Glynnis standing in the doorway, her blue silk gown and black curls shimmering in the hallway light behind her. "Everybody wondered where you'd gone."

"Courtney had expressed a wish to see the conservatory. So I obliged her," Dugan answered silkily with perfect poise.

Glynnis threw me a quick, inimical glance, then smoothed her features into a smile as Dugan reached her side. She looked up at him, head to one side, and said with a beguiling pout, "And there I was prepared to play and sing 'The Bonnie Scot' just for you."

"Och, aye? Perhaps you'll let me hear it now." They headed for the door, then Dugan speared me with a backward glance across his shoulder. "Well, aren't you coming with us, wo—Courtney?"

"I'll follow in a minute. These tiny orchids fascinate me."

"Keep the candle, then. There's enough light in the hall so we won't need it," Dugan said. "But be sure to close the door when you leave. The temperature in here must be kept steady. You'll be careful?"

Knowing that he meant tonight, I gave an emphatic, "Yes," and turned away to view the terrariums where fragile ferns, pink and purple orchids, Parma violets, and lily of the valley all thrived miraculously in this northern country hothouse.

However, my mind was not long on the tropical plants. Instead, Dugan's face swam before my vision, his expressions varying from distrust and impatience to a wary, new appraisal. Why did he still see me as a scheming, greedy woman? Did he think I was being deliberately provocative by wearing scarlet roses in the cleavage of my bosom? Angrily, I pulled the flowers out and flung them to the floor. It seemed that everything I did was subject to a suspicious questioning by this man. Did he have nothing better to do?

Why must my main problem—in itself so overwhelming—have to be continually compounded by Dugan MacInnis and his speculations?

15

I had to make a pretense of going to bed, and with that end in mind, I let Polly remove my clothes, brush out my hair, and lay out my night apparel. There must be nothing suspicious about my actions. Though, of course, nobody would expect me to have a rendezvous with the professor. If I was caught by any member of the household while flitting down the hall at midnight, they would be more likely to suspect a romantic interlude with Davy . . . or even Dugan . . .

I felt my face grow warm at the idea of being in Dugan's fierce embrace and gave a breathless laugh. What was I thinking! Why did I indulge in such fancies about a man I barely tolerated?

And yet tonight he'd spoken so strangely. Doubtfully. "Saint? Or sinner?" he had wondered. Then he'd started prowling toward me, his eyes riveted on mine with some dark question in their depths.

Did I regret the interruption of Glynnis's arrival? To be honest, I did. Since I had dreamed of Dugan's kiss, I was curious to know how his lips would feel pressed to my own. Though why I felt this way, I didn't understand since Dugan was not at all the type of man that I admired. He was overbearing, stubborn, opinionated, with a hard, closed face that might change to savagery when unbridled passion swept him.

And yet in spite of all these traits, perhaps he had another softer, warmer side. I had seen it when he was with Tommy or Meggie. Sighing with exasperation, I knew I dwelt too much on Dugan. Thoughts of him were prone to drive more pressing matters from my mind.

Impatiently, I flung off the covers and left my bed to check the French clock ticking on the mantel. It lacked only twenty minutes of the appointed time and I decided it would be a good idea to get there early. That way, the professor might not have a chance to prowl around and discover Dugan in his hiding place.

I wished Dugan had not wanted to be there albeit hidden. Suppose he sneezed? That would be the end of any collaboration or trust between the professor and myself. I hated the idea of working with the man, but since I had not come up with a single clue regarding the missing gold, I was getting desperate.

Drawing a deep breath, I donned my bronze and peach outer-robe and pulled a tight bow on the sash. The long hair streaming on my shoulders looked too provocative since I was in night apparel so I smoothed it back and confined it in a ribbon on my nape. Soft slippers went on my feet, a lighted candlestick in my hand, and I was ready.

Easing the door open, I peered up and down the hall, feeling rather uneasy at the darkness confronting me. Not a light shone anywhere, not even a glimmer of moonlight from the tall recessed windows. All was black, all was silent. Fear came very near the surface of my highly strung emotions.

I raised my candle and some of the shadows darted

back so I could see my way. Carefully, trying not to
tremble or breathe too loudly, I slid one slipper past
the other. Down the wide stone staircase I went,
through the main hall to the rear, then along a winding passageway.

As I opened the door leading to the moist dimness of
the conservatory, something creaked against the far,
glass wall.

"Professor Harden?" I faltered.

No answer.

Creeping forward, I approached the trellis and whispered, "Dugan? Are you there?"

Not a sound. I was alone.

What had made that noise, then? I held my candle
high and examined the room. When no one appeared,
I decided that a tree branch might have scraped
against one of the glass panes. I could feel a draft
against my face and realized that the wind outside had
risen strongly.

Still complying with Dugan's instructions, I sat
down on the wrought-iron bench and placed my candlestick on a nearby table. The wavering light made
the images of snaking vines and towering palm trees
more eerie as they alternately elongated and shrunk
away in the shadows generated by some air current.

My hands felt damp and I wiped them on my robe,
then pulled my neckline higher and tightened the sash
again. My eyes kept darting everywhere. I noted the
accelerated pounding of my heart and knew I must not
succumb to nerves. Breathe deeply, I told myself.
Think rationally. Nothing can hurt me here . . . can
it?

But where was Dugan? Surely he should have been
here by now. The thought that he had deserted me
started a slow anger building. Undoubtedly, he was off
with Glynnis, still involved in their "rendezvous."

Glynnis, who was so anxious to capture the wily Highlander, probably would try to keep him at her side all night. He evidently had completely forgotten me in Glynnis's clinging arms, the cad! When I saw him, I certainly would flay him with my tongue. I clenched my hands, an imaginary dialogue racing through my mind.

Well, Dugan, after all your talk about hiding here in case I was in danger—you never came.

Dugan then would say: *I thought you considered it rather unnecessary.*

I changed my mind. It was frightening, alone at midnight in the deserted conservatory, meeting a man who might be dangerous.

Sorry. I meant to come.

Admit it, Dugan, you were with Glynnis and my peril faded completely from your mind.

So engrossed was I with this imaginary conversation that when the hall door opened, I was completely caught off-guard and gave a stifled scream.

There stood Professor Harden, fully clothed, carrying a candle in a holder. "Mrs. Dunburn?" he called softly. "Ah, yes, I see you. Good, good. Now we can talk undisturbed."

"First, I have some questions," I blurted out, pleased that my voice was clear and remarkably steady.

"Wait a minute." He then prowled the length and breadth of the conservatory. If Dugan had been there . . .

I had to swallow hard and summon all my wits when the professor finally sat down beside me. I turned a little on the bench so that we faced each other but were not too close.

"Did you speak to me one night in London near the guest house on Walden Square?"

He hesitated fractionally. Then he nodded. "Yes, but

you seemed so terrified, I decided to come back in the daytime. Why were you so—"

"Never mind that," I interrupted. "What did you want?"

"I wanted an interview with Paul Dunburn. He refused to answer my letters and saw no one except for you. I watched, then decided to approach you and enlist your aid, so one night I followed you. But as soon as I spoke, you fled inside. The next day, you were gone."

"I soon married Mr. Dunburn," I said stiffly.

"Of course. That was to be expected when his attention to you was so constant."

"Then at last my husband agreed to see you."

He nodded. "I learned he was about to leave for Scotland so I sent one more letter telling him I had some valuable information for his book. We arranged to meet at his house. However, I refused to divulge my own ideas until he confided his theory to me about the gold. We argued and he became very agitated."

"That's when he threw you out."

"That's when I *left*. I could see there was nothing to be gained from such a fanatic so I turned to other avenues." His eyes rested coolly on my face, probably assessing my reaction. This man was very sure of himself and very sly.

It was time to strike deeper. I drew in a breath. "Then a few nights after my husband died, you invaded our home and ransacked the study like a common thief."

An angry color flushed his face. "What are you saying? I certainly did not!"

Ignoring his indignant (and I thought false) disclaimer, I went on. "I'm sure you stole my husband's manuscript. Now I want it back—or else I shall go to the police."

He smiled coldly, clasping his hands around a

drawn-up knee. "You didn't go before, I'm sure. Shall I tell you why? You had no proof. You still have none."

"We have some very suspicious circumstances. You were foiled by my husband in London. Now you're here and I think you followed me to see if I would be amenable to a collaboration."

His eyes slitted. "Well, *are you?*"

Before I could reply, his head jerked around and he leaped to his feet. "What was that?"

I hadn't heard anything and said so.

"I guess it was a branch or twig outside," he muttered, staring hard at the blank, black windows.

"Perhaps a dog or other animal." I shrugged impatiently. "Professor, let us be frank."

His glance quickened and he sank back down. "By all means. But I'll tell you this: I do not have your manuscript."

I let that pass for now and waved my hand. "My husband's book lacked an ending. He wanted to surprise the world with his discovery of Prince Charlie's gold, as you evidently are aware."

He seemed to pounce. He slid closer on the bench and leaned toward me with a hot gleam in his eye. "Did he know where it was?"

"Not exactly. He hadn't proved anything yet. He only had a theory. That's why he wanted to come to Castlecove before he submitted his book for publication."

"What was this theory? You can tell me that much, can't you? I assure you I am trustworthy with a well-known reputation. I'll even work with you on the ending, see that it goes smoothly. I fancy I am much more experienced than you as far as writing goes. All I want for my pains is a small acknowledgment at the end of the book."

Ha! That was an unlikely statement.

"I don't know what Paul's theory was. And I haven't

any clues myself. Everyone here is certain that the gold was taken long ago."

"Pshaw!" He rose and paced impatiently. "Paul Dunburn must have had a good reason to believe that the gold is still hidden here. He sent you here to find it, didn't he?"

I stared at him without answering.

He struck one fist into his palm. "Well, I believe in it, too. Just think—a fortune in golden sovereigns left by the Bonnie Prince. What a sensation that find would cause! And the book—how it would sell, eh? There could be an exhibition of the treasure, interviews in newspapers and trade journals . . ."

I knew that he could see himself as the literary lion of the hour, not me or Paul. I had no doubt that if he found the cache, he would rush to publish a paper on his discovery, claiming all the credit before Paul's book ever came to light. He might make a tidy sum from lectures on the subject, also.

He spun toward me. "Tell me where you've searched. Have you questioned everyone, including servants? Have you looked for old letters, diaries . . . ?"

"Yes, I've done most of those things, but—"

"Where exactly did you look? I want to know." He bent down and gripped my shoulders in big, strong hands. "This is the biggest thing to ever come my way. And I daresay the same applies to you. So let's not beat around the bush. Start talking."

I shoved him back. "For heaven's sake, calm down."

He straightened up, drawing a deep breath. "You must tell me exactly what ground you've covered. There may be things, places, that you've overlooked. After all, you are not a professional in unearthing historical matters. I am."

He was right about that. I was no professional. So far, I had made no headway at all. I debated swiftly, then decided that I had no choice. I would have to enlist the professor's aid. At least, if we were successful, I would have an ending for Paul's book and would try to whisk it off to the publishers as quickly as possible.

"Very well," I said. "Lady Margaret showed me some letters from clan members written when the prince was here. There also was a letter from the prince himself. It was sent from the Isle of Skye and told the family to disburse the gold among the widows of his followers. However, there seems to be no record of that ever being done."

"Because it never happened." He gloated. "What else? Tell me everything the prince mentioned in his letter."

"Well, he referred to his dog. He also spoke of the 'beloved place' and since he spent a lot of time in the old summerhouse—"

"A summerhouse?" he barked. "Is it still here?"

I nodded.

"Have you looked it over thoroughly?"

"Not yet. It's almost a ruin and they say it's quite unsafe. Everyone has warned me away so I haven't found a chance to approach it unobserved. Lady Margaret says her ancestors searched it thoroughly so—"

He waved a large, well-cared-for hand. "That means nothing. I will search it like a professional." He bent a stern gaze on me. "Anything else?"

"It's your turn. What about *your* information?"

He shrugged and stared at a spot above my head. "It seems that I know nothing more than you do. The prince was here, he hid the gold, went off to war, and was unable to return. I don't believe the gold was stolen, it probably was too well hidden. As for being disbursed, since the family has no record of it, I'm sure it never happened."

I stared up at him. "Well, there's not much more I

can do. The manuscript might have been some help if it hadn't been stolen."

"A pity," he said vaguely, "some jealous writer, no doubt." He picked up his candle, guttering low in its pewter holder. "Thank you, Mrs. Dunburn. This talk was most enlightening. Tomorrow I will begin my search."

"I think someone else may be searching," I said softly.

He whirled back. "Who? What do you mean?"

"All I know is that Dugan MacInnis's wife had a tower hideaway. I saw it, very rich and elegant, but things were torn and ransacked. I don't know when it happened. It seems to be a mystery. They say it might have been an angry servant who was discharged."

His eyes flickered and he chewed his thick, red lower lip. "Actually, two things might account for the destruction. As you say, a search for something. Or a vicious hatred for the former dweller in the tower. I'll try to find a way to look at it."

"I would like to come with you."

"Well, I don't know. You might be in the way. We don't want to draw too much attention to our activities, especially the search for gold. To all intents, I am here merely with an historical interest in the castle."

He turned away, then looked back over his shoulder. "Aren't you returning to your room?"

"No, not yet. I'll wait here a few minutes. We don't want to be seen together this late at night, do we?" I said in a determined voice. "Wasn't that the whole purpose of our meeting secretly in this manner?"

"Of course. You're very wise. Good night."

16

I heard the professor's footsteps fade away on the stone flags of the hallway. After that, there was no sound anywhere.

Alone in the conservatory, I rose, again noting a current of cold air. Frowning, I made my way closer to the windows where it definitely was colder.

Then I gave a startled exclamation. One hinged pane was ajar! Just a crack but enough for outside air to seep in, enough to harm the delicate plants nearby. *And also enough for voices on the inside to be heard.*

I closed the window; they simply pushed in or out as needed without a lock. It was entirely possible that somebody had stood outside listening to our conversation. Dugan instantly came to mind. He was probably the only person who knew about this meeting between myself and the professor.

Well, if Dugan had decided to eavesdrop outside instead of inside, it probably was a good idea after the way the professor had just inspected the conservatory.

I felt uneasy as I realized just how important the

Prince's Gold might be to others beside myself. But not to Dugan. He didn't believe that it existed; neither did the old laird or his lady. What about Davy? A young man of his type always had a need for money. Glynnis? Definitely. She had expensive tastes, was interested in Dugan's wealth, and seemed to have no present "protector," unless you counted the professor and, somehow, I didn't believe they were romantically involved.

Reluctantly, I added Miss Grey to my list of suspects because of her fanatical devotion to Prince Charlie's memorabilia. She, too, could certainly use the money. Servants? Well, Nora might be almost in that category, longing to escape from her drab life. But she was such a remote, aloof woman, seemingly wrapped up in household matters, that I dismissed her to the bottom of my list.

Wearily, I turned away. It was time to leave these questions for another day and seek my bed. However, as I approached the table where I had left my candle, I stopped dead and gave a little cry.

A man swayed in the doorway, his hands braced on either side, his cravat undone, red hair tumbling above glazed eyes.

"Dugan!"

"Come here," he croaked.

I stared at him in dismay. In this mood, the way he looked, drunken, belligerent . . . Suddenly, I felt afraid. I didn't know what he might do.

I decided to try a calm approach. "Why don't you sit down here for a minute? I saw the professor, you know." Gingerly, I slid back to the bench.

Dugan staggered drunkenly (there were no other words for it) across the tiled floor and dragged a chair in front of me. Straddling it, he crossed his arms on the back and rested his chin there. The nearby candle threw dark shadows across his face, adding to his menacing appearance.

His speech definitely was slurred. "Wha-what happened?"

I looked away, tightening my robe, which had a tendency to gape upon my chest. "The professor denied taking the manuscript, which was no surprise, and I don't believe him for a minute. He's the only logical suspect. He'd been to the London house before so he knew the layout of the room. It would have been no problem for him to unhinge a ground-level window and climb in."

"Aye," Dugan growled, rubbing thoughtfully at his chin.

"However, he offered to help me find an ending to Paul's book," I continued, "and I accepted. He plans to search the summerhouse. Among other things."

Dugan gave a sudden bark of laughter. "Good luck to him. The place has been searched for ages."

"He said he will do it professionally."

"Och, aye?" He sneered.

"There's something else. A window was ajar while he was here. I think someone was listening . . ."

"Why in b-blazes did ye no' in-investigate?"

"I did after the professor left. That's when I noticed a draft of air. Were *you* listening at the window?"

"No."

"Well, then, why weren't you here as promised?"

He ran his fingers through his tousled hair. "I—I fell asleep."

My lip curled. "You were intoxicated. And still are." I stood up. "Now, since I've told you everything, please excuse me."

The chair crashed backward and Dugan lurched to his feet, his hands catching at my shoulders. "Not so f-fast, my girl. For one thing, I'm not drunk. I n-never am." He straightened with difficulty and glared at me.

I tried to twist away. "Why don't you admit it," I

said furiously. "You went to Glynnis and loved and drank until—"

"I did not," he roared. "The only d-drink I've had this night was the remains of my b-before-dinner sherry." He put his face close to mine and whispered solemnly, "S-something was put into it."

"Who would want to do that?" I scoffed.

"The professor."

"Nonsense." But a little uncertainty crept into my voice. "I still think you're intoxicated and don't know what you're saying. Now, will you *please* let me go? What do I care how you spent the night!"

"Wait." He was breathing hard, but he managed to pull me close. He dropped his head down on my shoulder where the robe was pulled awry and I felt his fevered lips against my skin as he spoke in a harsh whisper. "When I p-promise to come, I do. I was not with Glynnis."

"All right, all right." My voice was oddly weak. So were all my muscles as I pushed feebly against him. I could feel the beating of his heart against my breast, the heat and heady male scent of his skin.

"Dugan—move away now—it's late—"

"The b-blasted room is going round. C-Courtney, can you help me to ma bed?" He raised his head and looked groggily into my eyes.

"I-I'll try," I answered, swallowing against an odd obstruction in my throat. "Put your arm around my shoulders. Can you hold the candlestick?"

We started out. His big hand dangled just above my breast, and during our wavering progress to his room, it frequently touched me. I glanced at him in quick suspicion, but his eyes were nearly shut, his breathing stertorous, so I staggered on as best I could, unable to shift our positions.

He indicated the way, and fortunately, his door

stood open. No servant waited for him and only one lamp flickered low.

At the big, four-poster bed, we stopped and Dugan blinked at me, managing to slide the candle onto a nearby stand. "Th-thank you, Courtney. Am I for—forgiven for not c-coming earlier to the conservatory?"

"Yes. It doesn't matter. No harm came to me. Good night." I turned to leave, but suddenly his arms reached out and pulled me back against his chest.

"Dugan! What are you doing? Let me go—" Helpless in his grip, I tried to squirm away.

"Be s-still." He shut his eyes with a quick catch of his breath. "I—I would n-not let you be hurt." The next instant, he caught my lips in his with a shocking, feverish kiss that seemed to go on forever, plunging deeper and deeper.

Emotions swirled through me like a searing fire. I felt surprise, then faintness, and finally an excitement that I could not control even if I had wanted to. Here it was at last. The thing I'd dreamed about now was a reality: Dugan's hot, strong lips on mine, reducing me to a weak and dazed, mindless creature, trembling in his grasp and making no effort to fend him off.

But when Dugan finally raised his mouth to gasp for breath, a flood of shame came to my rescue. "If—if you don't let me go this instant, I'll scream the house down!" No matter that my heart was hammering as fast as his or that I was so breathless I could hardly speak, I pushed against him, exerting all my strength.

He smiled slowly. "Aye, I think you would s-scream somethin' fierce. B-but it would be worth it."

Suddenly, his arms grew slack and he stumbled back onto the bed while I grabbed at a post to keep my balance. His eyes shut, his breathing became deep and hard. He didn't move a muscle. Evidently the drunken stupor had overtaken him. I watched warily, and when he didn't stir, I flung a portion of the bedspread over his prone figure. His face was flushed beneath the damp and straggling hair, but there was no softening of his rugged features. In sleep, they looked as hard as ever, probably just like the Highlanders the English used to call barbarians in days of old. They must have been a tough, strong-minded group. Men to be afraid of in a fight. Men whom women longed to conquer.

I turned and fled.

When I reached my room, my brain was whirling, my breathing rapid, my pulses still hammering. I must have been mad to allow Dugan to kiss me like that! What would happen next time we met? How on earth could I look him in the face?

With a moan, I crossed the room to press my fevered forehead on the windowpane. The lamps were not lit. I had left the room in darkness when I went to the conservatory and now I felt grateful for the cool and faceless shadows.

I clutched the drapes and peered into the night, seeking solace, seeking calmness. But then I noticed a light in the distant summerhouse and my attention quickened. Was the professor searching there already?

I wondered about him. If he found the gold ahead of me, would he simply abscond with it? Here was a new thought—and a worrisome one, pushing other matters momentarily from my mind. I certainly didn't trust Professor Harden. He was too smooth, too confident, with his rich clothing, affected, domineering voice, and the floridly handsome face with its touch of cruelty and coarseness.

As I watched, I saw the light go out, but though I waited, straining my eyes, no one appeared on the path leading to the castle. It was so dark, however, someone might have passed unseen.

At last, cold and weary, I dropped the curtain and crept, shivering, into my bed. For the first time, I fully realized what dangerous forces I was combating.

Much was at stake here: fame as well as fortune. And now two ruthless people had arrived: Glynnis and Professor Harden.

Just before I drifted off to sleep, I thought how comforting it would be to have a pair of warm, strong, male arms holding me throughout the night.

Dugan . . . I thought drowsily, against all reason. Dugan . . .

17

It was late when I awoke next morning, and for a
while, I stretched luxuriously, wondering why I felt so
strange . . . so different . . .

Then I remembered.

Dugan had kissed me. In a way no gentleman would
ever kiss a lady. A searing blush seemed to engulf the
whole length of my body as I recalled the shocking
episode. It had been like an invasion when Dugan
pushed my trembling lips apart. He had been intoxicated, of course, and his true, savage, passionate nature had emerged.

But he had sworn he wasn't drunk, and thinking
back, I couldn't recall a taint of liquor on his warm,
moist breath. No . . . none at all.

Was it possible that someone *had* dropped a drug
such as laudanum into his drink? He said he had left it
on the mantel before supper and must have finished it
off later on. But who would do such a thing to him?
And why?

Of course, the professor was the most likely culprit,

drugging the wine to keep Dugan from overhearing us in the conservatory. Perhaps he was aware that Dugan had been there in the London house when it was ransacked and might now suspect him of stealing the manuscript. The professor seemed to know a lot about our movements. Was it possible he had employed a spy?

I decided not to accuse him of tampering with the wine. He would deny it and right now I was committed to an alliance with him in searching for the gold. I could not endanger that.

When I was dressed, I went down to the breakfast table where I found that the professor and Glynnis were the only ones still present. It was quite late, of course, and Dugan must have been out in the fields. A great relief surged through me that I need not confront him for a while. How could I ever live down the fact that at first I had clung to him in soaring ecstasy, letting him kiss me as long as he desired? Dear heaven, how I prayed that his befuddled state would retain no memory of that encounter.

As I approached the table, Glynnis and her companion stopped their low-voiced conversation and looked at me. I couldn't help wondering about them. How well had they known each other in London? There didn't seem to be anything loverlike between them, glances were cool and indifferent. I would have dubbed them "casual acquaintances," but then one never knew.

They both greeted me, the professor with a smirk as he touched a napkin to his full, red lips. "Today, I have permission to cull a little background material on Prince Charlie by exploring portions of the grounds and castle. I must be up and doing. So—" He shoved back his chair and rose. "If you will excuse me, ladies—"

"Oh, Professor Harden, I would like to accompany

you," I said hastily, turning around from the sideboard with my cup and plate. "If you'll just give me a few minutes—"

He waved a plump hand, the diamond flashing in his signet ring. "I believe there are other plans for you today, dear lady." He started briskly from the room. "But I'll be in the garden for a while."

"You needn't wait for her, Max," Glynnis called after his retreating back. "I'm taking Courtney for a boat ride." Her head swung in my direction. "The children, too. Miss Grey will bring them here in a few minutes."

Was Glynnis trying to keep a path clear for the professor's investigations?

"Oh, I wouldn't care for a sail today," I said. "Thank you, perhaps another time." Quickly, I poured cream and sugar on my porridge and began shoveling it in, determined to seek out that wily Max Harden as soon as possible.

Glynnis's long, green eyes looked coldly amused as she took a sip of tea. "It was Lady Margaret's idea since Tommy was begging for a sail and the air is very still today so she asked if I would take the children out for a little while. She then suggested that you might also enjoy a boat ride and could supervise Tommy and Meggie."

"Can't you ask Davy to go with you? I really would like to talk to the professor."

"Davy took Nora shopping in the village. Tonight's the dinner party in your honor. Really, Courtney, how can you refuse to comply with a little request from your hostess?"

She was right, of course, I couldn't. Still I tried one more feeble excuse. "Won't you be nervous going out in the cove again after—after what happened?"

"Not a bit. We had gone farther out that day and it was windy. Besides, that was two long years ago and it's time to freshen up my capability on the water."

After that, I gave in, albeit uneasily, and as soon as I had finished eating, I went upstairs to fetch my wraps.

I met Polly coming out of Glynnis's room. Her usually good-natured face was marred this morning by a scowl. She sighed when she saw me. "Miss Courtney, would you be wanting any of your jewelry cleaned today? I have this basinful to do for Miss Glynnis so a few more pieces make no matter." When I said I only had a small amount of jewelry, but I would get it for her, she followed me into my bedroom.

She set the basin on a nearby stand and I rummaged in a drawer for my pearls and chain. Suddenly, someone shouted to her from the hall, and as she whirled around, the bowl of glistening gems tumbled to the rug. Polly gave a worried moan. "I'll be right back, miss."

I bent and swept the pieces up, unable to stop myself from admiring each and every one. They didn't look as bright as they had last night by candlelight, but maybe it was true they only needed washing.

There was a necklace of cabochon-cut rubies and pearls, lockets set in gold and silver filigree, a number of mixed rings, and two diamond bracelets. Some gemmed brooches had articulated pendants to make them quiver.

But then as I looked more closely, holding them up to the light, suddenly I realized that these stones were *paste!* Every one had gold paint on the back to increase the shine. I gave a short laugh, but I wasn't too surprised. Hadn't Glynnis indicated that she was interested in Dugan's money?

At last, however, I lifted up a silver chain that looked different from the rest, heavier, richer, with a huge blue sapphire in the center surrounded by real diamonds! It seemed familiar to me. And then I knew. *It looked exactly like the lavaliere worn by Aileen in her portrait.*

I caught back an astonished exclamation. Had she given it to Glynnis? It must be a family heirloom of undoubted value. Could it have been left here after Aileen died and then confiscated by Glynnis from a hidden cache up in the tower? It certainly puzzled me, and as soon as I donned a short wool cape and bonnet, I hurried to the hall of portraits. Yes, the jewelry was identical and I knew Glynnis's lavaliere was no paste copy, the hard glass of artificial gems. Here was another mystery and I determined to probe it at the earliest opportunity.

Glynnis was waiting by the front door, the children jumping up and down and shouting excitedly. Tommy actually was the more excited of the two, but Meggie's blue eyes sparkled and her face was flushed as she ran to me and grabbed my hand. "Oh, Miss Courtney, isn't this gr-rand? I love to go out on the water, don't you?"

"Yes, I do, but I've only done a little sailing."

Tommy caught my other hand. "*I'm* going to sail the boat and I want to leave *right now*. Come on!"

"Whisht, Tommy, behave yourself," Meggie said sternly. "Miss Glynnis said *maybe* you could hold the tiller for a wee bit."

Glynnis looked around with barely smothered boredom. "Shall we go? The day is perfect for a sail, but if the weather changes, we will have to come right in."

I caught Tommy as he took a flying leap. "One word, my little man. You must promise to obey your elders on this boat ride. Instantly! If there is any rambunctious behavior, you won't be going out in the near future if I have anything to say about it."

"I'll be very good, Mama Courtney." Tommy gave me his most winning smile and managed to jerk free. He and Meggie tore off at once.

I was glad that life at Castlecove had taken Tommy's mind from thoughts of finding the Prince's Gold. He found so many new things of interest, but I was afraid one of these days he would revert to treasure hunting and that might be a nuisance. I hoped he would continue to be intrigued by other things for a long while.

There was a great deal to be enjoyed here and this was indeed a perfect day. When blue skies and sunny light appeared in the Scottish Highlands, as they did today, everything seemed so brilliant, so full of vibrant colors and pungent, sweet aromas. It was enough to stun the senses with the heady mixture.

I found that, after all, I looked forward to being on the water and was filled with anticipation as Glynnis took the path down to the cove by means of flat wooden steps set into the hillside. However, the way was steep and rocky, there was no handrail, and we all proceeded cautiously. I forced Tommy to wait for me until I could hold on to the back of his short jacket.

When we reached the bottom, I looked about with pleasure. The cove waters were indeed calm, intensely blue, turning green farther out, and sparkling most invitingly. We crossed a narrow, gritty shingle to where a wooden pier extended and a small sailboat tugged at its rope as though anxious to be off. The children both yelled and pounded toward it so that Glynnis and I had to raise our voices and demand order in our sternest tones. Meggie immediately calmed down while Tommy capped his ebullience with difficulty. A little riffle of uneasiness went over me and I could see why it had been necessary for another adult to accompany Glynnis.

However, when we pushed off, the soft breeze sped our little craft along quite merrily and I relaxed. For a while, we sailed back and forth, admiring the views of cliffs and the many islands farther out, thickly crowned with stands of pine. Meggie told me that some were inhabitated, some not, while many had thriving industries such as weaving woolen cloth and distilling a well-known whisky they called "Scotch."

After a while, the children grew restless with this peaceful passage and Tommy finally prevailed on Glynnis to let him take the tiller while she watched and Meggie added her encouragement. It amused me to see that sober, little Meggie was becoming more like Tommy: bouncing, laughing, wanting Tommy to go faster. I had hoped that it would be the other way around and the older child would tone down the impulsive exuberance inherent in Tommy's nature. Where he got it from, I didn't know. Paul had been such a quiet man.

I wondered if Meggie would ever take after her mother. Right now, with Dugan raising her, it didn't seem at all likely. From all I had heard, Aileen had been a very frivolous, self-centered flirt who had to capture any interesting male she came across.

Davy seemed to be the only one who still sincerely mourned the red-haired beauty. How Glynnis felt— supposedly Aileen's best friend—it was difficult to tell. She might have been jealous of Aileen and resented the fact that she held on to Dugan when Glynnis wanted him for herself. That reminded me of the lavaliere and the other gems. I raised my voice a little as the waves were getting noisy. "Polly brought your jewels into my room this morning so she could clean my few pieces along with yours. I must confess I was awed by the beautiful things you have. Especially that lavaliere."

Glynnis turned abruptly, moving closer to me, leaving Tommy at the tiller. Her green eyes narrowed on my face.

"You examined them?"

I nodded, watching her closely.

I could almost see the wheels turning in her brain. Wondering. Speculating. Had I seen the lavaliere and compared it with the one in Aileen's portrait? I was sure Glynnis had not intended to display it. Somehow, the chain must have become entangled with her other jewels. But however she had come by it, greed had kept it close at hand.

I said nothing, looking back at her innocently. She could not be certain that I attached any significance to it, but the fact that she didn't mention receiving it as a gift from Aileen made me certain there was some reason for secrecy.

Her gaze stayed so sharp and inimical on me, I began to regret mentioning anything about the jewelry while we were in this little boat where an accident could easily overtake me. As it once had Aileen? I couldn't trust this cold-eyed woman who was staring at me.

But I was not the one who had an accident.

Tommy had been left too long at the tiller and he soon gleefully headed from the cove for rougher waters that would be more of a challenge. Straight in his path, an island loomed, rock-ringed. Too late, we saw the danger. Meggie shrieked and Glynnis spun around just as the boy panicked, making too sharp a turn. The boat dipped wildly, waves splashed onto the deck with a hard, chilled force. For a moment, all was confusion.

Glynnis slipped, made a futile grab for the rail, and went flying over the side into the water. I screamed and stumbled to the edge of the boat, clinging desperately to the cold, slippery rail. The spray blinded me temporarily, but then I saw her vanish out of sight. Terrified, I stretched out my hands and cried her name while Meggie screamed beside me.

The next second, Glynnis's head broke the surface and she shrieked, arms flailing. "Help, help—*I can't swim!*" Again the water closed above her.

"Glynnis, Glynnis!" I shouted, lunging as far over the side as possible. "Oh, God, where are you?"

Only the children had been put into the two mackintosh rubber life jackets, but there was a preserver underneath the seat and I yelled for Meggie to get it. I had never felt so helplessly terrified in my life. Should I dive into the water myself? I was a very indifferent swimmer, but perhaps I should try—

Just then, Glynnis's head resurfaced, water streaming from her black hair into her eyes. She choked and coughed. "H-help—help me!"

"Grab this," Meggie cried, and tossed the rubber circle neatly right in front of her.

Glynnis thrashed wildly, apparently panic-stricken, but then she clasped the ring and managed to get closer to the bobbing boat. Meggie and I reached down and caught her arms, and after considerable heaving and tugging, we were able to haul her aboard.

Glynnis flopped down like a stranded fish, choking and coughing up seawater. She shook in every limb. I knew she must be chilled to the bone and I tore off her skirt and jacket, flinging my own wrap around her.

Meanwhile, the boat was going in the wildest circles due to Tommy's frightened steering and I flew to take the tiller before we capsized. "Tend to Glynnis," I cried to Meggie. "Wrap her in that blanket underneath the seat."

I finally brought the boat around so that we headed back to shore, a sober, subdued little group, the only sound on board the chattering of Glynnis's teeth. Meggie held her in her plump little arms, rubbing briskly so the blood could circulate and warm her.

Thankfully, by the time we tied up at the dock, Glynnis was relatively calm, though still shivering beneath her wraps. She managed to express her appreciation to Meggie and me for saving her.

I sent up a prayer of thanks that this other boating accident had not been serious. I certainly was going to see that Tommy had some sailing lessons before he ever ventured out in a boat again.

We went as quickly as possible to the house where I

sent servants to bring hot water for Glynnis's bath and take her a heated alcoholic lemonade.

Nothing further was said about the jewels. What business was it of mine if Glynnis had the lavaliere? Even though I couldn't help wondering about it . . .

Then I suddenly recalled something else of equal mystery. When she was in the water, Glynnis had said, "Help, help. *I can't swim.*" Yet I had distinctly over-heard her in the garden telling Davy: "Aileen couldn't swim. I can."

18

T hat night, even when I was dressed and Polly had pronounced me "richt bonnie," I dreaded descending to the large dinner party consisting of curious strangers.

The near-tragedy in the bay today had not helped my peace of mind, and my stomach was so tied in knots I wondered how I would survive the endless courses. All I really wanted was a glass of sherry to calm my nerves.

Tonight I would be on display to a host of clan members who might view me with the same suspicion and antagonism that Dugan had first shown. Why did Paul marry someone English? they might wonder. And someone so much younger?

How fortunate I was that Sir Hugh and his sweet lady had welcomed me so warmly. They had shown nothing but pleasure in the fact that Paul had married me. And both had urged me to become a permanent member of the household.

When I finally surveyed myself in the long pier glass,

I knew that at least I looked my best in the new pink rep, and if my bosom and shoulders were exposed more than usual, I had seen pictures of Queen Victoria in much lower necklines than mine so I knew I had nothing to worry about. My hair shone from Polly's energetic brushing and she had drawn it back in a smooth coil, pinning on a circlet of rosebuds, which I had picked in the garden. A few matching sprays were attached among the ruffles of my skirt so that I moved in a drift of fresh rose perfume.

My spirits lifted as well as my chin as I picked up my fan and descended to the parlor. After all, I had done nothing to be ashamed of. Why not hold up my head and act the gracious lady? However, I was not so bold that I could make a conspicuous entrance so I went down early before any of the guests arrived.

The drawing room was already occupied by Sir Hugh in his wheelchair, Lady Margaret, and Dugan. The men in their Highland dress looked truly splendid. Sir Hugh wore black velvet; Dugan was in bottle-green adorned with silver buttons. Their white shirts had ruffles at neck and cuff, plaid kilts hung pleated to the knee, and at their waists, sporrans of fine otter had a silver trim. Lady Margaret was in a full white gown with a silken tartan sash across one shoulder and a parure of pearls and diamonds glistening on arms, throat, and hair.

This seemed like an occasion for elegance of manners, and as though I greeted royalty, I sank into a curtsy, murmuring their names. The men bowed. Lady Margaret inclined her head, eyes dancing with delight. "Och," she exclaimed, "what a bonnie sight you are."

"Aye." Her husband smiled. "And I see you are wearing my favorite Damask rosebuds. So fragrant. They suit you well, my dear."

Dugan examined me with his usual thoroughness, which made me wonder if my petticoat was dragging or a hairpin was slipping out of place. As I recalled our last encounter, I felt a warm blush sweep my cheeks. Was Dugan also remembering that passionate embrace?

However, he made no comment except to inquire coolly, "Have you recovered from your trouble in the cove today?"

"Oh, yes. Is Glynnis all right? Will she be down?"

"See for yourself," Glynnis trilled, advancing from the doorway. "I am perfectly well."

"Oh, I am so glad." My eyes went over her composed, thin face, which appeared to have been powdered. I even detected some skillfully applied coloring on cheeks and lips, evidently to disguise any ill effects caused by her fall into the sea.

"Your gown is beautiful," I exclaimed. The pale green *peau de soie* was overlaid with a lace skirt and train embroidered with pearls and crystal pendants. If this was a Worth original, it must have cost a pretty penny. I wondered if a Scot would admire the extravagant gown. As for Dugan, he seemed to be examining her other assets, staring frankly at the large amount of creamy flesh displayed. But when she whispered something in his ear, he shook his head, and, frowning, she moved away.

I saw her glance at me across her shoulder. Was she afraid of what I might have divulged regarding the lavaliere? She also must be aware now that I knew she couldn't swim. Her story about saving herself in the bay while Aileen floated off was very strange, to say the least.

At that moment, the other members of the household entered, the front door chimed, and immediately I was caught up in a hubbub of introductions and hearty greetings issued in round Scottish burrs. The guests were a merry, good-looking throng. Several couples with fresh, high-colored faces were in their middle years. The rest were in their twenties or thirties, all very well dressed, including some quite fine jewelry. The men as a whole wore Highland dress tartans and their wives had matching sashes over wide-skirted silken gowns.

Everyone acted extremely friendly to me and I soon relaxed and even enjoyed answering the same questions over and over.

"Do you miss London?"

"No, I have no ties there anymore, but unfortunately, I must return pretty soon."

"Did Paul finish his latest book about Prince Charlie?"

"Not quite, but I hope to find an ending for it. Then it can be published."

"Don't you think Scotland is bonnie when the sun shines?"

"The bonniest," I replied sincerely several times.

All the while, I was aware of Dugan close at hand, sipping from a crystal glass, listening and observing me from hooded eyes.

When I stood alone for a moment, he moved closer. "I must warn you not to go out in the cove again unless I'm with you."

"It was Miss Macrae who had the accident, not I. It seems your cove is rather dangerous."

He shrugged. "Glynnis was in no danger. She says that she can swim quite well."

I blinked at that, but I didn't feel like arguing. I turned away and it was then I noticed Nora looking better than I had ever seen her. She wore a full-skirted blue satin with a matching silky bow in the curls piled high on her head. Her thin, usually harassed face was suffused with color and animation tonight.

I wasn't long in discovering the reason. She was standing close to a stocky young man with a serious, dark mien. Her eyes on him were admiring, almost hungry. Had Nora found romance?

Lady Margaret, noticing the direction of my gaze, murmured in my ear, "You are observing Nora's transformation. And the reason for it. That young man is Malcolm Lorne, our local doctor. A while back, they were getting serious about each other until a serpent intervened."

Her voice had become cold and hard. I stared at her. Could she mean Aileen?

Lady Margaret sighed. "Let's hope they have another chance."

Just then, dinner was announced and there was no time for further comments. Though this was a country estate, it was all very formal tonight. Each lady had a designated escort into dinner. Mine was Davy. Dugan gave his arm to Lady Margaret.

At the table, there were place cards and beside each plate was a menu, which I read with awe.

Dinner
Potage St. Germain
Poached Scotch Salmon—Cucumber-Parsley Sauce
Croquettes of Chicken—Tomato Sauce

****

Roast Sirloin & Ribs of Beef—Horseradish Sauce
Baked Ham and Spinach—Sauce Madère
Vegetable Marrow—Cream Sauce—Carrots Julienne—Rice
Roast, Mashed, & Boiled New Potatoes

****

Plum Pudding—Sweet Sauce   Strawberry & Apple Tart
Cheese—Sweetmeats—Tea or Coffee

I took a little from each item offered and everything was so delicious, I found my usual appetite returning in full force.

All of the guests were very lively, much more so than English people, but Glynnis was the liveliest of all, laughing, flirting, accepting a number of refills in her wineglass.

"You would never know that Glynnis had fallen in the water today and nearly drowned, would you?" I remarked to Davy, who was sitting next to me. "She was very frightened—especially since she couldn't swim." I eyed him keenly, watching for his reaction.

"What do you mean?" Davy blinked a little in surprise.

"She cried out, saying something like: 'Help me! I can't swim.'"

He shrugged. "I guess it was the shock of going overboard, the icy water and so forth. Right then, she couldn't swim. That's what she meant."

"Oh," I answered blankly. Well, it was a possible explanation all right. I hadn't thought of that, proving again how inadequate were my powers of investigation.

I could hardly wait to see if Professor Harden had discovered anything today that might be of help to me. I had tried to track him down earlier in the afternoon, but was unable to find him.

When the gentlemen finally joined the ladies in the parlor after dinner, I started toward him, but was again thwarted, this time by Lady Margaret. Glancing around, she held up her hand for silence and announced: "It wouldn't be a true *ceilidh*—that's a Scottish gathering, Courtney," she whispered to me— "without a skirl or two on the bagpipes. So, everyone, let us adjourn to the rose garden."

A babbling group surged forward and I was swept along, soon finding myself outdoors beside the wheeled chair containing Sir Hugh in the lovely lavender light of "gloaming."

He looked up at me and smiled, reaching for my

hand. "Not everyone admires the bagpipes, Courtney, but it's a true flavor of our country and not to be missed."

A hush fell over the crowd as a long, wailing sound issued from the surrounding hills. On a rocky promontory, I saw a lone figure, the setting sun burnishing his hair, and I knew that Dugan was our piper.

It proved to be a moving experience. Among the many tunes, I recognized only Robert Burns's beautiful "A Red, Red Rose" and "Comin' Thro' the Rye," but all were equally enjoyable. Every face was lifted to the hills, as the company listened with smiles of pleasure. At last, amid the clapping and laughter, Dugan bowed, left his perch, and the guests began to reenter the castle.

This time, I managed to reach Professor Harden and held him back with a hand upon his arm. "I've been anxious to have a word with you all day," I said softly. "Did you examine the tower? The summerhouse? Has anything turned up?"

"Nothing," he answered curtly.

Evidently, he was annoyed by my persistence. How he must wish that I had stayed docilely in London instead of interfering in something about which I knew so little. If I should stumble upon the solution and rush to publish Paul's book, the professor might be ready to kill me—figuratively speaking, of course.

As I started to move away, he couldn't stop himself from a little bragging. "However, I am not discouraged. My search is just beginning and I am counting on the fact that I'll find clues that other untrained minds have missed."

"Good luck," I said, thinking what a pompous man he was. Pompous, maybe, but also shrewd, determined, and energetic. My only advantage was in being on the scene earlier and having worked closely with Paul, though I certainly wished he had confided more regarding his theories. I also had the prince's letters, Aileen's diary, and the confidence of Lady Margaret and Miss Grey. Though so far, I didn't seem to be any nearer the truth than Professor Harden.

Back in the drawing room, it seemed that Glynnis was about to perform again on the piano with Davy standing by to turn the sheet music for her. Evidently, the selections had been placed there ahead of time to circumvent any of Glynnis's music hall repertoire.

I settled down on a sofa, listening as Glynnis and Davy joined their surprisingly pleasant voices in duets, starting out with "Flow gently, sweet Afton, among thy green braes."

Suddenly, the springs creaked beside me and there was Dugan settling his large body next to me, so close I felt the warmth of his recent exertions on the hillside. I could smell the spray of heather thrust in his button-hole, as well as his own male, wind-fresh scent, which always stirred my senses regardless of how I tried to curb my reaction to him.

"Did you enjoy the pipes?" he asked under cover of the clapping for the performers at the piano.

"Yes, very much. It was quite dramatic."

"The pipes are used in wartime to inspire the troops. The Scots are mighty warriors."

"I can well believe that," I murmured. "I had no idea that you were so musical."

His eyes probed into mine. "There are a lot of things you'll not be knowing about me. Not yet." His large, warm hand squeezed my upper arm, then slid posses-sively down to enclose my wrist.

Startled, I jerked away, attempting to put a few more inches between us, and heard him give a mad-dening chuckle.

"The time will come, my fine lassie."

"For what?" I snapped, angry with him, as well as

angry with myself for wishing he still touched me. "I liked it better when you were antagonistic to me."

"Och, aye?"

"I know what you are attempting to do now."

"And what is that, pray?"

"You want to embarrass me."

"Now that is really daft." He rose lazily and gazed down at me with a sardonic smile, hands resting on his hips. "I still am antagonistic. Make no mistake that I am getting soft."

"Oh, go away," I hissed, fanning rapidly. "You're spoiling the music."

With a short laugh, he turned on his heel and headed for a table containing decanters of various strong spirits.

I quickly accepted a glass of syllabub from a passing maid. The wine and cream mixture was vastly soothing and I had just set down the empty goblet—when it happened. That astonishing event that was to change so many lives.

The music had ended and everyone was chattering and moving about when, suddenly, a servant approached Lady Margaret and whispered in her ear.

She immediately uttered a hoarse cry and staggered to her feet. "No, no! Oh, God, I can't believe it! Hugh! Dugan!"

Those close by turned to stare at her and exclaim: "What is it?" "What has happened?"

"Aunt Meg, what's wrong?" Dugan cried, and leaped toward her, his glass crashing to the floor.

Unable to utter another sound, his aunt could only gulp and point a shaking finger.

A terrible silence swept the room and every eye went to the arched doorway leading to the hall. A woman stood there in a long black cloak lined with fur. Dramatically, she swept it back and it fell behind her, a dark pool from which rose a voluptuous body draped in sapphire satin, a cloud of red-gold hair curling on bare white shoulders.

Cries rang out, some hoarse, some awed, all filled with the extremity of wonder.

Davy gave a strangled shout.

Somebody gave a hiss of hate.

I didn't need to be told that Aileen MacInnis stood before us . . . somehow, someway resurrected from her watery grave.

19

It was like an evil dream. A fantastic specter. Aileen was dead. Drowned in the bay two years ago.

Only she wasn't.

I felt faint, held immobile by stunned and reeling senses, as was everyone around me. Until, suddenly, cries broke out, exclamations, questions—but only Dugan moved toward the figure in the doorway. To my surprise, Aileen was staring—not at her approaching husband—but at Professor Harden.

"Everyone thought you were dead!" Nora's voice shrilled above the others, sounding harsh and strained. Hardly welcoming, a corner of my mind registered.

Then my attention swung to Dugan. How was he reacting to this astonishing occurrence?

He moved in front of Aileen, his eyes examining every inch of her. "Aileen—are you real?" he demanded hoarsely, his fingers digging into her white arms.

"Dugan, you are hurting me." She smiled slowly, coldly. "What a welcome! Aren't you going to kiss your resurrected wife? Or have you found solace in some-one else?"

He gave her a rather perfunctory kiss or perhaps merely dazed? He choked out something that I couldn't hear.

Her eyes traveled around the room and, to my sur-prise, settled on me. "Who is that stranger?"

Without glancing around, Dugan informed her tightly. "She's Paul's widow, Courtney Dunburn."

"Indeed?" Displaying no sign of further interest, Ai-leen's languid gaze transferred itself to Glynnis. "Well. So you survived."

Glynnis didn't speak. Her face was quite unread-able.

Then Davy seemed to throw off the spell that had descended on the room. He flung himself toward his sister, shoving Dugan to one side. "*Aileen!* My God, what happened? Why—? How—?" Tears rolled down his cheeks as he grabbed her in his arms.

Aileen's chilled, wary expression altered. "Ah, Davy, Davy, I'm sorry to startle you like this. I'll tell you ev-erything, but first—"

She swayed, then young Dr. Lorne, white of face, pushed closer and drew Davy away. "Let her sit down, lad. Fetch a glass of wine." He helped Aileen glide across the room to a large chair. She looked up at him and smiled, a secret sort of smile.

Lady Margaret seemed to make a supreme effort to regain her self-control. Drawing herself up, she spoke tremulously. "My dear friends, I wonder, could I crave your indulgence at this time? Would you mind—"

"Certainly, certainly." "We'll go." The naturally cu-rious and astounded crowd reluctantly withdrew after casting long glances toward Aileen and expressing gladness in her safe return, spoken in numb and shaken tones. Even Malcolm moved off slowly, eyes lingering on Aileen as though still afraid to believe his senses.

Aileen smiled wanly at them all from the depths of a velvet chair. Her shoulders looked like thick cream, her hair a shining halo against the dark upholstery. I thought she looked thinner than in her portrait, older, too, which was not to be wondered at considering what she might have been through. However, she was still a fascinating beauty.

The professor never took his narrowed gaze from her. He lit a cheroot as he leaned against the mantelpiece, and when I glanced at him, he didn't look surprised or impressed by this marvelous resurrection. But I imagined that his poise was seldom shattered. He was a man of dark, mysterious depths. He stayed in the background and so did I while the others crowded around Aileen to question her.

She sipped her wine and answered carefully and calmly. "Of course, I didn't drown. Though I very nearly did. When the waves swept us over the side, I went under and probably hit my head on the bottom of the boat. I must have floated a long way because when I came to, a fisherman had rescued me. At that time, I had no idea what had happened, where I came from, or who I was."

There were exclamations on every side, but Dugan's voice rose loudest. "Aileen, *what do you mean?*"

"It's true. I have had amnesia for the past two years. I was taken to a little island village and cared for. A local doctor was called in but he couldn't help me. So there I stayed. No one knew who I was. Then one morning I woke up in this little cottage belonging to the fisherman and his family . . . and I remembered everything."

"How did you get here?" Dugan demanded, his eyes sweeping her expensive gown.

"Someone brought me—I forget the name." Wearily, Aileen leaned her head back and closed her eyes.

Glynnis jumped to her feet. "My God! And I told everyone you were dead. I had no idea—"

Aileen raised her head. "Of course, you didn't. I'm glad you survived." A long, odd look passed between them that I couldn't fathom.

A babble of questions ensued that Aileen quickly fended off by moaning that she was exhausted. Lady Margaret immediately summoned a servant to prepare a bedroom. The maid appeared so promptly, she must have been listening in the hall.

Aileen accepted Dugan's arm, but when she reached the professor, she halted. "Well, Max, we meet again."

He bowed. "Congratulations on your survival."

Dugan's eyebrows rose. "You know each other? Harden failed to mention that."

"Only slightly," Aileen said. "We had mutual friends in London."

"What do you think about my wife's . . . adventure?" Dugan demanded of the professor.

He waved his cheroot. "I am as surprised as anyone by this strange tale, old chap." His full, red lips curled in an enigmatic smile.

Aileen now transferred her cool, blue gaze to me, evidently noting everything: my blond hair so much less dramatic than her own red-gold. My less than vivid eyes. Even the modest curves I had displayed tonight paled beside her voluptuous sensuality.

"I knew your husband," Aileen said to me. "Do I understand that you're his . . . widow?"

"Yes, he had an accident in London and died recently."

"So sorry. We'll talk later." She inhaled deeply, aware that both men watched her. "Dugan, take me to your—"

"A room has been prepared for you," he broke in curtly, "and a maid awaits you."

"Yes, that's best. For tonight." Her face held a strange, almost challenging expression. His, I couldn't read at all.

A rush of fierce emotion swept me as they left side by side and I gripped my fan so hard the ivory and lace spokes nearly snapped. I was jealous—*jealous!* And I knew it was because this ravishing and careless beauty had come back after all the anguish she had put her husband through and now she expected to step again into her role as the adored wife. And Dugan probably would let her.

The others started chattering among themselves, but the professor spoke for my ears only, echoing my thoughts so accurately I thought he must have read my face.

"I wonder how our stalwart Scot feels now? Will he forgive and forget?"

"How can he resist her?" I said bitterly. "She's the most beautiful creature I've ever seen."

"And one of the most selfish." He tapped his ash into the fireplace. "Even beauty such as Aileen's can turn sour when there is nothing behind it. Any man would want to sample her wares for a while, but after that—" He shrugged. "You, on the other hand, might possess a much more lasting allure. Not so obvious and blatantly displayed as Aileen's, but still . . ." His bold gaze traveled across my bare shoulders down to the swelling of my bosom.

Flushing, I put up my fan and moved away, not replying to his leering compliment, which I knew, of course, was a lie. I felt his remarks were out of place tonight and his ogling most embarrassing.

On the couch, Davy sat with his head in his hands. Beside him, Glynnis had her arm across his back. Lady Margaret and Sir Hugh held tightly to each other's hands. The old man's face looked waxen and I wondered anxiously if this shock would harm him.

But when Sir Hugh spoke, his voice was strong and unemotional. "Amnesia, now. How . . . odd."

"A convenient thing to have if one wants to play at games," Lady Margaret muttered darkly.

"What do you mean?" I blurted, not stopping to consider that I might be intruding on a private, family conversation.

Luckily Lady Margaret didn't seem to mind. She pressed her lips together before replying. "It was common knowledge that Aileen was not a virtuous wife. Now we must hear her out. I'm sure there's more to this than she is telling."

Sir Hugh and the others muttered in agreement. As for me, my mind churned with a dozen speculations. Would Aileen be able to convince her husband of her sincerity? Had she really had amnesia? Would she stay this time or wander off again?

I felt a deep pity for Dugan. In spite of our differences, I admired his strength of character and his sense of duty. He seemed like a rugged tower of dependability. Now he might be caught in a trap not of his making.

When Dugan returned to the drawing room, every head moved to observe him. His face was still a rigid mask of self-control.

"Is Aileen all right?" his uncle asked.

"Yes," Dugan answered wearily, slumping down on the sofa, legs thrust out before him.

"I'll go to her," Davy exclaimed, leaping to his feet.

Dugan stopped him with an upraised hand. "No, don't bother her tonight, lad. Tomorrow will be time enough to question her." He had discarded his velvet coat and the frilled shirt was unbuttoned at the throat. How tired he looked! A fallen giant. I filled a tumbler half-full of the spirits he liked called "Scotch" and handed it to him silently, although my hand was shaking and the contents sloshed against the sides of the glass. How I wished I knew the proper words . . .

He glanced up and covered my cold fingers with his own. "Dinna spill the bonnie brew." Then he added on a long breath, "Thank you."

I cleared my throat. "It's a miracle that your wife wasn't drowned, isn't it?"

"Aye." In two gulps, he downed the drink and held out the glass.

"More?"

He nodded. "Don't you need a wee dram yourself? This night has been a mighty shock for all of us."

Davy roused himself to fetch a drink for everyone and we all sat, sipping and conjecturing, still stunned almost past belief.

"This is a matter that requires a mort o' questioning," mused Sir Hugh.

"What are you thinking, Uncle?" Dugan asked.

"I'm thinking that amnesia must be hard to prove."

Lady Margaret frowned thoughtfully. "She claims that she drifted underneath the water for a way, then was rescued, while Glynnis saw nothing?"

"That's right." Glynnis spoke up firmly. "Remember, I was fighting for my life. High waves had come up suddenly making a strong current, the water was icy—"

"Yet Aileen survived," Dugan said. "Someone rescued her. Who? Where did she live all this time? I want to speak to this doctor who saw her. Why didn't the police—or somebody—put out notices?"

No one had an answer, but suddenly Davy sprang up shouting, "That's just like you, Dugan. Never giving her a chance to explain. Always suspicious—"

"I intend to hear her explanations. In other times, I have had good reason to be suspicious."

"Aye, that you did." Nora broke in harshly. "You put up with a lot." Her face looked white and strained, the knuckles standing out sharply on her clenched hands. "Because she was so beautiful, men made fools of themselves over my sister. We were not a wealthy family, but Aileen got everything my parents could scrape together for her: the best education, finest clothes, travel. . . . Davy and I had what was left."

"Now, now, old girl," her brother demurred. "Don't blame Aileen. She couldn't help her beauty nor the knowledge of how to use it."

"She was fickle, shallow, and false," Nora ground out. "And eventually she tired of every man once she had him at her feet. Including Malcolm."

No one spoke and I had to catch back a gasp of surprise. Aileen tempted even the young doctor, her sister's sweetheart? So that's what Lady Margaret had meant by a "serpent."

"Aye," Nora continued bitterly. "She turned her wiles on Malcolm after I had quarreled with him about the way he stared at her so much. Of course, I forgave *him*, but not my sister. She was cruel enough to brag that she could get him any time she chose."

"That's enough, lass," Dugan said wearily, passing a hand across his face. "We're all tired, stunned, and upset. Let's go up to bed."

They followed his advice, and accompanied by Professor Harden and Glynnis, the family stumbled to their feet, mumbling good nights.

I started to follow, but Dugan stopped me. "Bide a minute, Courtney. I need your calm, cool English presence."

I sank back down beside him on the couch. "I am far from cool or calm. Instead, I feel that I must be dreaming. Can all this actually be happening?"

"It's true enough that Aileen's back. Though I don't know—" He shook his head. "Do you believe her story?"

What could I say? Remembering the lavaliere and the accident in the cove when Glynnis proved she couldn't swim, I found it hard to believe any of it. How could Glynnis have been able to swim to safety? How could she not have seen the fisherman rescuing Aileen even if his boat was far away? Should I tell all this to Dugan? Perhaps, but not tonight. We had both been through enough.

Helplessly, I shook my head. "I don't know what to believe."

The embers had sunk to dark coals in the grate. The candles guttered low and shadows filled the room, turning Dugan's strong face into a mask of anguish.

"This will make some changes for you," I faltered.

"I had such dreams," he whispered, his voice breaking. As he leaned closer, his eyes devoured me, traveling from my face and hair down across my body. "You look so . . . pure and lovely."

Dreams? Perhaps, I, too, had dreamed. I couldn't help myself. Weakly, I leaned toward him, hardly knowing what I did. Whispering his name, I raised my arms.

With a smothered groan, he grabbed me close and our lips met in a surge of violent emotion, blinding, deafening, shutting out the world and all its problems.

He kissed my face, my throat, my bosom, with a fierce, searing hunger while I clutched him tighter and tighter—wanting more—wanting him to never stop—

Then, somehow, he came to his senses before I did and dragged my clinging arms down from his neck. I could only sob his name, the yearning for him still pulsating throughout all my being.

He stood up and looked down at me, raking back his hair. Though his hand shook, his voice was harsh and cold. "I won't be bothering you again. I have a wife now in the house. And we must both remember that."

Bewildered, stunned, and shamed, I fell back and watched him stride out of the room.

20

After I dragged myself upstairs and went to bed, I found it was a long time before I could get to sleep.

I knew now that I loved Dugan with all my heart and soul with a mature passion aching to be fulfilled. The feeling must have been there for a long time. I recalled the first night of my arrival at Castlecove when I had dreamed of Dugan kissing me. Amid all our differences, my annoyance over his suspicions and lordly domination, the attraction had been growing. Once he had said I would want to know the passion of a man someday. He was right. Dugan was that man.

I knew he felt desire for me, perhaps even love. But while I felt that I could give up everything for him, his rigid code was stronger than my weakness. More than any other country, Scotland frowned upon divorce. It was a scandal in England but much more so here.

So what was left? My departure, that was all. As soon as I could manage it. Scalding tears came then until I lay exhausted in the tumbled sheets and damp, twisted pillow.

Now my thoughts went to the mystifying appearance of Aileen and I forced myself to examine it. Just what was the truth behind her fantastic tale? It seemed that everyone—myself included—felt pretty skeptical about it all.

But if it wasn't true, what really had happened? *Had Glynnis tried to kill her?* Had Glynnis left Aileen to manage as best she could while saving herself and sailing back to shore? When Aileen didn't reappear, did Glynnis simply steal the lavaliere?

But why, then, didn't Aileen accuse Glynnis of leaving her to drown? Did Glynnis have some hold over her that ensured silence?

Aileen must have made a lot of enemies. It surprised me that she had even tried seducing Nora's sweetheart, Malcolm. Were there no limits to her wanton behavior? Only Paul seemed to have eluded her clutches and perhaps that was because Aileen had another interest in him, namely, the location of the Prince's Gold so that she could steal it and slip away.

I must talk with Aileen and try to find out what Paul had discovered that made him so sure the gold was here. Perhaps I could suggest that Aileen and I pool our knowledge. Cupidity might play as strong a part in her makeup as her appetite for men. Even though I planned to leave, I must make one more effort.

So many problems. So many questions without answers.

Finally, exhaustion claimed me and I fell into a dark, deep well of sleep from which I didn't emerge until Polly knocked at my door with morning tea.

She immediately informed me that all the servants were "agog." "Whisht, Miss Courtney, did you ever hear such a monstrous thing? Miss Aileen back from the dead!" She stared at me, wild of eye, her cap askew.

What a household this would be today! I hoped that

Nora would be able to calm them down. However, she had been pretty upset last night and still must have a mind of whirling, conflicting thoughts just like the rest of us.

I pushed up against the banked bed pillows and attempted to speak calmly to Polly while I sipped my tea. "Miss Aileen was not dead. Only stunned by falling in the sea. She has been ill for the past two years and couldn't return home."

"But—but the dear knows where she was," Polly cried, worrying her twisted apron. "Or what—or how—"

"It will all be made clear very soon," I said, hoping that was true. "Now, I want to bathe and dress at once. Have the children been told the news?"

"Och, ma'am, I'll not be knowing."

"Well, I'll see to them as soon as possible. Tell the servants—" Then I paused. What was I doing? It was not my place to give instructions to the staff. "Never mind. Just lay out my brown merino and attach the lace collar and cuffs with those beauty pins in my bureau tray. Are any of the family up?"

"Most are having breakfast in their rooms, but there's food ready in the little room as usual." Her excited eyes slid around to me as she shook out my dress. "I haven't seen Miss Aileen since she returned. Would you say, ma'am, that she looks the same as ever?"

"Well, I never saw her before, but she looks like her portrait. She's very beautiful indeed."

Eager to impart this latest information, Polly made swift work of my toilette and I followed her scurrying figure down to the lower floor.

Dugan and Nora were the only ones at the breakfast table and broke off a low-voiced conversation when I entered. Both greeted me briefly and I managed to respond though Dugan's presence made my heart pound with mortification and I couldn't meet his eye.

"Well, I must see to the kitchen," Nora muttered, rising. "The servants are all atwitter. It's going to be difficult for a while. Naturally, their curiosity is as great as ours."

When she caught my eyes on her, she smoothed her face. "Courtney, please don't misunderstand. We are all relieved that Aileen is back unharmed. Last night we were upset and said things better left unsaid. Isn't that true, Dugan?"

So that's the way it was going to be played.

Dugan merely nodded, his eyes brooding on the window as he held a cup of coffee between his hands, elbows propped upon the table. This morning, he looked more stern and tired than ever. I wondered what was going through his mind. Whatever it was, joy did not seem uppermost. And to my shame, that gave me a small satisfaction.

Before Nora reached the door, I called to her. "I will do anything I can to help. Would you like me to break the news to the children?"

"Yes, that would be a good idea. But say little to the servants."

"Little is all I know," I muttered underneath my breath.

Dugan sat silent while I ate. Perhaps he felt as ill at ease as I did though it was more likely that he was immersed in his own thoughts and oblivious to my presence.

At last, I could bear it no longer and shoved my plate aside while I mumbled to the air, "I'll see if the children are up."

Instantly, he was on his feet. "I'm coming with you. I must speak to Meggie."

We walked upstairs in silence, but when we reached

the upper hall, I swallowed hard and raised my head. "I think I should return to London soon. My search here is apparently useless. I'll just hand in Paul's book with a brief explanation that he was mistaken regarding the Prince's Gold."

Dugan put out his hand, then drew it back without touching me. "Not yet. Courtney, I want you to remain—"

I clasped my hands together tightly and looked away. "I—I can't."

"Why not?"

"I—I have to hand the book in to the publishers—"

"Blast the book! What about Tommy?"

"He'll be all right here. This is his place now. I promised Paul to look after him but Tommy has settled in so well he doesn't really need me."

"Courtney, look at me. About last night—how I acted when we were alone—if it's because of that, I give you my word that it won't happen again."

My face flamed remembering how I had actually made the first move toward him and then clung in abandoned ecstasy until he had dragged himself away.

I pressed my shaking lips together and cleared my throat. "Please—let's just forget about that. We were both upset—not thinking. I know there won't be any repetition of that episode. As you reminded me, your wife is here now."

"Yes." He drew in a ragged breath. "But will you just stay until things settle down? With Tommy and Meggie, for one thing. Personally, I don't know Aileen's plans at all." He stared, frowning at the carpet, his fists thrust into his jacket pockets.

A wave of pity swept me and I couldn't suppress the tenderness I felt for him, wishing I could comfort him, draw his head against my breast and kiss away the frown and heavy creases beside his hard, taut mouth.

"Very well," I answered, sighing tremulously. "I'll wait for just a little while."

He nodded without speaking and we turned into the nursery. The children were seated at a sunny table with Miss Grey, chalks and slates before them.

I could see at once that she knew what had happened. "I'm glad you came, Mr. MacInnis. And Mrs. Dunburn. Would you like me to leave you with the children?"

"Yes, please, for a few minutes," Dugan answered. "I'll take Meggie into the bedroom while you, Courtney, speak to Tommy."

Immediately, the children were on their feet, wide eyes going from one of us to the other.

"Papa?" Meggie quavered, uncertainty and alarm mingling in her round, freckled face.

Without another word, Dugan swung the little girl up into his arms and vanished from the room.

Tommy ran to me with tears brimming in his eyes. "Mama, Mama—who is dead?" he cried wildly, and buried his face in my skirts.

Of course, being so recently bereaved, the poor little fellow's thoughts had flown to death. Making comforting sounds, I sat down in a rocker and drew him up onto my lap. "No one died, love. It's just that . . . well . . . Meggie's mother came back last night."

"Wh-what! B-but she drownded!" His face was suffused with horror.

"No, no." I strove for calmness. "That was a mistake. She fell overboard into the sea, hit her head, and evidently floated a long way until some fisherman rescued her. They cared for her in a far-off village, but she couldn't remember who she was and no one knew her."

"Mama," he gasped. "She couldn't *remember*? But where did she stay all this time?"

"We don't know yet. Probably in someone's house

on one of the outlying fishing islands. Then, just recently, her memory returned and last night she came back."

Tommy absorbed all this. I could almost see his bright mind clicking in the facts. Then he picked on the most important point in his opinion. "Will Meggie be glad? Is her mama nice?"

"Well, everybody's pretty overwhelmed." I hedged. "But I'm sure her mama is nice to Meggie, she's such a lovable little girl."

"Whisht!" he said on a long-drawn sigh, using a Scottish exclamation while a week or so ago he would have used some English word. Soon he would grow up into his heritage, a true laird. And how I would miss him when I left! I hugged him tightly and he was still baby enough to let me.

"You won't go out in that cove again, will you, Mama?"

"No, and neither must you. Not until you've had some sailing lessons and then always with an older person."

"Yes, Mama—"

He didn't finish for Meggie and her father returned then. Her eyes were round. "Tommy, something's happened—"

"I know all about it, Meggie." He slipped down from my lap. "Are you glad?"

"Och, aye," she answered, matter-of-factly. "But my mama never paid much heed to me."

"She'll speak to you later when she's rested," Dugan said. "Now, here's Miss Grey. You've heard the news, ma'am?"

She nodded calmly, her face a studied blank. "My congratulations to all concerned."

"Oh, we were going to have tea up here today." I suddenly remembered, glancing at the governess. "Should we postpone it?"

"No, madam. This is a very good day for it, I think." Miss Grey sent me a speaking glance.

"Tommy," Dugan said, "be a good lad and take care of Meggie today."

"Right, sir." Tommy's small chest swelled.

"Hoots toots," Meggie cried. "I take care of *him!*"

"You do not," Tommy shrilled.

Things seemed to be getting back to normal, but I lingered after Dugan left, not favoring a long walk down the hall beside him. I still felt very self-conscious in his presence and knew, in spite of my promise, that I must leave as soon as convenient. Until then, I would have no peace of mind. Who knew when my feelings might again break the bounds of propriety and embarrass him?

Miss Grey set the children to a paint and paper project before she stepped with me into the hall, dropping her restrained manner to the point where I was "Courtney."

"This certainly was a surprise about Mr. MacInnis's wife. Are you not astounded, Courtney?"

"Indeed I am and most anxious to hear more details." We exchanged glances, but both of us were aware of the impropriety of gossip at this point.

"I hope to have a chat with her as soon as possible about another matter," I said. "She and my late husband often conferred in the summerhouse about the Prince's Gold."

Noting a lifting of her eyebrows, I hastened on. "I know that nothing could have distracted Paul from his search. Not even the most beguiling female."

She inclined her head. "I agree with what you say. But do you think Mrs. MacInnis will cooperate with you?"

"I don't know. Perhaps she might if I suggest we combine our information. I have a feeling she might still be interested in the gold. Not in the same way I am, of course, which is as a means of vindicating Paul's research."

Miss Grey narrowed her eyes thoughtfully. "Perhaps I have something that might help you. Lady Margaret gave me a letter written by dear Prince Charlie. I keep it under lock and key, but this afternoon I will let you read it." With a finger to her lips, Miss Grey glided back inside the room to her charges.

Somewhere a door closed, but when I whirled around, the only person in sight was Glynnis, vanishing down the rear hall staircase to the garden.

Without any clear thought, I hurried after her and called her name when we reached the brick path through the roses. She wore a fashionable black riding skirt today with a white silk stock and a tall hat with an emerald plume.

"Are you going riding?" I called.

"That's obvious, isn't it?" She turned around. "I hope to join either Dugan or Davy for a canter. They are both outside somewhere."

"Oh, I see." I moved up beside her, debating how to proceed.

She snapped her riding crop against her skirt. "Well, what is it? Are you wondering if I know anything more about Aileen's miraculous escape?" Her thin lips curled. "Though I really can't see why it should concern you."

When I didn't answer, she gave a crack of laughter. "Don't tell me this wrecks your hopes of snaring the wily Scot? Ah, your painful blush answers that question. Well, you can just forget your silly dreams, my girl. Why would a passionate, virile man like Dugan be interested in a pale little mouse?"

"How dare you?" I flamed, incensed that she had hit upon the truth. "I'm not after Dugan. Marriage vows are sacred to him—no matter how his wife behaves."

"You are incredibly naive. He can stay married for

all I care. For Dugan, I have other things in mind."
She turned on her heel and her laugh floated back, the
green plume on her hat seeming to add a mocking
wave as well.

I was not surprised by her boldness, only upset that
she had noticed how I yearned for Dugan. I prayed
that no one else had her sharp eyes.

I had not had an opportunity to question her about
Aileen, but as I turned back to the house, a sound from
up above alerted me, and there was the lady in question.

She stood gazing from an open window, clad only in
a gauzy night shift, her hair a tangled fire on her shoulders
and barely covered breasts.

Then I noticed somebody behind her as a plume of
smoke drifted past her head. I halted in my tracks,
staring upward. It couldn't be Dugan or Davy in her
room. They were both outdoors according to Glynnis.
That left only the professor.

Just then, Aileen looked down and saw me. A slow,
strange smile curved her lips. "Ah—Courtney, isn't it?
Come up. We can talk while I am getting dressed."
She dropped the lace curtain without waiting for an
answer.

I didn't hesitate. This might be a good opportunity to
find out how much she knew about the Prince's Gold.
She also might divulge the real reason behind her return.

Perhaps I was overly optimistic to think she would
discuss such matters with an outsider. On the other
hand, she might put me down as too insignificant to
matter, while she in turn, tried to discover just how
much I knew about the gold.

Of course, the professor would be gone when I arrived.

21

⁂

I was right. Aileen was alone in her room when I entered. But I could detect an aroma of tobacco in the air and I wondered how she would react if I said, "I had no idea you smoked cigars."

She was still in her gauzy negligee, and after frankly staring at me for a minute, she waved me to a chair. "Sit down while I get dressed." She turned to the bed, pawing through a sea of lace-trimmed white silk garments.

"Where is that stupid maid? She's taking hours to iron one dress." Aileen pulled viciously at a bellpull on the wall. She then proceeded to divest herself of the pink chiffon wrap and wriggle into undergarments.

"How long do you intend to stay at Castlecove?" she asked abruptly.

I kept my eyes averted, repelled by her lack of modesty, and answered coolly, "I am trying to find an ending for Paul's book. The sooner I am successful, the sooner I can return to England." That might prove an incentive for her to contribute some information. Even if Aileen didn't consider me much of a threat, she probably wanted to abolish *any* competition. Especially as she was on rather shaky ground with Dugan.

"I thought perhaps you might be able to help me," I added.

Before she could reply, a red-faced, frightened maid slid into the room, her arms filled with silken ruffles. Aileen turned an angry tirade on the girl until she had helped Aileen into the full-skirted day dress in two shades of lilac, elaborately puffed and bowed.

The maid quickly departed with another armful. Aileen evidently wanted every item in her wardrobe freshened. It struck me, then, that no one had questioned her perfect attire when she arrived. Another mystery!

Smoothing her sleek waist and pulling down her neckline, which was already lower than usual for daytime, Aileen looked at me in the pier glass. "How on earth could *I* help you? Why should I know more about Paul's book than you do?"

"Sir Hugh mentioned that you and Paul did a lot of research in the summerhouse trying to find the location of the gold left here by Bonnie Prince Charlie. That was to be the ending of Paul's book—the discovery of the treasure."

"Yes, I knew that." Aileen's blue gaze narrowed as she whirled around. "But he didn't have an ending when he left here, did he? What conclusions had he reached in London?"

Helplessly, I shook my head. "I only know he was sure the gold was hidden at Castlecove while the prince was staying here. Paul intended to return and test a theory that he had. But he was killed before that could happen. Just before he died, he asked me to carry on his work if at all possible."

"So, what have you found out?" Aileen asked, apparently indifferent as she snapped some gold bangles around her wrist.

"Nothing so far. Do you have any idea why Paul was so certain the gold was still here?"

"Where else could it be? It was never found, was it? The instructions to the family for its removal were left by the prince in a kind of . . . code, I think, that no one understood."

My interest quickened. "What was this code?"

Aileen shrugged. "Paul hadn't discovered that when he left for England. He intended to do a lot more research, but evidently he still hadn't figured it out. Perhaps no one can."

I didn't tell her that at the end Paul had been sure of his theory, which, unfortunately, he hadn't divulged to anyone. Not even me.

I stood up, feeling I was not much further along. "If you remember anything else, I would appreciate it if you would tell me so I can clear this up and leave as soon as possible. Your husband has made my stay most pleasant, but Paul's publisher is anxious for his book."

"So Dugan's been . . . attentive?"

"Indeed. He even came to London to escort Tommy and me to Castlecove. We had a lovely trip. Dugan—that is, Mr. MacInnis—is so very charming when he wants to be."

"You think so, do you. Well, now that I am back, Dugan will have his hands full taking care of me."

I gave a forced trill of laughter as I opened the hallway door. "You must seem rather like a stranger to him after two years of believing you were dead."

She didn't argue that. But before I could leave, she stopped me. "Wait. In one of Prince Charlie's letters, he mentioned 'remember the beloved place' in connection with the gold. I imagine he meant the summerhouse."

Alas, this was something I already knew. "Is there any more that you recall?"

"No, I fear my brain is not at its fullest capacity yet. I have just come through a terrible ordeal, you know."

I hovered on the brink of asking her some pertinent questions about her experience, but I lost my nerve, and murmuring my sympathy, I moved into the hall with Aileen at my heels.

Meggie and Tommy spied us at once and ran forward, Miss Grey vainly cautioning them on their behavior. This was a time, however, when discipline could not prevail. Curiosity was all. It was even there on the governess's thin face as her eyes traveled swiftly to the beautiful woman who stood facing us. Aileen's expression was one of impatience barely held in check.

Poor Meggie stared at her mother with a brief flare of expectation and put out her hands. But when Aileen planted a swift, small kiss on her child's forehead and then stepped out of reach, Meggie's face settled into its usual stoic calm.

"How are you, Mama?"

"I'm fine. What a great, big girl you've become. More freckles than ever. And this must be Thomas, Paul's son. How do you do?"

"I'm pleased to meet you." Tommy's eyes surveyed her admiringly. "You *are* beautiful. Drowning didn't hurt you, did it?"

Aileen warmed a little. Compliments from males could probably always sway her. "I didn't drown! You're very good-looking yourself. I knew your papa."

"Do you know where the gold is?" he asked bluntly.

She laughed shortly. "No, not yet. Now, children, I must go."

Meggie moved closer. "Mama, what happened in the water? Where have you been? Why didn't you—"

Aileen swept up her skirt with an impatient exclamation. "So many questions! Don't be tiresome, Meggie. I've explained it to your father and that's sufficient. Now run along. I'm going to my tower in a few minutes."

"Can we come, too?" Tommy piped.

"Nobody goes up to my tower unless I invite them personally."

We watched her violet ruffles swish away as she called imperiously to a maid. Then Meggie turned her solemn gaze on me. " 'Tis verra strange. How could it be that she was saved?"

"Why, just like a fish." Tommy chortled. "She floated. A fisherman caught her in his net and took her home."

Meggie quickly caught his mood. "There he saw she was a bonnie lass and fell in love with her and—"

"Naw." Tommy was not interested in love. "He treated her like a pet. A pet fish."

Giggling and chattering, the two children scampered back to the nursery.

Miss Grey and I moved behind them slowly. "Wait until she sees the condition of her 'hideaway,' " I murmured. "Then we'll hear some screams."

"Perhaps they repaired the damage," Miss Grey ventured.

"Perhaps. But no one expected her to return, remember."

"It's a hard tale to swallow, but think, Courtney, suppose it all is true. The amnesia, everything . . ."

"I guess it's possible," I said slowly, "though rather fantastic."

As we halted by the nursery door, a maid came hurrying toward us. "Please, which is Miss Aileen's room? The mister wants her in the library."

"She may have gone up to her tower."

Aileen evidently had not made her way yet up the tower stairs because a minute later she appeared from the upper floor behind the maid. The beauty's face was white and set and I wondered if she was afraid of Dugan's anger? The questions he would now fire at her. I couldn't blame her for being trepidatious, but how I wished to be a fly upon the wall when Dugan confronted her.

Miss Grey gave a discreet cough. "I will see you at teatime, then?"

I nodded. "Perhaps by then a little more light will be shed upon this new mystery."

I wandered out into the garden, my footsteps somehow leading me to the rhododendrons crowding around the library windows, which unfortunately were shut. All I could hear were angry, upraised voices, until finally a door slammed.

As I was about to scurry away, Dugan suddenly flung wide one of the windows and called to me. "I could see you hovering out there. Come in and I will set your overwhelming curiosity at rest—at least as much as possible."

"I assure you, I was not trying to overhear your conversation," I lied, drawing myself up haughtily.

"Oh, come in here," he barked impatiently.

When I entered the library, he was sprawled in a big leather chair, chin in his hand, moodiness apparent in his heavy-lidded eyes and outthrust lower lip.

I took a place in the nearby padded window seat, and when he didn't notice me, I stirred restlessly. "Well, Dugan, speak, for heaven's sake."

He glanced at me, then sat up straighter. "Very well. I'll tell you. Make of it what you can.

"First, I charged her with deceit and snarled at her that she never would have spent two years in a village hut. She answered that it wasn't a hut but a comfortable home and everyone was very kind, especially a handsome young fisherman. I asked if he'd made love to her and she laughed and said, 'I can't remember. Why should you care? You haven't wanted me for years.' I said to her, 'That's true. Your gluttony for men and roving eye soon repulsed me.' She got angry then and accused me of bringing her to a dull, isolated place. I told her she knew where I lived when we got married. She shrugged and said that a castle had seemed grand and at first she liked my lovemaking. I reminded her that hadn't lasted long. She always wanted someone new. She didn't reply to that, and after a few minutes while my anger and resentment grew, I said to her: 'If you think you can come back here and live and still pursue your wanton ways now that Meggie is older—'

"She asked with a sneer what I would do about it and I said: 'I will get rid of you.'

"Then she slammed out of the door. And that was all. Now, my cool-headed Englishwoman, what do you think?"

My hands were clenched in my lap and I felt far from cool. What did he mean by that last threat to Aileen?

He stared beyond me out the window and muttered, " 'Tis more than a man should have to bear."

I shuddered away from the terrible expression on his face and also turned my eyes to the garden. Clouds now streamed upward through the sky and the sun was gone. How swiftly the weather could change in this Highland country. Like Dugan, it could be violent and unpredictable.

I couldn't add to his strange mood, which almost frightened me, even while I understood it, so I told him: "Dugan, it may all be true. Perhaps we cannot judge—"

His eyes had turned to me even before my words were cut off abruptly by a sudden shriek.

After a startled pause, we both jumped to our feet and rushed into the hall. The screams were coming from high above and I didn't need Dugan's choked exclamation to tell me it was Aileen.

22

Several people ran into the hall as the screams continued. They seemed to be coming from the tower. Had Aileen gone up and viewed the destruction there? But these cries seemed more pain-filled than even the tower room could have evoked.

Dugan and I raced to the top floor and there I saw Davy push open the door leading to the twisting stairs. "Oh, God," he yelled. "She's fallen—get help! Quick!"

Now I could see Aileen, a white-faced, crumpled violet heap. Not moving. No longer screaming.

"What's happened?" Dugan cried.

Davy already had his sister in his arms and headed for her bedroom. "Aileen fell down the tower steps," he jerked out. "Her ankle—I—I don't know what else—"

"Send for Dr. Lorne," Dugan barked to one of the hovering maids.

Davy laid his sister gently on her bed. A crowd gathered in the doorway of Aileen's room, but Dugan asked them to disperse, except for me. "Courtney, you can help me undress her. The rest of you wait somewhere until the doctor sees her."

"Will she be all right?" Davy faltered, edging out reluctantly.

Dugan quickly felt her arms and legs, checked her back. "I think it's just her ankle."

I moved up beside him and removed Aileen's velvet shoes, seeing the swelling bruise. I noticed there was something greasy on the soles of her slippers before I placed them on the floor. When Aileen was down to drawers and camisole, Dugan drew up the sheet and dropped into a nearby chair.

"What will happen next?" he muttered, running his fingers through his hair.

"Should we try to rouse her?" I stared uncertainly at Aileen's open mouth, fluttering a little, her blue-veined lids. At least she was breathing.

"We'll wait for the doctor. When she comes to, she'll start screaming. She never could stand much pain. You should have heard her at Meggie's birth."

"She probably will have a lot of bruises," I murmured, thinking how Aileen would deplore the marring of her milky skin. "I wonder how she came to fall? Was she alone in the tower?"

Dugan looked at me from half-shut eyes. "What are you saying? Do you imagine someone shoved her down the stairs?"

I bit my lip uneasily, then blurted out, "There was grease on her shoe."

"Grease? Something that made her slip? That could just have been an accident. Something spilled—"

Or it could have been done on purpose. "I'm going to take a look at those stairs."

"If there's any grease, they could be dangerous. Stay off them."

Reluctantly, I sat down and we both waited silently. Finally Aileen moaned and Dugan rose up quickly as her eyes flew wide. She uttered a wild cry. "Oh, my ankle—it's on fire! Help me, Dugan—" She tried to sit up, catching at his arm. "I want some drops—get the laudanum—"

As Dugan hesitated, Davy burst into the room. "The doctor's here!"

Malcolm Lorne shoved past him. "Aileen—they said you fell." There was deep concern on his rugged face. Probably he still cared for this capricious beauty.

With an expanded audience, Aileen grew almost hysterical, tearing at her hair, shoving back the covers, screaming loudly.

"Clear the room. I must examine her for other injuries." Malcolm bent over his medicine bag and extracted a bottle. "But first, my dear, this will relieve your misery."

I followed Dugan from the room as his wife's cries subsided. I glanced back and saw her flushed face looking upward as the doctor bent down and tenderly brushed back her hair.

Poor Nora. I didn't think she stood a chance.

"Let's look at those tower stairs," Dugan said to me in a low tone and I nodded anxiously.

When we reached the pie-wedge steps, the slippery sheen was plainly visible. Dugan leaned over and rubbed his finger back and forth, then sniffed. "Candle grease," he said, straightening. "I don't know how high up it goes. Probably not too far or she would have been hurt worse, even killed."

"Do you think it was deliberate?" I whispered.

He stared downward. "If so, it must have been applied after Aileen was in the tower. And fairly recently: the wax hasn't hardened yet. Courtney, summon a maid to clean this up at once with hot water, soap, and vinegar. We want no more . . . accidents."

"Do you think we should show it first? Question people?"

"Who would admit to such a thing?" He grunted and strode down the hall.

I hailed a passing maid and gave her the instructions from Dugan. Then I followed him back to Aileen's room.

I was just in time to hear her protesting shrilly, "I didn't see a soul! Someone called to me, said they had something that I wanted. I started down the stairs. And fell."

Her voice rose to a wail. "Malcolm, don't go yet." She was now draped in a lacy shawl, her foot swathed in a wet towel, resting on a pillow.

The doctor smiled at her gently. "I must attend another patient, my dear. You'll be all right. I'll look in on you tomorrow."

He snapped his bag shut and looked across the bed at Dugan. "It's just a sprain, painful but it soon will heal. Nothing else is wrong. No broken bones, thank heaven. A few bruises on her side and back."

"They *hurt*, Malcolm," Aileen wailed, giving him a pouting glance.

"The sedative will work soon and you'll sleep. Keep cold cloths on your ankle and stay off it for today."

She caught his hand. "Th-thank you." Her eyes drooped, her speech beginning to slur, but she looked very seductive in her tousled dishabille, her leg bare to the knee, and her upper body easily glimpsed beneath the lacy shawl.

Malcolm's face flushed as he looked at her and he tugged at his cravat before dragging his eyes away. I saw Dugan watching him with a slight, cynical smile.

When the doctor left, Dugan and I turned to follow, but Aileen stopped me. "Wait—I want you to stay with me, C-Courtney. Dugan, do you know what m-made me fall? And who wrecked my tower room?"

"I don't know anything about the tower," Dugan

said. "But someone spilled grease on the tower stairs—"

She let out a fishwife scream. "Did you do that? Are you t-trying to get rid of me, like you said? You m-monster!"

"I had nothing to do with any of it," he ground out, and headed for the hall. "I'll send your maid to care for you."

Before I could follow him, Aileen reared up anxiously. "Courtney, don't leave me alone!"

I sat down reluctantly and she sank back on her pillows. I couldn't like this woman. Everything about her was repulsive to my nature, but I felt sympathy for her pain. I thought how she had wasted her life with indiscretions. Here she had a man who would have loved and cared for her, a wonderful castle to live in, a healthy, lovable child, plenty of money for clothes, travel, parties. But it apparently was all meaningless to her. She wanted more, diversion, change, and always would. What a vain, foolish, selfish woman.

Suddenly, with closed eyes, she spoke quite clearly. "Well, Courtney, if I were out of the way, you could go after Dugan, couldn't you? Or have you already started?" Her lids flew wide. "Don't give me that indignant gasp. I'm warning you—I told the doctor if anything else happened to me, there were several people here who would like to see me dead. And I named them."

I sprang to my feet. "You really are the most impossible woman I have ever met. How dare you suggest that I would try to kill you? Do you suspect your dearest friend? The professor? Your brother or sister? Your husband?"

"You left out Lady Margaret."

I whirled away. "I refuse to stay another minute and listen to such rubbish."

"Stop—I don't want to be alone!" she shrieked.

"Your maid will be here in a minute," I said callously, and with that, I left.

A storm arose that afternoon, battering the garden, tossing tree branches so that leaves flew thickly through the air. The windows shook and the wind moaned through the cracks.

I sat by my fire and considered Aileen's fall, which I felt, somehow, was no accident. Someone had tried to harm her. I felt certain it had not been Dugan in spite of the good cause he had for hating his immoral, cheating wife. The grease on the stairs was not his type. It was too sly, too nasty—more apt to maim than kill.

I had to consider other people and I felt very suspicious of Glynnis. She might be jealous of Aileen and even have tried to kill her in the bay. There was something very strange between them and I couldn't figure it out.

Nora? She might have hated Aileen because of Malcolm. But they were sisters, after all. Max Harden? He and Aileen could be lovers and perhaps he wanted her to leave Dugan and she refused. However, it was hard to see the self-possessed, sophisticated professor committing such an act as greasing stairs.

I had to give it up. Too much of my remaining time was being taken up with matters that really didn't concern me. I must concentrate on finding a clue to the Prince's Gold or else I would have to return to London and let it remain a mystery for other generations to ponder over.

First, I spread out Prince Charlie's letters, then I withdrew Aileen's diary from beneath my mattress. Looking down at it, I felt a jolt of guilt. What was I doing, reading the confidential words of a woman who was not dead as I'd supposed but very much alive? Aileen's fury would know no bounds and it would be justified. Before I did anything else, I must return the journal to the tower. I flung a shawl around my arms, holding the book hidden against my body. The stairs should be cleaned by now and safe enough.

I met no one as I scurried through the halls. The door leading upward to Aileen's tower stood open, and when I bent down to eye the steps, I found every vestige of the danger had been removed.

For a few grim moments, I stared thoughtfully, then I started upward. Proceeding with the utmost caution, I crept along, one hand pressing on the rough, stone wall. I didn't draw a full breath until I reached the landing and turned the knob.

The tower room was empty, but signs of Aileen's recent efforts here were obvious. Ruined articles had been piled into the center of the floor, the bed stripped, undamaged pictures and bric-a-brac straightened. All of this was work that she would not allow a maid to touch—so jealous was she of her secluded bower.

I knew I must not tarry, so with a quick glance around, I returned the diary to its hiding place and wiped my soot-stained hands on a pocket handkerchief.

As I made my way back across the room, it struck me that Aileen might have discovered that the diary was missing and when the person called her to come down and get something that she wanted, she might have expected to be given the book. In her agitation, she would have been heedless of her safety on the steps.

As for myself, I exerted the utmost caution when I went down, step by step, until I could run along the hallways to my room.

The rain still thundered, wind tugged at the draperies, and shivering from nerves as well as drafts, I climbed beneath my covers until teatime.

23

I slept at last, skipping lunch, and woke in time to
dress for tea, which I was taking with Miss Grey and
the children. I donned a fresh cream muslin with a
double skirt and a shock of broad blue ribbon tied at
the waist, the fringed ends falling to the hem. I wound
my hair into a crocheted snood, inserting a matching
ribbon bow.

On my way to the nursery, I first knocked softly at
Aileen's door. The maid, Mary, answered me and whispered: "Miss Aileen is sleeping like the dead." The sim-
ile made me shudder. I nodded hastily and hurried on
my way.

Miss Grey greeted me with a cautious expression
slanted toward the waiting children. "I hear there's
been an accident. How fares the lady?"

Meggie and Tommy, scrubbed and combed, wore
clean white cottons: his, a sailor suit, the loose trousers buttoned to the blouse. She dressed in piqué covered by a pinafore. Both had evidently heard some
rumors and surveyed me anxiously.

I smiled reassuringly. "She's doing fine. A sprained ankle, that is all. The stairs to her tower are rather dangerous, being so steep and narrow, which I guess Aileen had forgotten. She's sleeping now. I just looked in. A maid is by her side."

Immediately, the children relaxed and drew me toward the tea table, making sure I was apprised of all its goodies. Miss Grey evidently had obtained special treats from the kitchen and the dishes held Scotch eggs (which were hard-boiled, wrapped in sausage, and then fried), oyster patties, tomato sandwiches, and for afters little iced oatmeal cakes and various fruit tartlets topped with whipped cream. A jug of lemonade stood ready as well as a pot of strong, dark tea accompanied by a pitcher of milk, which seemed to be enjoyed as much in Scotland as in England.

Since I had missed lunch, I felt ravenous. Miss Grey also displayed a hearty appetite barely held in check by her innate good manners. She probably had teas of a much more frugal nature as a rule.

The fire crackled merrily, the storm abating to a mere pattering on the windows that served to emphasize our own secure warmth while we ate and laughed and talked.

At last, with every crumb demolished, Meggie and Tommy sprawled on their stomachs by the hearth, a picture book spread out before them. Miss Grey and I retreated out of earshot, and pulled two cushioned chairs close together.

"Did you find an opportunity to speak with Miss Aileen before her accident on the tower stairs?" Miss Grey whispered.

"Yes, but I learned little. Not a thing about what happened in the cove. When I questioned her about the gold, she only reiterated what I had already learned from the family letters shown to me by Lady Margaret."

Miss Grey gave a quick glance at the children and then withdrew a piece of paper from her capacious pocket. "This is not the original envelope—that was lost—but the letter inside was written by the prince himself so you can imagine how I treasure it. Dear Lady Margaret gave it to me in celebration of my twenty-year service with the family; I was formerly employed by her sister. Unfortunately, the first page is missing, but the gold is mentioned so I wish you would read this part and tell me what you think."

"Oh, thank you." With careful reverence, I unfolded the fragile paper and read the faded brown writing in a whisper:

"I feel it is wise to hide the sovereigns in what I term 'the beloved place.' My sweet young pet Goldie was too young to die, but I feel her soul will guard the money until I return. The battle looms and I must make haste to lead us all to victory."

Goldie! The first mention of the pet's name sounded like a clarion in my brain. *Was this the clue Prince Charlie left?* Suddenly, my eyes widened. "The grave— *Goldie's* grave—could the money have been hidden there?"

Miss Grey shook her head. "There was no grave for Goldie. I have asked, wishing to view anything connected with my dear prince. The grave does not exist."

I could not believe this. The dog would surely have been buried someplace. This last letter of Miss Grey's confirmed the theory about the gold being secreted in a "beloved place." And the favored dog had been named "Goldie." I felt certain there was a connection. I couldn't take Miss Grey's conviction that there was no grave; I would have to find out for myself.

The children joined us then, begging for a game of

"Hide the Thimble," and so we crowned our tea party with energetic cries of "hot—warm—cool—cold."

When I returned to my room, I noticed that the storm had subsided and a feeble sun rimmed the scudding purple clouds. There were two things I was anxious to pursue outdoors. First, a search of the summerhouse. Second, a few words with Auld Angus. Perhaps I could jog some old, dim memory in his stubborn mind. I felt certain the grave was somewhere on the grounds although now it might be completely covered by a century of earth and weather. I was getting desperate and could not afford to pass up any lead, no matter how slight or unlikely.

I donned a warm cape and a pair of vulcanized boots, which I thought would be adequate since the rain had stopped and only the ground was wet.

To my surprise, when I stepped out the front door, I met the old gardener right away. He was hurrying along, pushing a cart of sodden leaves and battered petals. He halted reluctantly when I hailed him.

"Mr. Angus, I would like to ask you something."

"*Auld* Angus," he snarled. "Nae *meester.*"

"Very well, Auld Angus. Have you ever heard of a grave hereabouts for Prince Charlie's dog, Goldie?"

"Nae," he grunted, and started away.

"Wait. Didn't your father or grandfather ever mention it? I've heard they worked here, too." I hurried to his side. "You know who Bonnie Prince Charlie was, don't you?"

"Aye, aye."

"He stayed at Castlecove long ago and had a little dog named Goldie. In one of his letters, he mentioned that the animal was buried here. Have you forgotten that?"

His grizzled head reared angrily. "Nae! Ma mind's as keen as iver. I recall now. They say the doggie was buried nigh the wee house lang, lang—"

"It must still be there," I cried excitedly.

He seemed to fly into a rage and shook his fist almost in my face. "Dinna be sae daft. 'Tis gang, I say, all gang. And I'm warnin' ye, stay awa' from yon wee house!" Baring his snags of yellow teeth, he picked up speed and rattled off across the yard.

I turned away until he was out of sight, but then I made my way once more toward the summerhouse, mulling over Auld Angus's words. Evidently, the grave had been searched for and then given up as lost. Yet Paul believed the gold was here and he had mentioned the summerhouse with his last breath. How could I go without searching it as well as the surrounding area?

But I soon saw that someone else had the same idea. And being very enterprising, the professor had appropriated a long iron bar from some shed and was busily poking holes all around the ground adjacent to the summerhouse. I wondered what Auld Angus would say to that!

The immaculate, dandified professor was spattered with mud and his eyes were filled with frustrated wrath.

"Are you having any luck?" I called sweetly.

He flung his long rod violently across the yard. "Well, if ever there was treasure buried here, it's been washed away. Perhaps over the cliff into the sea."

"Are you giving up?"

"I see no alternative. How about you?"

"I suppose so." My spirits had dropped considerably. With all that digging, if there had been a grave, the professor would have struck the stone somewhere. It seemed that my last hope had just vanished.

He clumped toward me on the path, his boots thickly caked with mud, which he tried unsuccessfully to stamp off. "Well, you can write in Paul's book that there was an untested theory about the gold. But after all this time, there is no earthly way to prove it." He gave a crack of bitter laughter. *"Earthly!* There's a joke!"

I didn't smile. My disappointment was very keen. But I still wanted to look inside the little house. I was curious to see the place enjoyed so much by Paul and Aileen. Not to mention the Bonnie Prince. This might be the last chance I would have. Nobody would be apt to see me since the weather was so inclement with the constant threat of another downpour.

The professor didn't wait to see if I was following, and as soon as he was out of sight, I hurried through the weed-choked path and mounted the sagging steps. Even though the porch was newer than the little house, it also had succumbed to the harsh elements. Everywhere I saw peeling paint, dirt-encrusted eaves, and boarded windows. Perhaps it had been sorely neglected after Aileen disappeared.

There was an old-fashioned latch upon the door as well as a blackened brass knob. I lifted one and turned the other. My pulses quickened as I pushed my way inside.

The far windows on the sea side were uncurtained and not boarded up, but since the day was so dark, very little light came through. Fortunately, right by the door stood an oil lamp and a box of lucifers on a table. As soon as I had it lit, my eyes stared avidly in every direction.

The single room was completely furnished with a crimson carpet, a satin-covered sofa, and two padded armchairs. Oddly there was very little dust. I crossed to the opposite window and stared outside. Now I could see that the house really was in a very dangerous location, right on the edge of the badly eroded cliff. At any time, a storm might send the whole place washing over the side where, far below, the rocks rose sharply like a giant's teeth waiting with deadly hunger.

Shuddering a little, I turned away, wondering if

there was anything I could discover after all this time? The professor evidently had examined everything, but if he had found any clues, it was not apparent.

I still decided to look around. When I tugged open a cupboard, to my surprise I found that a bowl held sugar biscuits, another contained fresh fruit. There even was a dustless bottle of red wine. Someone had been staying here, eating, and perhaps sleeping. I noticed that the fireplace showed signs of recent ashes.

Next, my eyes went to the satin sofa, cozy and inviting in a corner of the room. When I moved closer, I saw that it was piled with tufted pillows and a ruby velvet spread, padded and warm. Had Aileen ever slept here? Had Prince Charlie? The furniture looked old but surely had been renovated sometime in the past. Ghosts . . . the summerhouse seemed filled with ghostly memories.

At last, I sighed and turned to leave. It had been interesting, but there were no clues here. I had done all I could and nothing was left except defeat. Forgive me, Paul . . .

I had almost reached the door, when I heard a board creak on the porch and the gruff muttering of a Scottish accent. Could it be Auld Angus checking on the little house? Quick as thought, I sped across the room and dived beneath the cover on the couch, pulling it taut above my head.

I heard the door's rusty hinges protest as it was opened. Then the gardener's voice: "A licht! What fulc left that? And dug yon ground?" With growling and muttering, he must have turned off the lamp and then prowled around the room. "This be *her* place. Guid siller she gae me to keep it so. Aye . . ."

Finally, the steps receded and the door shut smartly with a loud clang of metal. For a long moment, I held my breath and didn't move. Then I peeked out through a slit. The room was dark, deserted. Drawing a deep breath, I pushed free of the cover and stood up. I ran swiftly to the door, tugging the knob, then twisting when it didn't yield. It took several minutes for me to realize what Auld Angus had just done. *He had latched the door.*

At the same moment, thunder crashed, the loudest I had ever heard, seeming right above my head. Then light flashed from the seaside windows. The storm had returned and here I was, trapped in a place where no one would ever think to look for me. Fear swept me like a cold wave from the sea and I cried out for help, pounding on the door until I lost my breath and my bruised knuckles stabbed me with pain.

No one answered and no one came and I realized that it was doubtful anyone could hear me over the fiercely raging elements. The wind moaned and howled, the rain shot against the panes like bullets.

What should I do? It might be quite a while before the storm abated, perhaps days. Then I was aware of a new danger. The house began to quake and it seemed that the very floor shifted underneath my feet. With a sob of terror, I flung myself howling and pounding on the door.

Would this be the storm that would sweep the summerhouse into the sea? I had a terrible vision of the house splintering, crashing, as it broke upon the vicious rocks below.

Desperately, I took deep gulps of air. I knew I must get hold of myself and find a way out of this place. I ran to the far windows. Thank God, they could be opened! When I pushed them up, I could see that a ledge ran along the back of the house. It was not more than two feet wide and with thunder crashing, lightning flashing, and rain pouring down in sheets, it was a daunting prospect.

But I felt the house shake again and it seemed to rattle a terrible warning I could not ignore. The ledge was my only hope. From there, I should be able to edge around the side of the house and get to safety.

Before I could dwell on it any further, I swung my legs outside and dropped to the ground, immediately becoming drenched with rain. It was fortunate that I still clung to the windowsill as the wet earth was as slippery as oil. I had to scrabble wildly for a foothold. It was a hideously long way down the bare hillside and the rocks below looked more menacing than ever in the flickering stabs of yellow light that shone on the killer bay, dark gray with violent waves and spewing foam.

For a moment, I held on, staring downward, unable to tear my eyes from the terrifying spectacle. How could I leave my perch, unhook my fingers from the sill, and move around the house along that oily ground? Beyond the window, there was nothing but a blank wall. No rocks, no bush to clutch, no handhold of any kind. Just the splintered, flaking boards buffeted by wind and rain. And beyond the ledge—the drop.

But I had to move. The house might start to slide at any moment.

Then I heard it. Someone shouting. Calling me. "Courtney, Courtney, where are you?"

The voice was coming closer and I answered with all my strength. The door burst open inside the house, and as I peered desperately through the window, I saw Dugan stride toward me, water pouring from his yellow oilskin cape.

"My God," he yelled when he reached the window. His hands gripped my waist and dragged me through the opening. Sodden, shaking, and sobbing, I fell against him. He clutched me for a moment and there was some round Gaelic cursing.

Then he held me off. "Are you all right? What in heaven's name are you doing here, woman?"

"Searching for the gold. Oh, Dugan, I'm so glad you

came—I wanted to see this place, but I was t-trapped—''

His hands clamped on my shoulders. '' 'Tis no sense you're making. Did I not warn you of the danger here? You daft, stubborn creature! What were you doing out on the ledge?''

"Someone locked me in and I—I had to try and escape through the window. I called and called but—''

"Who would lock the door with you inside yelling like a banshee?''

"Auld Angus came and I hid in the sofa so he wouldn't see me. When he went away, I found the door was locked. Ohhh, let's get out of here before the house slides into the sea. Don't you feel it shaking?''

"Come on,'' Dugan said grimly. He tucked me against his side beneath the cape and we staggered out of the house into the drenching rain and keening wind.

"How did you know where I was?'' I shouted at his ear.

He answered something about the professor having last seen me near the summerhouse.

By the time we reached the house, I felt like sinking down on the warm floor and never leaving. But Dugan peeled off our capes and hustled me upstairs, shouting for the maids to bring hot water to my room. I was too cold and exhausted to argue, and when my numb fingers couldn't manage the buttons, he ripped my dress from me and kicked it across the floor.

"What are you doing?'' I cried, hugging myself. "Do you intend to try and put me in the tub yourself? Get out!''

"Such ingratitude,'' he growled, and strode out of the room just as Polly and another maid entered with the cans of steaming water.

24

When I finally emerged from my hot tub, I was disconcerted to discover that Dugan had again entered my bedroom. I stopped abruptly and stared at him.

He had changed his clothes and now wore a casual, white woolen shirt without a cravat or jacket. He sat before the fire, gazing with moody concentration at the leaping flames.

Aware that I was covered only by an outer-robe, with my unbound hair streaming down my back, my lips parted on an angry question. But then they closed, the words unspoken as I saw the worried lines around his mouth, more deeply grooved than ever, the bitter frown between his heavy-lidded eyes.

His misery was apparent; however, I couldn't help wondering what he was doing here, waiting in my room. What did he want from me? Uneasily, I tightened the sash around my waist and closed the opening higher on my chest; certainly I was clad in a very compromising manner to be alone with a man.

Halfway across the room, I halted and cleared my throat. "Dugan? What is it? Why are you here?"

Slowly, he turned his head, the still-damp russet locks gleaming darkly in the firelight. "I wanted to be sure you were all right. You nod a bit reluctantly. Are you too tired for a bit of a talk? I won't stay long."

There was something oddly pleading in his glance and I took the chair across from him at once. "How can I refuse? You just saved my life and I don't think I've thanked you."

He waved his hand. "No thanks are necessary. You don't know how glad I am that I found you." There seemed to be a double meaning in his taut words and the intensity of his gaze became unnerving.

"How is your wife?" I asked, hoping to remind him where his duty lay.

"Sleeping peacefully. Her ankle looks almost completely normal." He leaned back in his chair, eyeing me sardonically. "We haven't had a recent chance to talk, but if you think she would mind my being here, you don't know how little morals matter to Aileen."

However jealousy might matter. Even though she might no longer desire Dugan (and I was not at all sure about that), I imagined that she clung viciously to what was hers.

"I have a feeling she will not stay long at Castlecove," Dugan continued somberly. "Only until she gets what she came back for."

"And that is—?"

"I don't know yet. I have reached the point where divorce seems like the only answer. When I agree to that, and offer her a very large amount of money for support, she may depart."

"The scandal—would it hurt the family?"

"Of course, that's why I've hesitated. Divorce in Scotland is not easily obtained and I would hate to place the stigma of divorced parents upon Meggie's future. But would it be any worse than having her become increasingly aware of her mother's immoral conduct with all and sundry?"

He stood up and leaned his hands against the mantelpiece, gazing downward at the leaping flames. "Before the accident I wanted to avoid divorce. I hoped that as Aileen grew older, she would settle down. A foolish hope! Now, however, there is another reason why I must be free."

He turned abruptly and swung me out of my chair, holding me taut before him. *"Don't you understand?"*

"Dugan," I gasped, trying to steady myself against his rigid arms. "No, I don't. What are you saying?"

He clenched his teeth and the burr came strongly in his voice. "Ye ken fine! Don't play the innocent with me, woman!"

The next instant, he jerked me hard against his body, his lips plundering mine like a starving fire that must consume all in its path.

A whirling chaos engulfed me and I clung to him, all sense, all reason lost. Nothing remained but the hunger. Feverishly, I returned him kiss for kiss, my hands tugging at his hair.

At first, with the leaping of my instant response, I barely noticed the bed beneath my back. But when his mouth closed on my breast, a sharp flame darted through me and I uttered a wild cry.

He raised his head, a drugged glaze in his eyes. His breath dragged hard and deep as he propped himself upon his hands. "Do you see? How long can we avoid this—?"

"I thought I heard a cry," Glynnis said, opening the door. "Are you all right?"

For a moment, neither Dugan nor I could move or speak. Then both of us stumbled to our feet, he raking back his hair while I gasped and covered up my breast with shaking hands.

A terrible anger swept over Glynnis's face as she took in the equal dishevelment and scarlet faces of both Dugan and myself. I had never felt such utter, all-enveloping shame!

"So this is why I've made no headway with you, Dugan," Glynnis hissed, her head outthrust like a venomous asp. "She's gone after you herself—no doubt telling about Aileen's lavaliere that she saw in my possession—implanting lies so you would turn from me."

"I didn't, I never—" I choked out.

Dugan's face was sharp as flint. "There never was a thing between you and me, Glynnis. Suppose you explain further about that lavaliere. I wouldn't want to condemn you unheard."

Agonized, I melted into a corner, tightening my robe. It was astonishing how quickly Dugan had regained his poise and I felt a little resentful of the fact.

Glynnis sent me a furious glance and she pointed an accusing finger. "I wondered how much you would tell Dugan—you little sneak! Pawing through my jewels! Dugan, what has she told you?"

"I never told anyone," I cried, shrinking back as far as possible.

Both of them ignored me. "I'm waiting for your explanation, Glynnis," Dugan grated.

"Well, I assure you I didn't steal it." With her usual arrogance returned in full force, she lifted her orange silk skirts and plumped down in a chair. "I guess you might as well know the truth. It doesn't matter now. I certainly don't want to be falsely accused."

"Go on," Dugan growled.

"Aileen wanted to get away from here, but you had warned her after her affair with Malcolm that you wouldn't tolerate any more escapades." She gave a taunting smirk. "You didn't know that Max had met her in London some months before and they became lovers. He asked her to remain as his mistress, but he was also interested in her knowledge of the Prince's Gold—perhaps more than anything."

Dugan moved in front of her, fists clenched on his hips. "So then you cooked up the lie about her disappearance in the sea?"

Glynnis smiled, clearly enjoying herself. "We hired a fisherman to help us. He got me ashore, then took Aileen to a remote island where she stayed for a week or so until the search died down. Max arranged the rest. After staying with him until their money almost had run out, he insisted she return to Castlecove. We all knew that Paul's widow was here and might be on to something about the gold. Max managed to give Aileen money for a gown and the price of a hired carriage, telling her to make a grand entrance when there was company here. That way you could hardly refuse to take her in with all those people looking on."

"My God," Dugan breathed.

"But she actually came back earlier, didn't she?" I exclaimed. "And stayed in the summerhouse? I think she listened outside the conservatory when I had a meeting with Professor Harden."

"Aileen probably didn't altogether trust the professor. Liars never believe anyone else," Dugan said coldly. "I wonder that she trusted you as much as she did. Just what did you get out of all this, Glynnis? Only a lavaliere?"

"Two things. She gave me her sapphire and diamond jewels. And I wanted her out of the way so I could get to you, Dugan." She rose and stared at him boldly.

"I have not the slightest interest in you, Glynnis. And never had." Dugan eyed her up and down distastefully. "Now everything is clear and it was a vile, insensitive plot. What about the pain it caused Davy, Meggie, and others to think she had drowned?"

Glynnis's lip curled. "I didn't think it would cause you much pain."

"Of course it did. I have never wished for Aileen to suffer."

"Not even now when she stands between you and . . . her?" Her angry glance swept over me.

"That's enough." Dugan spat the words. "I want both you and the professor out of Castlecove."

Glynnis's aplomb wavered then and her glance went to the rattling, storm-drenched windows. "Not tonight, surely?"

"No, but as soon as the weather clears, a carriage will be at the door. Make certain you both are in it."

Glynnis cleared her throat. "I'm sorry things turned out this way and I know I have no right to ask a favor, but perhaps it would be better all around if you refrain from divulging this knowledge about Aileen until—"

"Until you are well away and Aileen can't demand that you return the lavaliere?" Dugan sneered.

Glynnis turned her face away, but pride kept her head high even while she pleaded. "Believe this or not, but my main reason for helping Aileen was the hope that you would turn to me after she had gone."

There was silence in the room, then Dugan answered heavily, "Nothing will be said until you have left Castlecove."

Glynnis nodded and left the room.

Slowly, I moved forward and Dugan turned to me with narrowed eyes. "Well, what do you think of that? Are you surprised?"

"I'm amazed. However, I knew that Glynnis had the lavaliere and it looked like the same one Aileen wore in her portrait. But Glynnis didn't explain and I thought it might be just a copy. Anyway, I felt that I had no right to probe into the matter."

"She's a difficult woman to understand. I hope she keeps quiet about what she saw when she burst in on us."

I inhaled deeply, feeling the blood stain my face. "I realize you were upset, not thinking clearly when you began making love to me. This is a terrible time for you a-and you have my sympathy."

He grunted. "Is that what you think I wanted from you? Comfort?"

"Partly. And also proof that you still are physically attractive to some female."

Anger flashed across his face. "Woman, you are so—so—" He clamped his lips together.

"What else could I think? You tore into me, pulling down my robe. Not a word of please or may I or—or love."

"Do you expect dainty speeches from a Highland *barbarian*, as you call me?" he ground out between clenched teeth. "Besides, without any words from me, you were allowing it, enjoying it. Didn't I tell you that someday you'd want passion from a man?"

The truth was overwhelming and I averted my flushed face. "Yes, I agree that I was weak. But remember that I had nearly lost my life. How could I think clearly? Perhaps I needed comfort, too."

He gave a grating laugh. "Och, aye? Comfort doesn't take the form of things that we were doing. That has another name."

Suddenly, I could bear no more and put my face down in my trembling hands. "Oh, leave me, will you? Go away!"

He hesitated, then came close and brushed back my hair, planting a full, soft kiss upon my neck. "That's comfort, lass," he murmured, then went out the door.

25

When I thought it over, Glynnis's revelation actually made more sense than Aileen's tale about amnesia and two years spent living in a simple cottage on an island. Nobody really had put much faith in that story and now perhaps the truth would not elicit great surprise. Repugnance at Aileen's deception was another matter.

In fact, I felt unable to face any other members of the household that night and ordered my supper on a tray.

Thoughts of the arrogant professor filled me with uneasiness. I sensed that his ruthlessness would sweep any obstacle from his path without the slightest compunction.

Glynnis was equally malicious, a hard, cold woman devoted entirely to self-satisfaction. She must hate me after seeing that lovemaking in my bedroom and probably still blamed me for her lack of success with Dugan. There was no telling what she might do now to gain revenge.

Aileen, of course, was appalling. Utterly immoral, selfish, and greedy, her appetite for men seemed unquenchable. If Glynnis told her what she had witnessed between Dugan and myself, Aileen might also seek retaliation.

And, lastly, there was Dugan, whose dangerous company I must try to avoid at all costs. I knew now that I loved him deeply. How could I bear never to see that decisively chiseled, proud face again? Never to hear his rolling, Scottish burr, or feel his bruising arms and urgent, searing lips. "Never" was a black pit of despair and it yawned before me without any hope. When my tray came, I had to push it away, half-eaten, and climbing into bed, I cried myself to sleep.

It was late when I awoke next morning and the storm still raged. I scarcely felt refreshed, but after I had dressed, hunger overcame me, and since I had eaten very little of my supper, I made my way to the breakfast room, believing that by now most of the family would be finished and gone.

To my relief, only Nora and Lady Margaret were still there, sipping tea and conversing in low tones. They greeted me and we spoke about the weather while I filled my plate with sausage, eggs, fried potatoes, an oatmeal roll, and then poured myself a cup of strong coffee for a change.

"Are Glynnis and the professor still here?" I asked, trying to make the question sound offhand.

"Yes, but Dugan said they would be leaving as soon as the weather permits." Lady Margaret glanced uneasily at the rain-slashed windows. " 'Tis many a long day since I've seen such a fierce, enduring storm. And so late in the spring, too. All the blossoms in the orchard will be down and—" She broke off at a sound from the doorway and I heard Nora give a smothered gasp.

"Good morning," Aileen caroled. "Is there any breakfast left?"

Malcolm, rather red of face, held Aileen in his sturdy arms. He carried her to the table and she slid into a chair, tilting back her head to murmur, "Thank you, Doctor," with a little catlike smile.

I stared at her, willing my face not to show the disgust I felt. What a cruel, scheming hussy she was with her lies and adulterous behavior. And now she was working her treacherous wiles on the susceptible Malcolm. Just for a momentary diversion I was sure. A local country doctor was not likely to have enough money for a long-term affair.

But for now, Malcolm was a gasping fish upon her hook. He nervously greeted everyone at the table while he smoothed his ruffled hair and straightened his coat. "Well, I think I'll just be away on my rounds now—"

"No, no, wait," Nora cried. "You must eat something first. Sit here, I'll fill your plate." She sprang up and grasped his arm, propelling him to a place beside her and away from Aileen, who looked fresh and lovely in a gown of yellow muslin topped by a morning sacque of cambric and blond lace.

Malcolm, still protesting, albeit reluctantly, sat down. He was seated right across from Aileen and lifted his eyes to her as though she were a magnet. "May I get you something to eat?" he asked her.

"Yes, please," Aileen cooed, and ordered practically the same menu as I had, but took tea instead of coffee.

"How are you this morning?" Margaret asked her stiffly. "I trust your sprained ankle has mended?"

"Yes, thank you. It's just the stairs I can't manage on my own. After Malcolm examined me this morning, he said I could walk anywhere. But of course, I will avoid the tower."

Her vivid blue eyes narrowed as she took a sip of tea. "Dear sister, I wonder how grease came to be there on the steps? Since you are the housekeeper, surely you should have kept them cleaner?"

"Yes, how do you suppose they got that way?" Lady Margaret exclaimed. "So dangerously slippery?"

Nora flushed an ugly red. "I don't know. Perhaps a careless maid dripped candle wax. I can't be everywhere."

Aileen took a forkful of scrambled eggs with sausage and chewed thoughtfully. "But it does seem very strange. No one used to go to that tower room but I."

"It was just an accident," Malcolm muttered, hunching over his plate. "Perhaps a maid took a wrong turn and started up the steps before she realized where she was and spilled the grease. Thank heaven, the accident was not more serious."

"And you knew just what to do, Doctor dear." Aileen smiled at him beneath half-shut lids. "You have such good hands for stroking away my pain."

I thought Malcolm was about to choke with embarrassment. A picture formed in my mind of him helpless before Aileen in her lacy wrap and unbound hair . . . I doubted if she would have had the least compunction about seducing him.

Then bitter guilt assailed me. Had I been much better? Submitting—nay, *reveling*—in Dugan's forbidden embrace? He was a married man, Aileen's husband, bound to her by laws of church and state. I dug my fingernails into my palm. I must get away from Castlecove! But until that time, I prayed my conscience would keep me from a mortal sin. However, I was no weak creature, subject to fits of abandonment. My mind was sound, my will could be strong, too. Almost defiantly, my backbone stiffened and I concentrated on my breakfast.

A little later, I was about to excuse myself, when Aileen spoke, her confident, bright glance sweeping around the table. "I've invited Malcolm to dinner tonight. It's been so long since I have seen him. And since Glynnis and Max are leaving shortly, I thought a little celebration was in order. Lady Margaret, I hope that you don't mind?"

"Why . . . no. Of course not. We're always glad to have you, Doctor." Lady Margaret stood up hurriedly. "If you will all excuse me, I must see to my husband. You will be back later with his medicine then, Malcolm?"

"Yes, I'll bring it tonight. Thank you. And now I must be on my way."

Nora rose, her hand upon the doctor's shoulder like a statement of possession. She glanced at Aileen with a cold defiance. "If you're finished, Malcolm, I'll see you to the door."

Suddenly, Aileen flung out her hands, tossing back the curls upon her shoulders. "Malcolm, first you have to carry me up to my room."

Nora folded her arms. "I'll wait in the hall."

Malcolm looked helplessly from one demanding woman to the other. He was a fool to get involved again with Aileen, I thought. He didn't look weak, but he was. Aileen didn't love him. She could only love herself. But she would toy with him for her own amusement, pushing him into a frustrated turmoil. And Nora, with her possessiveness, would suck him dry. He should avoid them both and seek another life somewhere else. But I didn't believe he would.

I spent the rest of the day on two projects. First, I wrote an epilogue to Paul's book. I explained his theory and how he had been unable to test it due to his untimely death. Then I wrote about the impossibility of locating Goldie's grave. My last sentence was: "So the mystery of the Prince's Gold must forevermore remain just that—a mystery." Though I felt sad, I was rather proud of my writing. It sounded almost professional. Perhaps I had absorbed something from copying so much of Paul's erudite prose.

My second project was even more depressing. I had to pack my clothes and plan to leave. Not with Glynnis and the professor, but right after. As I spread out the gowns and cloaks, the hats and warm gloves that Paul had so generously purchased for me, I felt tears slide down my cheeks. I had been happy when the three of us were preparing for our trip to Scotland. Paul with his high hopes of locating the Prince's Gold; Tommy with his eagerness to see his grandparents and the Scottish heritage he would have someday.

I could have had a pleasant life with Paul. I would have been warmed, comforted, and loved. In time, I might have loved him, too. Oh, not in the way I felt about Dugan. Now I knew the difference between a gentle affection and the wild ecstacy of shared passion. Now I knew what it felt like to love a man. It was weakness and elation, a searing, breath-stealing fire. A joy such as I had never dreamed of . . . almost an agony of bliss.

At last, the stormy day lengthened into nightfall and it became time to dress for dinner, something I scarcely anticipated with any joy. Indifferently, I donned one of the gowns I had not worn before. It was almost plain with its oyster-colored double skirt edged in pleated gray silk ribbon, the sleeves modestly demi-long, only the corsage dipping low to reveal my shoulders.

My face flushed with embarrassment when I glanced at Dugan, but he only nodded coolly when I entered the drawing room. Quickly, I turned my eyes away.

Everyone except Sir Hugh was assembled and I immediately noticed that Aileen had taken much more care with her own toilette than I had. She dominated the scene in her low-cut azure silk and rippling red-gold curls threaded with pearls and artificial roses. Davy, Malcolm, and the professor couldn't take their eyes off her. Only Dugan remained aloof, sipping his "wee dram" of Scotch and gazing down into the fireplace.

There was a coolness in his manner toward Glynnis and the professor and they both must now be aware that the hospitality of Castlecove had been withdrawn. Fortunately, manners and custom held their conversation flowing easily.

At the dinner table, Aileen kept up a constant teasing of her two illicit lovers, flirting openly with first one and then the other. It made me nervous to see how jealousy raged in Malcolm's face as she touched the professor and leaned boldly against him, whispering in his ear behind her lacy fan.

Then she would turn and cling with equal abandonment to Malcolm on her other side so that the professor's face grew watchful, his eyes narrowing with a cruel thoughtfulness. I didn't think he was a man who would take kindly to being made a fool.

Only Davy seemed unaware of any hidden nuances and hung around his sister after dinner, talking to her eagerly whenever he found an opening. Though everyone else made casual conversation, eyes kept turning to the little drama being enacted by Aileen and her swains.

Finally, Glynnis was prevailed upon to play the piano. Under cover of the music, I saw Dugan slip away. He did not return until the evening was drawing to a close. Then he suddenly appeared in the doorway, water gleaming on his hair. "The road to the village is impassable. Malcolm, you will have to spend the night. You can't go home."

"Oh, I think I better have a try at it," Malcolm exclaimed, struggling to his feet.

Aileen grabbed at his arm, shaking it playfully. "Don't be stubborn, you silly man. Why should you rush out into the storm with all these beds available?"

"Well—er—" he faltered. "I don't want to be a bother."

"You won't be," Lady Margaret stated, but her eyes were rather cold.

"That's settled, then," Aileen cried. "Now, Doctor, please carry me up to my room."

"I'll do it," Dugan grated, stepping forward.

"Faugh, you have rain upon your clothes. Do you think I want my lovely silk dress ruined?"

As Malcolm swung her up, his tortured eyes avoiding Dugan, Aileen slanted a provocative glance back over the doctor's shoulder. "Aren't you going up to bed now, Max?"

"In a few minutes. I want a cigar before I retire. Sweet dreams, Aileen."

She answered with a mocking laugh.

I let the others precede me from the room, and was just about to start after them, when I found the professor at my side. "That lady plays a dangerous game, methinks."

I didn't have to ask him whom he meant. "It's hardly any of my business," I said shortly, gathering up my skirts.

"There's violence in the very air."

I threw him a startled glance. "From whom?"

He shrugged his massive, elegantly tailored shoulders. "We have here many candidates with motives involving jealousy, desire, frustration . . . years of smoldering hatred from all directions. Even the protective love of Davy might be a danger to someone. Where will it explode? And when? I'll tell you. Here. And soon. Thank God, I will be gone."

Without thinking, I burst out scornfully, "So your love affair with Aileen is all over?"

He gave a sardonic laugh. "Aha, you've heard the story now? Though what we had was scarcely 'love.' We're quite alike, you know, Aileen and I. Immoral, selfish, egotistical . . . If she fancies the doctor now, I wish her joy of him. He won't last long."

There was something very unpleasant in his voice, and I turned quickly. "Good night, Professor. And good-bye."

His hand shot out and caught my arm. "Not quite so fast." His eyes swept me up and down with an almost cruel, insulting assessment. "In fact, like Aileen, I'm ready for a new diversion. When you return to London, I think I'll call on you, my pale blond beauty."

I flashed him a haughty glance. "Pray don't bother. I intend to be fully occupied with my husband's book."

"Indeed? Perhaps I can help you get it ready in a more professional manner. Would you like that?" His thick fingers moved up and down my arm with a double meaning.

I managed to jerk away. "I would not. I don't need your help."

"London can be a lonely place, m'dear, and I have many friends. Under my protection, you would be introduced to a whole new sort of life, exciting and stimulating. Writers, artists . . . you might even learn how to write a book yourself. With my tutoring, of course."

"I haven't the slightest interest in becoming a professional writer. Nor have I any interest in your so-called 'stimulating' world."

"I see. Perhaps you think Dugan will eventually seek you out." His voice had grown thick with barely suppressed rage. "I can tell you that he will have a long, difficult time obtaining a divorce in Scotland. And by then, your meager charms will be just a dim, lost memory. Don't waste your youth waiting for something that will never happen."

"I didn't ask for your advice. I will run my life the way I want without any help from you. This is good-bye, Professor, and I trust we never meet again."

He didn't answer as I sped out to the hall and up to bed. But that night, I slept with a chair wedged beneath the doorknob of my room.

26

I passed a restless night, hearing the rain stop and a moaning wind supplant it. My mind went over and over the professor's warning: violence. Here. And soon.

Surely not from Dugan . . . so strong, honorable, and upright. Yet he certainly had provocation, especially if Aileen refused to cooperate about a divorce. She might decide it was more to her advantage not to leave Castlecove, at least not until she had found a new, wealthy "protector." Someone with more money than Professor Harden.

The next most likely suspect was Malcolm, whose mind seemed to be in a state of frustrated turmoil. I sensed that "hole-in-wall" affairs were not his style, yet he appeared to yearn hopelessly for Aileen's love. I had seen his distress when she flirted openly with the professor. Malcolm was so besotted with Aileen, I wondered if he could be rational right now.

Then I had another thought. Perhaps the violence would not strike at Aileen. Someone driven by jealousy might attack Dugan. Or the professor. Or even Malcolm.

I tried in vain to clear my mind of all this useless speculation, but my sleep was sporadic at best. It was gray dawn when a loud noise brought me upright, my heart pounding with the fear that had beset me throughout all the night. I heard a door slam below. Caught in a blast of wind, it continued banging back and forth as I hurried to the window and peered outside.

Everywhere, trees tossed wildly, branches cracking as leaves flew hither and yon in a mad, abandoned dance. Dark clouds raced along the sky, carrying away the storm.

And someone raced just as swiftly down the garden path. A purple velvet cloak edged in marten, red-gold hair streaming like a fire around her head.

I pushed the window wide and shouted. "Aileen, where are you going?"

She didn't stop. She reached the summerhouse and her cry came back on the wind. "Malcolm! I got your note. Open the door. I'm here!"

A light gleamed from the summerhouse as she disappeared inside. What was this? A rendezvous with Malcolm? So early in the morning?

I gripped the window ledge and seconds later, I heard a scream. It was almost as though I had been expecting it.

I didn't hesitate. Stepping into shoes, I pulled hard on the servant's bell, flung a cloak around my shoulders, and tore into the hall and down the stairs. Before I reached the back door, a maid emerged from the rear quarters and I cried to her, "Get Mr. MacInnis to the summerhouse! At once!"

I had no idea what might have already happened. I had less idea of what was *about* to happen.

Before I reached the tangled cliffside garden with its

ancient summerhouse, something shook the ground. Stunned, I grabbed a nearby tree. *Was this an earthquake?* But as I stared ahead, a paralyzing terror gripped me. Sick and unbelieving, I could hardly grasp the awful scene.

A portion of the earth suddenly broke off and fell down toward the sea, and the summerhouse, splintering and shattering, slid from its base. Walls burst out, windows broke, bricks from the chimney rained everywhere, partially obscured by clouds of dust. I hid my face, shuddering, sick with shock as the remains toppled over the cliff.

Around me I heard pounding feet, screams, the constant roar of a dying, two-hundred-year-old house. When Dugan called my name, I raised my head. "Aileen—" I managed to croak, and pointed ahead. "She —she was in there—maybe others—"

He cried out in horror and tore away. A crowd gathered and every face looked stunned. People came from all directions. There were cries, questions, exclamations. "Someone's been killed! Aileen was there!" The message raced back and forth. I never will forget the look on Davy's face as he ran along the cliff, shouting his sister's name.

Even the children and Miss Grey appeared, wraps thrown over nightclothes. I put my trembling arms around Tommy and Meggie, holding them close.

"Courtney," Miss Grey asked hoarsely. "Was anybody in the summerhouse?"

"I only saw Aileen, but I heard her call to someone." I had to clear my throat, which was filled with stifled tears. "Children—will you please go back inside—"

"I can't. I have to stay," Meggie said through stiff, white lips.

"Me, too," Tommy whimpered, arms tight around my legs.

Amid all the noise and shouting, I finally saw Dugan

climb into view, his face a mask of horror. He spoke briefly to the crowd as he pushed through to us.

Meggie immediately grabbed his hand. "Papa, is Mama dead—this time?"

He knelt down and enfolded her tightly. "Yes, little one. She died at once. No suffering. Can you be brave about all this?"

She nodded, then sobbed, her face hidden on his shoulder.

Dugan looked at me and expelled a shaken breath of purest agony. "Nora, also. Both dead. Flung clear of the rubble."

Nora!

Meggie cried even harder and Tommy joined in. Miss Grey exclaimed aloud, a trembling hand across her lips.

Dugan stood up wearily and wiped the wetness from his eyes. "Children, go wait in your room. I'll be in shortly and we'll have a talk together." He gave me a blind glance, then went back to the cliff where he vanished out of sight.

Miss Grey took a child in each hand and silently moved away. I saw Lady Margaret run back to the castle, presumably to be with her husband. Dimly, I was aware of Malcolm's sudden appearance; he was running toward the cliff where cries and shouts continued and a brown cloud of dust still mounted to the sky.

But nothing really registered in my brain. I only was aware of a deep sorrow and tears streaming down my face. Two young lives—gone in an instant!

I put my head down in my hands. Suddenly I heard the professor's voice. "Didn't I tell you this would happen? Violence came—even sooner than I thought. And not from any human intervention after all. At least . . . not all of it."

I looked up, blinking the wetness from my eyes. "What do you m-mean?"

"Nora was there waiting in the summerhouse for Aileen. Perhaps she struck her just before the house broke loose. There was blood upon a candlestick gripped in Nora's hand—even in death. I have drawn my own conclusions." He shrugged.

I gave a cry of consternation. "Are you sure? I heard Aileen call out: 'Malcolm! I got your note.'"

He shook his head. "I saw Malcolm coming from the stables. A note from him must have been a ruse to lure Aileen into Nora's clutches. She probably intended to shove her in the sea after she had killed her."

I gripped my hands together and said hoarsely, "Did Nora really hate Aileen that much?"

"Of course. It's obvious she greased the tower stairs. She was insanely jealous. And who else had a better motive? Dugan and Lady Margaret may have despised Aileen, but they live by a rigid code. And as for Glynnis —Aileen didn't matter that much to her. Glynnis is only concerned with herself. In fact, she's now casting lures in my direction." He gave a grunt of dry amusement.

"Well, she and I will leave this morning. I don't wish to be involved in all this trouble. Back in London, I think I can write quite an interesting article about Castlecove for a lecture tour. Good-bye, Courtney. I guess this ends our erstwhile 'collaboration.'"

I stared grimly after his departing figure. What a cold-blooded individual! Not a word of sorrow about the recent catastrophe. Aileen had been his mistress for two years and he brushed away her memory like a squashed fly. Suddenly, I remembered how I had spurned him last night. That, also, seemed to have been erased from his mind.

Everything else was drawfed by the awfulness of this landslide. I groaned and turned back to the cliff, the scene of so many things . . . the ruined foundations where once a little house had stood. It had been a place beloved by a young prince, as well as Paul and Aileen and countless other generations.

I found a handkerchief in the pocket of my cape and wiped the tears from my face. Then I sorrowfully picked my way among the remnants that had not crashed into the sea: broken glass, splintered boards, bricks from the chimney. . . . Even the porch had been uprooted and lay upon its side, the ground underneath exposed and raw.

Afraid to go any closer to the cliffside, I was just about to turn away when I saw it.

A ray of early sun struck something in the earth and led me like a pointing finger. I saw a gaping hole where once the porch had stood. Then, as I crept closer, a tiny, dirt-encrusted slab of marble and a broken, rusted box.

And spilling from the box, a pile of golden coins. Purest gold that doesn't rust or tarnish.

Was this . . . could it be . . . *the Prince's Gold?* My heart thundered in my ears as I crouched low, held immobile for a long moment while I simply stared, hardly daring to believe my eyes.

But I knew what it was. Soon a cool canniness enfolded me. Quickly, I glanced all around. Everyone was still down below the cliff. I reached into the hole, collected the coins and box, and hid them deep in the folds of my cloak. The pathetic little marble slab I buried nearby underneath a sturdy bush. Nobody must find this yet. It would start a hue and cry and many questions. I didn't want to lie regarding my discovery, but the professor must be far away before I made my disclosure.

After that, I hurried to my room, took a long, gloating survey of the treasure, then finally hid it underneath the packed clothing in my satchel. Tomorrow, when some of the turmoil had died down, I would show my discovery to the family.

As soon as possible, I must rewrite the ending to Paul's book and journey to London with all speed. If this would turn the professor's article into a grave error, I didn't care. Hadn't he said our collaboration was at an end? There was not a thing he had done to aid in my discovery of the gold. Every praise and honor must go to Paul's research and strong beliefs.

But in spite of my exultation, I had an ominous feeling that the professor was going to be very angry.

27

All day long, everything was in a feverish commotion. Polly told me that the professor and Glynnis had departed, and soon after that the rector arrived along with several officials who declared the deaths a "freak of accidental nature." Perhaps the professor was wrong about Nora's deadly intentions. At any rate, not a word was mentioned in my presence and I never would repeat what Max Harden had told me. The family had enough to bear.

Most of the time I stayed out of the way, requesting a light tray in my room at suppertime. Far into the night, I heard the sound of voices, bells ringing, clattering footsteps, the pounding of a fence being installed along the landslide.

I awoke the next morning determined that it was time to show the family what I had discovered. Perhaps it would help to divert some of their anguish.

Carrying the heavy box beneath a shawl, I sought out Miss Grey and the children in the nursery. Tommy, as Paul's son, must be among the first to know.

The three of them were seated close together, making no attempt at lessons. Tommy and Meggie, red-eyed and overwrought, flung themselves on me with cries and questions.

"Mr. MacInnis tried to subdue them." Miss Grey shook her head. "But as you see, they still are very upset."

"Perhaps I have something that will help." I gave a mysterious nod. "But it all must remain a secret between us for a while."

Silence engulfed the room as everybody stared at me.

"Is it a nice secret?" Tommy quavered uncertainly.

"Very nice. My dears, draw up your chairs around the table and I'll show you what I've found. But first—do I have your promise not to breathe a word of this?"

Eyes widened but heads nodded solemnly, including Miss Grey's. However, I noticed that her face grew scarlet and I wondered if her quickened breathing indicated she had guessed.

When we all were seated, I slid the rusty box in view, raised the lid, and poured the sovereigns out upon the table. "Behold—the Prince's Gold!" I whispered.

"Dear heaven!" Miss Grey shrieked softly, and clapped her hands upon her chest.

"Ohhh—ohhh, the Bonnie Prince's Gold," breathed Meggie.

"Where—how? Oh, Mama, am I dreaming?" Tommy cried, reaching for the coins.

"Shhh . . . Listen, and I'll tell you all about it." Nobody ever had a better audience. There were constant smothered cries, exclamations, and a great many questions. I had to repeat the story several times while they all marveled. It did my heart good to see the strain and horror eased from their faces to be replaced by ecstatic wonder and delight.

Miss Grey's eyes held tears of joy. "My dear, you are a heroine! The world must be made aware—"

"No, no. It's really all Paul's discovery. He's the hero. It was his research, his conviction that the 'beloved place' was somewhere near the summerhouse—"

"But you had the conviction that the grave must still be here," Miss Grey interrupted. "And that it held the secret to the treasure. So I'd say the honors go to both of you."

"Thank you, but I want all the public credit to go to Paul. He's the deserving one in my opinion. However, this discovery must be kept secret until his book is published. A leak could ruin everything."

"I agree," Miss Grey said firmly. "You can trust our silence in this matter. Can't she, children?"

They nodded eagerly.

This was not the time to tell them I would soon be leaving so I put the coins away and we ordered some food as, suddenly, we all felt hungry. And when the chicken sandwiches, ham croquettes, and fruit salad came, we devoured every bit, chattering in low tones about the treasure. Every other topic was pushed aside and for that I was deeply grateful. As for Glynnis's revelations about the past two years, that was not for me to mention. The family must make their own decision in the matter. I imagined Tommy and Meggie would not be told for a long time.

After we had eaten, I took the gold to Sir Hugh and Lady Margaret. They both seemed shaken and aged by the two terrible deaths, but I knew that in time the memory would be eased. Now I had the satisfaction of seeing amazed excitement fill both faces just as it had the children's when once again I told my tale of finding the long-lost gold.

"How wonderful! Now you can finish Paul's book

just the way he wanted," breathed Sir Hugh, gloating over the pile of coins gleaming on his counterpane.

"Indeed, I will. I must return at once to London and take the manuscript to Paul's publisher so the news of the gold's discovery can't leak out before the book is ready. I've sworn everyone to secrecy and tonight I'll do the same when I tell Dugan. He's the only other person who must know."

Sir Hugh nodded. "I agree."

Tears filled Lady Margaret's eyes as she embraced me. "I knew it was a good thing when you came here. You'll come back soon, won't you? To stay?"

"Och, aye," Sir Hugh exclaimed, reaching for my hand. "There must be a gathering of the clan when the book comes out, ceremonies, decisions about the gold . . ."

A lump rose in my throat and it was hard for me to speak. "I'll write." That was all that I could promise.

"Someone must go with you. A lass can't travel by herself so far," Lady Margaret said. "Would Polly do? She's very loyal and likes you . . ."

I protested, but to no avail, and so it was decided that Polly would accompany me and stay in London as long as needed. *Until I returned*, they both insisted.

I packed the rest of my belongings, and just before the dinner hour, I sought out Dugan in the parlor. He was sprawled wearily on the sofa, a glass untouched beside him. He was so deep in thought, I had to call him twice.

"Dugan, may I have a word with you? I'm so very sorry about . . . everything. I really don't know what to say . . ."

"Och," he muttered, shifting a little. "What can a body do or say now? Was it my fault? Should I have tried harder to make her happy?"

I took a seat beside him and shook my head. "No, Dugan. What could you have done? Her whole life led,

I think, to that one fateful hour." A fate induced by Nora? I didn't say what I was thinking. He had enough tragedy to bear. Instead, I tried to turn his mind to other matters not so painful.

"Dugan, I have something to tell you. Something that I'm sure you will be glad to hear."

He turned his heavy-lidded gaze on me without much interest, though he seemed to be making an effort.

"Dugan, I have found the Prince's Gold," I said in a low vibrant tone.

Astonishment swept across his face and he jerked upright. "Wh-what's that you say? How? Where?"

When I had explained it all, the grimness had left his face and a spark of lively interest now shone in his eyes. "What an incredible thing to happen!"

"Of course I must return at once to London and get Paul's book into the hands of his publishers in case the news gets out somehow. Such things can happen."

"I wish I could go with you, but there is so much that I must attend to here." He sighed and ran a long hand through his hair.

"I know there is a lot for you to do. I can manage all right. Polly is going to accompany me."

He stared at me, almost with a touch of awe. "This really is the most astounding thing—your discovery of the gold. You should be very proud of yourself."

"Oh, I haven't done so much. It was all due to Paul and his research."

"Aye, but also due to your own determination to keep on searching."

Lady Margaret and Sir Hugh appeared just then, saying Davy would not be down to supper. I felt very sorry for the young man, who had been so full of life. He had loved Aileen deeply. More than anyone else, I believed that he would feel her loss for a long time.

* * *

The next day, everyone converged outdoors to see me off. I was glad the sun was shining for I felt very gray inside. Even the satisfaction of discovering the gold could not completely lift the pall cast by the recent tragedies or dull the wrench I felt at leaving Castlecove, not knowing when, if ever, I would return. Perhaps I could arrange for Tommy to visit me in London. Meggie, too.

I bent down to Sir Hugh in his wheelchair and pressed my cheek to his. "Thank you for making me so welcome."

He took my hands in his. "Dear child, it was a blessing to have you here. And now you have the undying gratitude of everyone for your part in discovering the treasure lost for all these years." To my astonishment, he then put one of the prince's sovereigns into my hand and waved away my sputtered thanks. " 'Tis little enough. It will just be a souvenir for you. Now, lass, take care of the arrangements for Paul's book and then return to Castlecove as soon as possible. This is your home now and don't forget that."

Lady Margaret said much the same thing, as did Miss Grey, both of them promising to write. Davy shook my hand and tried to smile.

"I hope you'll soon feel better," I told him softly.

He sighed. "I think I'll travel for a spell. Perhaps discover a new life."

"That's a very good idea."

Next, I turned to Tommy and hugged him close while he tried hard not to cry—and so did I. "You'll send me letters, Mama?"

"Constantly, my darling. And every night before I sleep, I'll think of you." I blinked rapidly and cleared my throat. "Be a good boy, now."

"Come back verra soon," Meggie said. "We'll keep watch for you." She gave me a smacking kiss and squeezed me tightly.

My trunk and bags were loaded on top of the carriage. Polly, who was almost incoherent with excitement, waved to all the envious servants as she popped inside.

Then, somehow, the others fell back so that I was left alone with Dugan. He looked at me solemnly, sorrow still graven deep upon his face. "Take care, lassie. I will miss you."

"I'll miss you, too."

"The time will pass."

What did he mean? I looked up at him expectantly. But he said no more and didn't attempt to kiss me or even touch my hand.

The carriage drove away to a chorus of farewells, and when I craned my head out of the window to wave once more, Dugan still stood there on the driveway, staring after me.

28

I was very glad to have Polly's company on the long journey back to London. She had been a good-natured, well-trained maid at Castlecove. Now she proved to be dependable, intelligent, and invested with a new self-confidence. She told me that Sir Hugh had supplied her with funds and instructions for us to spend a night at the Caledonian and for a private compartment on the *Flying Scot*. Her wages were to be mailed from Castlecove as long as necessary.

All this was corroborated by a letter from Sir Hugh, which he had instructed Polly to hand me after we were on our way. In his message, Sir Hugh insisted that these financial arrangements were but a small repayment for my discovery of the family treasure. He begged me to let him know if there was anything else that he could do for me.

His solicitude was very heart-warming and there was nothing for me to do but accept graciously.

When we reached Scotland's capital city, I wired a message to Mrs. Barker apprising her of my imminent arrival and requesting that a room be made ready for my temporary maid. I also sent a letter to Sir Hugh and his wife with many thanks and enclosed a note for Tommy and Meggie.

Should I write to Dugan at this time? I finally decided that he had too much on his mind. It would be better to wait until I reached London, then I would send him a brief, calm note. Perhaps he would reply, perhaps he wouldn't. I felt sure that any feeling he might have had for me was now drowned in the wave of Castlecove's recent tragedies. The only way for me to survive my own heartsick yearning was to turn my thoughts to other matters.

After the weeks in Scotland, London struck me with a sense of unreality when we arrived and started home in a hired hansom cab.

Polly, however, was all agog, exclaiming with enthusiasm over everything she saw and heard: the cobbled streets crowded with carriages and carts, the vendors hawking umbrellas, toys, hot potatoes, coffee . . . She loudly admired the men in top hats and satin waistcoats, the fashionable ladies in hooped skirts and flowered bonnets, the glass-fronted shops bulging with so many wondrous things.

Though I smiled at Polly, I really couldn't share her joy. My own eyes dwelt wearily on the ragged urchins, gutters filled with filth, the soot-blackened buildings. I found the heavy, acrid air and stench of mud flats from the Thames a sad reminder of the fresh cleanness in the Highland glens.

As we rattled along the busy streets, Polly's head craned around at every gaudy poster, asking questions about the many tea gardens, fairs, and music halls that were advertised. I determined that she must be taken at least to Cremorne Gardens in Chelsea before I sent her home. And that brought up another matter.

I knew Polly's wages were to be paid, supposedly, until I returned to Castlecove. But I felt in my heart there was no likelihood of that in the near future. My own funds would not stretch far to include her keep as well as Mrs. Barker's if Polly stayed on indefinitely. I was loath to dismiss Mrs. Barker. I didn't care to live completely alone and she had been so devoted to Paul, I knew he would want me to engage her as long as possible.

"Do you think you will be homesick?" I asked Polly.

"Oh, no, ma'am, not at all. This is the most exciting thing that's ever happened to me. But I'd like to keep in touch with those at home if you could please get me some penny stamps? Sir Hugh will be sending on my wages so there's no worry for you at all about that."

I was thankful that I wouldn't have to send Polly back right away. She was a tie to all the things in Scotland that I'd just left so reluctantly.

Mrs. Barker gave both Polly and me a hearty welcome when we arrived, and even though it was so late, she had a hot supper waiting. She took my bags upstairs, then carried Polly off to see her own room and have a bite in the kitchen.

Here in Paul's little house, his loss smote me anew and I felt tears fill my eyes. At least, I hoped that he knew his dreams about the Prince's Gold finally had come true.

However, London no longer seemed like home to me. My heart was in the Highlands now and scenes of the glen and castle filled me with sick longing. The friendly faces of Sir Hugh and his sweet lady . . . the dear children . . . the roses, the hills, the deep blue skies . . .

But most of all, I yearned for Dugan, whose rugged strength hid such a passionate nature. He must be miserable after the two recent tragedies and the sense of guilt he claimed to feel. He had had years of a bitter, disillusioning marriage and might never want to try again. As for me, I knew there never would be a man like Dugan MacInnis in my life. And I would never look for one.

My only hope was to turn my thoughts and energy to Paul's book. With that in mind, next day I finished the last chapter, then dressed carefully in a walking gown of fawn brocade, three-tiered. Over it, I put a short green velvet cloak and matching bonnet edged in black lace with a wreath of moss roses underneath the brim. With Paul's manuscript tied in a stout box, I took a cab to the publishing offices of Mr. Holt.

The gray-haired owner proved much less austere than on my previous visits, perhaps due to my elegant attire and air of confidence, or perhaps because Paul's book now was in his eager hands.

When I told him about my discovery of the gold, it was gratifying to observe his reaction. He fell back against his leather chair, gaping at me, eyes reflecting his astonishment. He tried hard not to stutter. "D-dear lady, this is incredible news!"

He went over and over the last pages I had written and then nodded with deep satisfaction. "Very well done, indeed. I cannot tell you how greatly this ending will affect the book's sales. The whole literary world will be taken by storm. We must rush for immediate publication."

I nodded. "That would be an excellent idea. A certain Professor Max Harden has also been searching for the gold. He tried to enlist my late husband's help and when that failed, he followed me to Castlecove. He was most unpleasant, I might add."

He stared. "Is that a fact! I've heard of the man. A rather unsavory character by all accounts, though he manages to insinuate himself in certain groups for lectures and articles, not always hewing to the exact truth. I trust you have been discreet about your discovery?"

"Yes, indeed. I've only told the immediate family members at Castlecove. Then I placed the gold in Sir Hugh's hands for safekeeping and traveled here with all speed."

He beamed at me. "Very good. As soon as the book is published, you will be the lion of the hour—or should I say lioness? You will be feted and interviewed and—"

"No, no, please! The fame must all go to Paul."

"Oh, most assuredly. But you actually found the gold, held it in your hands and can describe the curious circumstances. . . . Believe me, your public appearances will be very important and greatly aid the book sales. You hardly can refuse, dear lady."

His eyes traveled over me with surprising warmth. "And of course, your attractiveness and elegance will prove invaluable."

"Oh, no, Mr. Holt, I have never done anything in public. I certainly cannot give a lecture. It would be a dismal failure, I'm convinced. Please excuse me from any part in this." Nervously, I drew on my glacé gloves and prepared to leave.

He sprang from behind the desk. "Mrs. Dunburn, I will help you every step of the way. Trust me in this matter. I think very soon you will enjoy your popularity. I've seen it happen—"

"No, no," I repeated, and waved my hand at him.

He caught my fingers and held on tightly. "Then at least allow me to take you out to dinner this evening. We have a great deal to discuss, my dear. About the book, you know."

"Why—why—" I cast around for an excuse, but none came readily to mind. It probably was true that there was a lot to settle about Paul's book. Mr. Holt might even increase the advance now that there was such a wonderful ending. As graciously as possible, I accepted.

That was the beginning of what soon became a regular event for me to dine frequently with Mr. Holt on some business matter. He did add greatly to the book's monetary advance and soon I found it pleasant and diverting to wear my finest apparel and be seen in the company of such a well-known and attentive gentleman. We even began to attend evenings at the theater or a stroll through a tea garden where lights and laughter, crowds and entertainment flourished. He treated me with the most perfect manners, and when they began to assume a warmer character, I put it down to his endeavor to win me over to making public appearances in the near future.

Polly, however, became overtly suspicious and muttered queries about his "intentions" being strictly honorable. I had to admonish her frowning greetings to him more than once and began to think about returning her to Scotland even though I found her a great help. She cared for my wardrobe, did my hair, ran errands for Mrs. Barker, and mailed my letters.

I wrote frequent short notes to everyone at Castlecove and had many in reply. But to my disappointment, it was always: "Dugan sends his regards." There was nothing from him personally. At last in desperation, I sent him a letter that required—nay, demanded—an answer.

Dear Dugan:
I wish that you would write to me, even though I hear the news from others. Still, I worry. Can you tell me how the children really are? How Sir Hugh and Lady Margaret are bearing up? And how you feel by now.

Paul's book will be out soon and the publisher and I are working closely on matters that concern it.

Though it occupies me, my thoughts are often with all of you and I pray that things are going well.

To my satisfaction, Dugan wrote back promptly, though more formally than I would have wished:

Dear Courtney:
Thank you for your letter, but do not worry about us. Time has eased the pain. The children and everyone else have grown into a calm acceptance. Davy has gone off on a trip and is greatly sobered. We are also planning to send Miss Grey and the children to visit Edinburgh. The new housekeeper is well trained, more of a true servant than poor Nora but just as able.
  I am glad to hear about Paul's book and look forward to reading it.
  I remain, your obedient servant, Dugan MacInnis.

Alas, there was not a word about missing me or any question as to when I might return. After my first flush of joy that Dugan had finally written to me, a feeling of dejection set in. He probably had no intention of ever seeing me again. At any rate, it seemed that his brief flare of passion for me had faded.

In desperation, I agreed to Mr. Holt's plans for some public appearances and interviews. He began to coach me diligently as the book now was ready to come off the press. We started slowly with small gatherings of publishers, editors, writers, and journalists. I was almost faint with nerves at first, but Mr. Holt stayed at my side and gradually my self-assurance grew. Under his tutelage, I bought some rather dashing clothes, and when his personal attention intensified, I did nothing to discourage him. It became a kind of balm for my misery over Dugan.

A few weeks later, we were making our way through

a crowd of people who had come to hear me speak and I had to pause frequently to sign my name in copies of Paul's book and respond to a great deal of fulsome praise.

Mr. Holt's arm was about my waist, ostensibly to assist me through the throng. Then his clasp tightened and he put his lips close to my ear. "Courtney, will you accompany me to Cremorne Gardens tomorrow night for supper and the fireworks show?" When I glanced at him to murmur my acceptance, his face was filled with a possessive admiration. Perhaps he considered my success was his own creation. He was right.

I smiled at him with amusement, then my features froze. Beyond Mr. Holt, another face appeared. It was Professor Harden, his eyes on fire with anger, his thick, red lips curled downward.

I didn't make a move. Neither did he until the next moment when he was swallowed up by the jostling throng.

I turned away to answer someone at my elbow, and in a little while, my rapid heartbeats subsided and I had pushed the unpleasant moment from my mind.

29

The next evening at Cremorne Gardens proved to be both a beginning and an ending.

It started out pleasantly enough. Mr. Holt had reserved an alcove table in his name near a grove of trees. It was secluded enough for conversation yet close enough for us to observe the passing scene.

The place had originally been part of Lord Cremorne's estate and was set in delightful surroundings between the Thames and King's Road in Chelsea. Tonight it looked like fairyland with lanterns among the trees glimmering on rustic paths and banks of flowers. People from every walk of life strolled informally: clerks, students, aristocrats, fashion plates of both sexes. And, of course, the "dippers," who kept a sharp eye out for the country bumpkin's purse.

A program announced fireworks, a balloon ascent, a concert, as well as "Constant Dancing to All the New and Fashionable Music."

What more could anyone need? Yet Mr. Holt seemed

high-strung and strangely indifferent to his surroundings. Before our supper arrived, he had consumed several glasses of port wine and edged his chair so close to mine, I felt his knee.

Then began the compliments. He certainly had changed from the cool, stern-faced publisher of our first acquaintance.

"You look wonderful tonight," he purred, sliding off my purple velvet cape so he could stare at my bare throat and arms. "Each day you seem to grow more vibrant and exciting. Your success as a speaker is quite phenomenal."

Pleased, I gave a little laugh. "Well, I find the prince's story so exciting, I quite forget myself when speaking."

"Didn't I tell you that you would do well?"

"You have been a big help to me."

"I hope so. I truly believe you could become a writer —with my assistance." His hand crept over the table to enclose my fingers while he eyed me over another glass of wine. "I would like you to call me Harrison. From now on, we must work very closely. There are many other paths where I can lead you."

What were these "other paths"? . . . I cleared my throat uneasily. I knew then that Polly was right. She had guessed immediately about Holt's direction. I hadn't wanted to believe in his ulterior motives, my sudden popularity was too pleasant.

"Do you agree?" he asked, raising up my hand toward his wine-stained lips.

Before I could reply, however, a roughly dressed man halted at our table, tugging at his cap. "Are ya Mr. Holt?"

The publisher glanced at him in annoyance. "What do you want?"

"A chap gave me this note fer yer. Said tell ya there was trouble at the book place."

Hastily, Mr. Holt scanned the folded paper and gave a startled cry. "Fire! At the publishing house! Who gave you this note?"

But already the messenger had vanished in the crowd. Mr. Holt rose hastily. "Good lord! Courtney, come, I'll put you in a cab. I fear I must—"

"No, no, I'll stay a little longer unless there's something I can do to help?"

He chewed his lip while he adjusted his top hat. "Well, if you really want to stay—"

"I do. I've never seen a balloon ascent. After a while, I'll have a waiter hail a cabby for me. I certainly hope your publishing house will be all right."

He groaned. "A fire is the greatest fear of every publisher." He flung some bills on the table, and with a strained smile in my direction, vanished in the throng.

Being on my own did not cause me to feel ill at ease. When the waiter brought my supper, I ate quickly. It was nearly time for the ascent and the crowds had thinned considerably as they streamed toward a wide grassed site.

Just as I was about to follow them, a well-remembered voice spoke in my ear. "Ah, Courtney, here you are in all your sophisticated finery. The toast of London's literary circles—taking the place that should be mine!"

Max Harden stood behind me in the grove, a snarl of hate upon his lips. He looked dangerous and angry and I knew why. A stab of fear shot through me when I realized how alone we suddenly had become. Could I placate this man?

"Wh-what a surprise to see you. Y-yes, Paul's book is quite successful."

He stepped close, gripped my arm, and pulled me to my feet. "Come with me. We must talk."

"Sit down, then—"

"Not here. Back through these trees." He jerked me forward.

"My escort will soon be looking for me," I faltered, attempting to halt our rapid progress in the grove.

"I think not. Holt will not discover he's been hoaxed for quite a while."

"You sent that note?" I gasped.

He didn't answer, but when we reached the river wall, we stopped. The trees surrounding us were thick and quite deserted. Far below, the inky Thames swept onward to the sea in silence. No boats, no voices anywhere, only a distant hum of music from the gardens. Clouds alternately hid and then revealed the feeble moonlight.

Max Harden's hands tightened on my arms and he thrust his reddened face close to mine. "Why didn't you confide in me about the gold, you deceitful vixen! You knew it was there and didn't tell me. *Didn't you?*" He shook me violently.

"No—no! Not until after the landslide," I choked out. "By that time, you had gone—"

"Why did you never give me any credit for helping in the discovery?"

"Because you didn't do a thing to help me," I cried out.

He rushed on, ignoring my words. "I punish those who try to make a fool of me. Just as I did Aileen." To my horror, his hands slid up around my throat.

"Wh-what d-do you m-mean?" I clawed desperately at his tightening fingers.

"I waxed those tower stairs after Aileen said she was through with me and intended to remain at Castlecove. She taunted me—said there was Malcolm now and many others. She said I was old, fat, worthless." His voice rose shrilly.

"Tell me how—how you—" I swallowed hard,

counting on his bragging nature. Sure enough, his fingers eased a little and a cruel smile curved his full, red mouth.

"I sent that note to her and when she entered the summerhouse, I struck her down, intending to fling her body in the sea. Unfortunately, Nora was there hiding in hopes of catching Aileen in another indiscretion."

"Good God, you killed them both? Before the landslide?"

"I did. Their bodies were so destroyed, there were no clues. I barely managed to escape myself. And now, you little devil, it's your turn!"

"Wait! L-let me make amends—I swear—"

"Your death will make amends. I'll take over with my own version of how you swindled me out of all the credit. Oh, yes, they'll believe me. I'm well known. Who ever heard of you before?"

I let out one stupendous scream and clutched his coat. Cursing obscenities, he tried to pry me loose while forcing me over the river wall. I felt the beast's hot, panting breath as once again he tried to choke the air out of my body.

Then, in the blackness settling over me, a miracle occurred. I was released and fell to the grass. As my vision cleared, I thought I saw Dugan struggling with the professor. Then a scream issued from the roiling waters and Dugan knelt alone to gather me into his arms.

"Dugan," I cried, clinging to him with a sob, "am I dreaming? Is it really you?"

"Aye, love. Are you all right?" When I nodded, he released me to peer over the wall into the river far below.

"The professor?" I croaked, rubbing my sore throat muscles.

"No sign of him. I'll alert the patrol to search for

him." Dugan came back to me and knelt down, shoving back my hair. "For heaven's sake, lass, what was he trying to do to you?"

"Kill me. As he killed Aileen and Nora."

"Dear God, what are you saying? Tell me." He drew me into his arms, hugging me fiercely.

"Later," I whispered. "But first, just take me home."

That night we sat in the little parlor for a long time, close together on the sofa, a fire crackling in the grate, while we talked and talked.

I told Dugan everything that the professor had confessed and there ensued some round Gaelic cursing. "I hope they never find him," Dugan grated. "I might take vengeance into my own hands."

"Now it's your turn, Dugan," I said. "How did you happen to be there in Cremorne tonight?"

"Well, Polly had made me anxious about you and Mr. Holt. She feared—"

"*Polly?* How—"

"She wrote to me each week as I had ordered her. You see, I had so much to say to you, but I was determined to wait a proper interval."

"Oh, Dugan, what did you want to say?" I asked in quick delight.

"Whisht, woman, let's take things in order. First, Polly got me so worried I had to come and find out if that publisher and you were serious."

"Not I. But he—tonight—"

Dugan nodded. "Aha, 'twas a strong feeling I had about it all. A true touch of 'the Sight,' you might say."

"Go on."

"Well, Polly told me where you'd gone. I was directed to Holt's table and there lay your purse and cloak. A waiter then said the lady had gone into the grove with a different man, but he couldn't describe him. Anyway, I started searching through the trees and then I heard you scream."

I touched my tender throat. "Another few minutes and I might have been dead."

"The villain tried to escape after I hit him. We fought fiercely, I can tell you. But, suddenly, he fell over the wall and I imagine the river finished him off."

(As it turned out, we never heard of Professor Harden again. He might have drowned and been washed out to sea. Or he might have emerged somewhere as another person. But he was gone completely from our lives.)

For a long moment we were silent, gazing somberly into the flames. Then our heads turned toward each other and the next instant our lips and arms were joined.

"I love you," Dugan said huskily. "Will you come home with me and be ma wife? For ever and aye?"

"Of course!" Delirious with joy, I kissed him back, then settled comfortably into his arms. "Now tell me when you first discovered that you loved me."

"If that isn't like a woman! Och, well, perhaps it started when you lolled out of the window that first day."

"Dugan, I've told you—I *didn't loll*."

We both began to laugh helplessly.

That night was the beginning of another life for me, a wonderful long life filled with loving and laughter. And, of course, occasional heated quarrels as my Highlander never was completely tamed.

And for that I was eternally grateful.